跟他學 部落格
職場生活英語

　　本系列套書共分《跟**她**學部落格職場生活英語》及《跟**他**學部落格職場生活英語》兩冊，兩冊皆以辦公室所發生的事情為主題。內容寫實、饒富趣味性。

　　為了增加本系列套書的可讀性，我們在編排上做了這樣的設計：

本　　　文：也就是部落格的內容，用字簡短、洗鍊並具實用性。美籍編輯特別用了許多時下流行的俚語及慣用語，裨與現代英語接軌。

這麼說就對了！：在這個專欄中，我們將本文所涵蓋的俚語或慣用語加以精細解說，使讀者明瞭這些俚語或慣用語的意思及用法，提升讀者口語及寫作的能力。

字 詞 幫幫忙！：在這個專欄中，我們將本文所有的重要單詞或片語陳列出來，並附上音標及例句，方便讀者學習這些單詞或片語的正確用法。

　　讀者從以上的編排設計就可看出我們編輯本系列套書的用心。我們另外聘請 ICRT 電台的美籍專業廣播員將本系列套書的內容錄音，方便讀者跟著朗讀，提升讀者閱讀及聽力技巧。

祝大家學習成功！

目 錄　TABLE OF CONTENTS

The Couch Surfer

Index \ Links \ about \ comments \ Photo

July 20

I got an email today from one of my online **buddies**, and he said he was going to come to Taiwan to **rip it up** with me next week. This is the first time I'll meet anyone I met online **in person**. He asked if I **knew of** a cheap hotel near my house, but I told him not to be **silly**. He's going to be a couch surfer and sleep at my house during his visit.

About me

Tom

Calendar

◄   *July*   ►

Sun	Mon	Tue	Wed	Thu	Fri	Sat
		1	2	3	4	5
6	7	8	9	10	11	12
13	14	15	16	17	18	19
20	21	22	23	24	25	26
27	28	29	30	31		

Blog Archive

- ▸ July (20)
- ▸ June
- ▸ May
- ▸ April
- ▸ March
- ▸ February
- ▸ January
- ▸ December
- ▸ November
- ▸ October
- ▸ September
- ▸ August

Tom at Blog 於 July 07.20. PM 08:26 發表 | 回覆 (0) | 引用 (0) | 收藏 (0) | 轉寄給朋友 | 檢舉

沙發客

July 20

　　我今天收到一位網友的電子郵件，他說下星期準備到台灣來找我一起玩。這是我頭一次與網路上認識的人面對面接觸。他問我是否知道我家附近有沒有便宜的旅館，但我告訴他別傻了。他在來訪期間會在我家借宿，就睡在沙發上。

About me

Tom

Calendar

◀　　　*July*　　　▶

Sun	Mon	Tue	Wed	Thu	Fri	Sat
		1	2	3	4	5
6	7	8	9	10	11	12
13	14	15	16	17	18	19
20	21	22	23	24	25	26
27	28	29	30	31		

Blog Archive

- ► July (20)
- ► June
- ► May
- ► April
- ► March
- ► February
- ► January
- ► December
- ► November
- ► October
- ► September
- ► August

Tom at Blog 於 July 07.20. PM 08:26 發表 | 回覆 (0) | 引用 (0) | 收藏 (0) | 轉寄給朋友 | 檢舉

couch [kaʊtʃ] 是『沙發』，surfer [ˋsɝfə] 則是『衝浪者』，而在沙發之間穿梭衝浪的 couch surfer（沙發客）其實是指『借睡人家沙發過夜的人』。

couch surfer（沙發客）這個詞來自其同名的網站 Couch Surfer（沙發衝浪）。『沙發衝浪』的運動是由一個美國年輕人所創。有一次他買到一張前往冰島的便宜機票，就先找了一份當地學生的通訊錄，並發了 1,500 封電子郵件詢問是否可借宿在對方客廳的沙發上，結果一天內有數十封回信願意幫忙，讓他度過一個美好的假期。於是 Couch Surfing 網站 http://www.couchsurfing.org/ 於 2004 年成立，讓會員們彼此接待，於是『沙發衝浪』就成了『借宿』的代名詞了。對自助旅行的人來說，當沙發客除了體驗住當地人家裡，另外就是可以省下住宿費，是個很不錯的選擇。

例: I'm traveling all through Europe and not staying in one hotel. Instead, my goal is to be a couch surfer the whole time.

（我要一路玩遍歐洲，而且不要住在旅館。我的目標是在這趟旅行做個沙發客。）

以下補充和 couch 相關的俚語：

a couch potato　　成天在沙發上看電視的人

couch potato（沙發上的馬鈴薯）其實是指『成天坐在沙發上看電視的人』，這種人什麼事都不做，整天躺在沙發上邊看電視，邊吃垃圾食物，日久體型就長得像圓滾滾的馬鈴薯一樣，所以稱為 couch potato。

例: Ted has become a couch potato ever since he got married.

（泰德自從結婚後就成了電視迷。）

rip it up　　尋歡作樂

rip [rɪp] 是『撕；扯』之意，網誌中的 rip it up 並非『把它撕個粉碎』，而是『尋歡作樂』的意思。

例: My friends love to rip it up on New Year's Eve.

（我的朋友喜歡在跨年夜狂歡作樂。）

除了 rip it up，還可以用 paint the town red 表『狂歡作樂』。

paint the town red 字面意思是『把城鎮塗成紅色』，紅色往往代表喜悅、興奮或歡慶，因此 paint the town red 就被用來表示『（到酒吧、夜店等）飲酒作樂、盡情狂歡』。

例: David and Helen planned to paint the town red on payday.

（大衛和海倫計劃在發薪日那天出去盡情狂歡。）

1. **buddy** [ˋbʌdɪ] *n.* 好朋友，死黨
= **pal** [pæl] *n.*
   例: I spent a whole week with my buddies in Kenting.
   （我跟死黨們在墾丁玩了一整個禮拜。）

2. **in person**　　本人；親自地
   例: I've seen the president on TV, but never in person.
   （我曾經在電視上看過總統，但從沒見過本人。）
   You'd better explain it to the boss in person.
   （你最好親自向老闆說明這件事。）

3. **know of...**　　獲悉 / 知曉……
   例: Do you know of any good burger restaurants in this neighborhood?
   （你知道這附近有沒有好吃的漢堡店嗎？）

4. **silly** [ˋsɪlɪ] *a.* 愚蠢的；可笑的
   例: My nephew looked silly when he dressed as Spider-Man for Halloween.
   （我外甥在萬聖夜扮成蜘蛛人的模樣看起來很可笑。）
   ＊nephew [ˋnɛfˌju] *n.* 外甥；姪兒
   　niece [nis] *n.* 外甥女；姪女
   　Halloween [ˌhæloˋin] *n.* 萬聖節前夕，萬聖夜

The Arrival

July 21

When Chuck finally arrived, he looked **exactly** like the picture he **posted** online, and I was sure we were going to <u>**have a blast**</u>. Since the **flight** was so long, Chuck had a serious case of **jet lag**. We took the bus back into the city, stopped at a small restaurant for some dinner, and then I showed him my apartment.

About me

Tom

Calendar

◀ *July* ▶

Sun	Mon	Tue	Wed	Thu	Fri	Sat
		1	2	3	4	5
6	7	8	9	10	11	12
13	14	15	16	17	18	19
20	**21**	22	23	24	25	26
27	28	29	30	31		

Blog Archive

▸ July (21)
▸ June
▸ May
▸ April
▸ March
▸ February
▸ January
▸ December
▸ November
▸ October
▸ September
▸ August

Tom at Blog 於 July 07.21. PM 10:52 發表 | 回覆 (0) | 引用 (0) | 收藏 (0) | 轉寄給朋友 | 檢舉

網友駕到

July 21

查克終於來了，他看起來就跟他放在網路上的照片一樣，我肯定我們一定會玩得很開心。由於飛程漫長，查克有嚴重的時差。我們坐巴士回到市區，在一家小餐館裡吃晚飯，然後我便帶他參觀我的公寓。

About me

Tom

Calendar

◀ *July* ▶

Sun	Mon	Tue	Wed	Thu	Fri	Sat
		1	2	3	4	5
6	7	8	9	10	11	12
13	14	15	16	17	18	19
20	21	22	23	24	25	26
27	28	29	30	31		

Blog Archive

- ► July (21)
- ► June
- ► May
- ► April
- ► March
- ► February
- ► January
- ► December
- ► November
- ► October
- ► September
- ► August

Tom at Blog 於 July 07.21. PM 10:52 發表 | 回覆 (0) | 引用 (0) | 收藏 (0) | 轉寄給朋友 | 檢舉

blast [blæst] 原指『爆炸、爆破』之意，可作名詞和動詞，作名詞時意同 explosion [ɪk`sploʒən ]，作動詞時則等於 explode [ ɪk`splod]。

例: It's estimated that 200 people were injured in the huge blast.

（據估計有 200 人在那場大爆炸中受傷。）

＊It is estimated + that 子句　　據估計……

They decided to blast the big rock that was blocking the road.

（他們決定把擋路的大石頭炸掉。）

但網誌中所提的 have a blast 可不是指『有爆炸』，blast 在此引申為『歡樂而刺激的經歷』。因此若說某人 have a blast，其實是指某人『玩得很開心』。類似的說法尚有下列：

have a ball　玩得很開心

= have a lot of fun

= have a good time

= have a great time

= have a wonderful time

＊ball [bɔl] *n.* 快樂的時光

例: We had a blast at Lucy's birthday party last night.

（我們昨晚在露西的生日派對上玩得很開心。）

Frank promised that we would have a great time going surfing with him.

（法蘭克向我們保證和他去衝浪一定會玩得很盡興。）

字 詞幫幫忙！

1. **arrival** [ə`raɪv̩] *n.* 抵達（不可數）；抵達的人或物（可數）

例: A lot of reporters were waiting at the airport for the movie star's arrival.

（許多記者在機場等候那位影星的蒞臨。）

New arrivals at the company will be given a short orientation on their first day.

（公司在新人上班的第一天會對他們做簡短的新生訓練。）

＊orientation [ˌorɪɛn`teʃən] *n.* 新生訓練

8

2. exactly [ɪgˋzæktlɪ] *adv.* 確切地

例: Do you know exactly what time the train leaves?
（你知道火車離站的確切時間嗎？）

3. post [post] *vt.* 張貼，貼出

例: Emma posted her funny stories on her blog and received a lot of feedback.
（愛瑪在她的部落格上張貼她的趣事獲得很大的迴響。）

＊feedback [ˋfid͵bæk] *n.* 回饋，反應

4. flight [flaɪt] *n.* 班機

a domestic flight　　國內班機 / 航班

an international flight　　國際班機 / 航班

＊domestic [dəˋmɛstɪk] *a.* 國內的

international [͵ɪntɚˋnæʃənḷ] *a.* 國際的

例: You'd better hurry up, or you'll miss your flight.
（你最好快點，不然會錯過班機。）

It is almost impossible to find cheap international flights during summer vacation.
（要在暑假時找到便宜的國際班機簡直是不可能的事。）

5. jet lag　　時差

jet [dʒɛt] *n.* 噴射機（是 jet plane 的縮寫）

lag [læg] *n.* & *vi.* 落後，拖後

lag behind　　落後

＝　fall behind

例: Try not to sleep too much while on the flight. Otherwise you'll get jet lag.
（試著不要在飛機上睡太多，要不然你會有時差。）

Billy lagged behind in the race.
（比利在賽跑中落後了。）

Danshui Delights

Index | *Links* | *about* | *comments* | *Photo*

July 22

Chuck felt much better the next day after getting some sleep, so I decided to take him to Danshui. First, we **took a boat ride** and the **breeze made us feel as comfortable as an old shoe**. Then, we had some **fish balls**, squid, iron eggs, and **freshly**-caught fish with **sweet and sour sauce**. Chuck loved the food and made me **swear** to take him to Danshui one more time before he left Taiwan.

About me

Tom

Calendar

◄ *July* ►

Sun	Mon	Tue	Wed	Thu	Fri	Sat
		1	2	3	4	5
6	7	8	9	10	11	12
13	14	15	16	17	18	19
20	21	22	23	24	25	26
27	28	29	30	31		

Blog Archive

- ► July (22)
- ► June
- ► May
- ► April
- ► March
- ► February
- ► January
- ► December
- ► November
- ► October
- ► September
- ► August

Tom at Blog 於 July 07.22. PM 09:43 發表 | 回覆 (0) | 引用 (0) | 收藏 (0) | 轉寄給朋友 | 檢舉

淡水逍遙遊

Index | *Links* | *about* | *comments* | *Photo*

July 22

　　查克睡了一覺後，隔天感覺好多了，所以我決定帶他去淡水。我們先去搭船，吹著微風讓我們感到很舒服愜意。然後我們去吃了魚丸、魷魚、鐵蛋和用現抓的魚做成的糖醋魚。查克很愛這些吃的，還叫我發誓在他離開台灣前，一定要再帶他來一次淡水。

About me

Tom

Calendar

◀ 　　　 *July* 　　　 ▶

Sun	Mon	Tue	Wed	Thu	Fri	Sat
		1	2	3	4	5
6	7	8	9	10	11	12
13	14	15	16	17	18	19
20	21	22	23	24	25	26
27	28	29	30	31		

Blog Archive

▸ July (22)
▸ June
▸ May
▸ April
▸ March
▸ February
▸ January
▸ December
▸ November
▸ October
▸ September
▸ August

Tom at Blog 於 July 07.22. PM 09:43 發表｜回覆 (0)｜引用 (0)｜收藏 (0)｜轉寄給朋友｜檢舉

11

這麼說就對了！

與好友出遊，享受美食、美景，實在是再享受不過的事了！搭著小船、微風輕拂，這種愜意的感覺就好像腳穿著一雙多年的舊鞋那樣舒服自在，所以英文裡才會有 make sb feel as comfortable as an old shoe 的說法，我們可想而知，舊鞋穿起來一定比新鞋舒適，因此這個片語就用來形容『讓人感到非常舒適』，感覺是不是很貼切呢？

例: Soaking in the hot spring after hiking all day made us feel as comfortable as an old shoe.

（健行一整天後泡在溫泉裡，讓我們覺得非常舒適愜意。）

as comfortable as an old shoe 也可以用來形容事物，此時就等於 relaxing [rɪ'læksɪŋ], soothing ['suðɪŋ] 或 cozy ['kozɪ] 等形容詞。

例: The hotel room was so cozy that we wanted to stay for one more night.

（這飯店房間太舒適了，讓我們想多住一晚。）

關於 old shoe 還有另一個常見的用法是 as common as an old shoe，指的就是『很一般的、很普遍的』之意，相當於 normal ['nɔrml]。

例: In this city, seeing a superstar is actually as common as an old shoe.

（在這座城市裡，看見超級巨星其實是很稀鬆平常的事。）

字詞幫幫忙！

1. **delight** [dɪ'laɪt] *n.* 樂事（可數）；愉快（不可數）

   take delight in...　　喜愛……

   To one's delight, S + V　　令某人高興的是，……

   例: Marvin takes delight in telling bedtime stories to his daughter.

   （馬文喜歡為他女兒讀床邊故事。）

   To my delight, John came back safe and sound from his expedition.

   （令我高興的是，約翰安然無恙地探險回來。）

   ＊expedition [ˌɛkspə'dɪʃən] *n.* 探險

   　safe and sound　　安然無恙的

   　此處的 sound 表『健全的』或『身體沒有受到傷害的』。

2. **take a boat ride**　搭船

   take a(n) + 交通工具 + ride　搭乘……（交通工具）

   例: Kelly decided to take a taxi ride to the restaurant.
   （凱莉決定要搭計程車去餐廳。）

3. **breeze** [briz] *n.* 微風

   shoot the breeze　聊天，閒扯（口語）

   例: Instead of studying, Mark shot the breeze with his friends.
   （馬克非但沒有唸書，反而還跟他的朋友閒聊。）

4. **a fish ball**　魚丸

   squid [skwɪd] *n.* 魷魚；烏賊

   an iron egg　鐵蛋

5. **freshly** [ˈfrɛʃlɪ] *adv.* 新鮮地；最近地

   例: The farmer treated his guests to freshly-picked fruit.
   （這位農夫用現摘的水果招待他的客人。）

   Wally sat on a freshly-painted bench.
   （華利坐在剛油漆好的長椅上。）

6. **sweet and sour sauce**　糖醋醬

   sour [saʊr] *a.* 酸的

   sauce [sɔs] *n.* 醬汁

7. **swear** [swɛr] *vt.* 發誓

   三態為：swear, swore [swɔr], sworn [swɔrn]。

   swear to V　發誓要（做）……

   swear + that 子句　發誓……

   例: Kevin swore to help me if I ever needed him to.
   （凱文發誓只要我有需要，他就會幫助我。）

   James swore that he had nothing to do with the bank
   robbery.
   （詹姆士發誓他和那起銀行搶案毫無關聯。）

   *robbery [ˈrɑbərɪ] *n.* 搶劫

Chuck's New Language

Index | Links | about | comments | Photo

July 23

I taught Chuck some simple Chinese phrases so he could **engage in** <u>small talk</u>. We went to the **nightclub**, and he wanted to **show off** his skill. The first person he talked to couldn't understand a word he said. Chuck felt **embarrassed** and a bit **frustrated** with his new language skills. But then, he met someone whom he could **communicate with**—a pretty girl named Monica. Soon, Chuck <u>**sweet-talked**</u> Monica into taking him around Taipei without me.

About me

Tom

Calendar

◄   *July*   ►

Sun	Mon	Tue	Wed	Thu	Fri	Sat
		1	2	3	4	5
6	7	8	9	10	11	12
13	14	15	16	17	18	19
20	21	22	23	24	25	26
27	28	29	30	31		

Blog Archive

- ► July (23)
- ► June
- ► May
- ► April
- ► March
- ► February
- ► January
- ► December
- ► November
- ► October
- ► September
- ► August

查克的中文初體驗

Index | Links | about | comments | Photo

July 23

　　我教查克一些簡單的中文片語，好讓他可以和別人簡單地聊上幾句。我們去了夜店，而查克想炫耀自己的語言能力。他第一個交談的對象完全聽不懂他在說什麼。查克覺得很尷尬，對自己新語言的表達技巧感到有點挫敗。但是接著他遇到可以溝通的對象 —— 一個叫莫妮卡的漂亮女生。很快地，查克就用花言巧語哄莫妮卡帶他去逛台北，沒叫我陪著去。

About me

Tom

Calendar

◄　　　*July*　　　►

Sun	Mon	Tue	Wed	Thu	Fri	Sat
		1	2	3	4	5
6	7	8	9	10	11	12
13	14	15	16	17	18	19
20	21	22	23	24	25	26
27	28	29	30	31		

Blog Archive

▸ July (23)
▸ June
▸ May
▸ April
▸ March
▸ February
▸ January
▸ December
▸ November
▸ October
▸ September
▸ August

Tom at Blog 於 July 07.23. PM 11:20 發表 | 回覆 (0) | 引用 (0) | 收藏 (0) | 轉寄給朋友 | 檢舉

網誌中所用的 small talk 指的是『閒聊、談天』的意思，為不可數名詞，內容多半是一些無關緊要的事情。

例: Ed and Al stood there making small talk while waiting for the guest of honor to arrive.

（艾德和艾爾站在那邊閒聊，等待貴賓的到來。）

　＊a guest of honor　　貴賓，主客

Let's skip the small talk and discuss the important issues at hand.

（我們略過寒喧，直接討論手邊重要的議題吧。）

　＊skip [skɪp] vt. 跳過

　　at hand　　在手邊

而網誌作者的友人查克用他新學的中文成功搭訕一個女孩子，所用的動詞 sweet-talk 是表『用甜言蜜語或花言巧語來哄騙／勸誘』之意。此外，sweet-talk 去掉兩個字中間的 "-"，形成 sweet talk 就是名詞了。

sweet-talk sb into + V-ing　　用甜言蜜語／花言巧語來哄騙／勸誘某人做……

例: My daughter can sweet-talk me into doing anything she wants me to do.

（我的女兒可以用甜言蜜語來讓我做任何她要求的事。）

Your sweet talk wouldn't persuade me to marry you.

（你的甜言蜜語不會說服我嫁給你的。）

字 詞幫幫忙！

1. **engage** [ɪnˈgedʒ] vt. & vi.（使）從事；（使）忙於

　engage sb in talk / conversation　　與某人攀談；使某人加入談話中

　engage in...　　從事……

　例: Jack acted distant when I tried to engage him in conversation.

　　（我想要跟傑克攀談時，他表現卻很冷淡。）

　　＊distant [ˈdɪstənt] a. 冷淡的；遙遠的

Gary is a busy man; he engages in all kinds of business.
（蓋瑞是個大忙人；什麼行業他都幹。）

2. **nightclub** [ˈnaɪtˌklʌb] *n.* 夜總會；夜店
   pub [pʌb] *n.* 酒吧（= bar），夜店

3. **show off (...)**　　　炫耀（……）
   例: My brother likes to show off his new sports car.
   （我哥哥喜歡炫耀他的新跑車。）

   Ignore what Holly said. She just likes showing off.
   （別理會荷莉說的話。她只是喜歡炫耀而已。）

4. **embarrassed** [ɪmˈbærəst] *a.* 感到尷尬的
   embarrassing [ɪmˈbærəsɪŋ] *a.* 令人尷尬的
   embarrass [ɪmˈbærəs] *vt.* 使尷尬，使難為情
   例: I felt embarrassed when I forgot my lines.
   （我忘了台詞時感到非常困窘。）

   It is very embarrassing to attend a formal party in jeans.
   （穿牛仔褲去參加正式場合是一件非常尷尬的事。）

   What you did really embarrassed me in front of my friends.
   （你所做的事讓我在朋友面前很尷尬。）

5. **frustrated** [ˈfrʌstretɪd] *a.* 感到挫敗的
   frustrating [ˈfrʌstretɪŋ] *a.* 令人洩氣的，使人沮喪的
   frustrate [ˈfrʌstret] *vt.* 使感到灰心，使挫敗
   例: Michael feels frustrated because he cannot find a good job.
   （麥可因為找不到好工作而覺得很挫折。）

   It's really frustrating that I failed the test even though I
   studied so hard.
   （我那麼用功還是考不及格真的很讓人洩氣。）

   The difficult math problem frustrated the students.
   （那道困難的數學題讓學生們感到挫折。）

6. **communicate with sb**　　　和某人溝通
   communicate [kəˈmjunəˌket] *vi.* 溝通
   例: Mrs. Lin finds it difficult to communicate with her teenage son.
   （林太太發現跟她青春期的兒子難以溝通。）

Beauty Is Only Skin Deep

Index | Links | about | comments | Photo

July 24

When I got home from work today, Chuck was **browsing through** the pictures on my computer. He said that by looking at my ex-girlfriends, he could tell I was **superficial**. I was hurt. I had had a lot of beautiful girlfriends, and maybe some of them weren't so smart, but I never felt superficial. Now, I **can't wait for** Chuck **to hit the road**. He's starting to **wear out his welcome**.

About me

Tom

Calendar

◄　　　*July*　　　►

Sun	Mon	Tue	Wed	Thu	Fri	Sat
		1	2	3	4	5
6	7	8	9	10	11	12
13	14	15	16	17	18	19
20	21	22	23	24	25	26
27	28	29	30	31		

Blog Archive

- ► July (24)
- ► June
- ► May
- ► April
- ► March
- ► February
- ► January
- ► December
- ► November
- ► October
- ► September
- ► August

Tom at Blog 於 July 07.24. PM 10:36 發表 | 回覆 (0) | 引用 (0) | 收藏 (0) | 轉寄給朋友 | 檢舉

膚淺的外在美

Index | *Links* | *about* | *comments* | *Photo*

July 24

　　我今天下班回到家時，查克正在瀏覽我電腦裡的照片。他說看完我前女友們的照片，就知道我很膚淺。我很難過。我交往過很多漂亮的女生，其中也許有些人不是很聰明，但我絕不膚淺。現在我等不及要查克動身離開。他已經逗留太久，不再受歡迎了。

About me

Tom

Calendar

◀　　*July*　　▶

Sun	Mon	Tue	Wed	Thu	Fri	Sat
			1	2	3	4	5
6	7	8	9	10	11	12
13	14	15	16	17	18	19
20	21	22	23	24	25	26
27	28	29	30	31		

Blog Archive

▸ July (24)
▸ June
▸ May
▸ April
▸ March
▸ February
▸ January
▸ December
▸ November
▸ October
▸ September
▸ August

Tom at Blog 於 July 07.24. PM 10:36 發表 | 回覆 (0) | 引用 (0) | 收藏 (0) | 轉寄給朋友 | 檢舉

hit the road　　動身離開，上路

hit 當動詞時，意思是『打、擊』。不過 hit 在此則表『去某地方』，hit the road 字面上的意思是『去馬路上』，意味說話者想要離開，故這個俚語可引申為『動身出發』。

例: Let's hit the road. If we go now, we'll be in Taichung by noon.

（咱們上路吧。如果我們現在出發，中午就可以到台中了。）

下列是一些有關 hit 的重要用法：

hit the nail on the head　　一針見血

＊nail [nel] *n.* 釘子

這是一個口語的用法，字面上是說『打中釘子的頭部』，其實意思就是『正中要害』或『一針見血』。

例: You hit the nail on the head when you said the boss is under too much pressure.

（你說老闆壓力太大，真是一針見血。）

hit the roof / ceiling　　大發雷霆，氣得跳腳

＊ceiling [ˋsilɪŋ] *n.* 天花板

hit the roof / ceiling 並不是指『撞到天花板 / 屋頂』。想像一下，如果一個人往上跳，碰到了天花板或屋頂，那他一定是氣炸了，才會有如此的爆發力，因此 hit the roof / ceiling 是指『大發雷霆、氣得跳腳』。

例: Sam hit the roof when he found out his sister crashed his new Porsche.

（山姆發現他妹妹撞壞他的新保時捷時大發雷霆。）

　　＊crash [kræʃ] *vt.* 撞壞

hit the sack　　上床睡覺

= go to bed

= turn in

sack [sæk] 原指『麻袋』，美式俚語中則指『床』，因此 hit the sack 表『睡覺』。

例: Ted was so tired that he hit the sack as soon as he got home.

（泰德累得一回到家馬上倒頭就睡了。）

字 詞 幫幫忙！

1. Beauty is only skin deep.　　外在美只是膚淺短暫的。（諺語）

例: Beauty is only skin deep. It is intelligence and spirit that count.
（外在美只是膚淺短暫的，智慧與心靈才是最重要的。）
＊intelligence [ɪnˋtɛlədʒəns] *n*. 智慧

2. browse through...　　瀏覽／隨意翻閱……（書刊、雜誌等）
browse [braʊz] *vi*. 瀏覽，隨意翻閱

例: Every day, my brother browses through the classifieds to find a better job.
（我弟弟每天都會瀏覽分類廣告看看有沒有好一點的工作。）
＊classified [ˋklæsəˏfaɪd] *n*. 分類廣告（原為 classified advertisement，此處省略 advertisement）

3. superficial [ˏsupɚˋfɪʃəl] *a*. 表面的；膚淺的

例: Vicky is so superficial that she only cares about a person's looks.
（薇琪很膚淺，她只在乎一個人的外表。）

4. can't wait for sb to V　　等不及要某人（做）……
can't wait to V　　等不及（做）……

例: I can't wait for Janis to visit me. We haven't seen each other for three years.
（我等不及珍妮絲來看我。我們已經 3 年沒見過面了。）
I can't wait to go fishing this weekend.
（我等不及要在這個週末去釣魚。）

5. wear out one's welcome
磨損某人的受歡迎度，衍伸為『因停留太久而不再受歡迎』
wear out...　　磨損……

例: After three weeks, Aunt Tracy has worn out her welcome.
（住了 3 個星期後，崔西姑媽就不再受歡迎了。）
You'd better replace the tires on your car because they are all worn out.
（你最好把車胎換掉，因為全都磨損了。）

Breaking the Silence

Index | *Links* | *about* | *comments* | *Photo*

July 25

When I got home the next day, Chuck was watching TV on the couch. We got some food but didn't speak a word. Finally, I **broke the ice** by saying, "What's the matter? **Cat got your tongue**?" Both of us laughed and tried to **clear the air** a bit. He **apologized** for calling me superficial, and I realized he only had one day left for his trip. I didn't want him to go home **bitter**, so we decided to go out for one last night of fun.

About me

Tom

Calendar

◄ *July* ►

Sun	Mon	Tue	Wed	Thu	Fri	Sat
		1	2	3	4	5
6	7	8	9	10	11	12
13	14	15	16	17	18	19
20	21	22	23	24	25	26
27	28	29	30	31		

Blog Archive

- ► July (25)
- ► June
- ► May
- ► April
- ► March
- ► February
- ► January
- ► December
- ► November
- ► October
- ► September
- ► August

Tom at Blog 於 July 07.25. PM 9:21 發表 | 回覆 (0) | 引用 (0) | 收藏 (0) | 轉寄給朋友 | 檢舉

打破沈默

July 25

　　隔天我回到家時，查克正在沙發上看電視。我們吃了點東西，但是一句話也沒說。最後為了打破冷場，我說：『怎麼了？啞巴了嗎？』接著我們倆都笑了，試著想化解不愉快的氣氛。關於說我膚淺一事，他向我道了歉，我也意識到他的旅程只剩下一天。我不想他回家時心裡有疙瘩，所以我們決定在最後一晚出去找樂子。

About me

Tom

Calendar

◄　　　July　　　►

Sun	Mon	Tue	Wed	Thu	Fri	Sat
		1	2	3	4	5
6	7	8	9	10	11	12
13	14	15	16	17	18	19
20	21	22	23	24	25	26
27	28	29	30	31		

Blog Archive

► July (25)
► June
► May
► April
► March
► February
► January
► December
► November
► October
► September
► August

Tom at Blog 於 July 07.25. PM 9:21 發表 | 回覆 (0) | 引用 (0) | 收藏 (0) | 轉寄給朋友 | 檢舉

標題的 **break the silence** 是『打破沉默』之意，但網誌中提到的 break the ice 卻不是『打破冰塊』的意思。break the ice 原指『破冰開航路』，後來引申為『打破僵局』或『打開話題』之意。而 icebreaker [ˋaɪsˌbrekɚ] 原指『破冰船』，可用來形容『打破僵局的事件』或『化解冷場的發言』。

例: The speaker told a joke to break the ice at the start of the lecture.

（演講者一開始就說了個笑話來打破冷場。）

It is common for people to break the ice by chatting about the weather.

（大家通常會聊天氣來打開話題。）

The children's innocent question became an icebreaker for the couple who hadn't talked for two days.

（孩子天真的問題打破了那對夫妻兩天沒說話的僵局。）

＊innocent [ˋɪnəsənt] *a.* 天真的，無邪的

"Cat got your tongue?" 字面表『舌頭被貓吃掉了嗎？』其實是比喻『舌頭打結了嗎 / 怎麼不說話了？』通常用在對方一時之間不知該說什麼，這時就可以用開玩笑的口吻來這麼詢問對方。

例: Darren: What did you think of this horror movie?

  Lizzie: Uh...

Darren: What? Cat got your tongue?

  Lizzie: It scares me to death.

（戴倫：妳覺得這部恐怖片如何？）

（莉茲：呃……）

（戴倫：什麼？怎麼不說話？）

（莉茲：嚇得我屁滾尿流啦。）

另外，要形容一個人啞口無言，或是舌頭打結的常用說法尚有下列：

speechless [ˋspitʃlɪs] *a.* 一時說不出話來的

tongue-tied [ˋtʌŋˌtaɪd] *a.* （因緊張、膽怯）說不出話來的

be at a loss for words 啞口無言，不知該說什麼

例: Tammy got tongue-tied during the job interview, so she didn't make a good impression.

（泰咪在工作面試時緊張到說不出話來，所以沒留下好印象。）

＊impression [ɪmˋprɛʃən] *n.* 印象

After six years apart, Rebecca was at a loss for words when she ran into Eddy again.

（分開 6 年後，芮貝卡再遇到愛迪時一時不知該說什麼。）

＊run into... 偶然遇見……

1. **clear the air**　　化解不愉快的氣氛；消除隔閡

   clear [klɪr] *vt.* 清除

   例: Kelly cleared the air between us by explaining the situation.

   （凱莉將情況說明白而化解了我們之間的不愉快。）

2. **apologize** [əˋpɑləˌdʒaɪz] *vi.* 道歉

   apologize for sth　　　　　　為某事道歉

   apologize to sb for sth　　　為某事向某人道歉

   例: I think Rita should apologize for her rude behavior last night.

   （我覺得莉塔應該要為她昨晚無禮的行為道歉。）

   The shop's manager apologized to the customers for their negligence in person.

   （店經理親自出面為他們的疏失向顧客道歉。）

   ＊negligence [ˋnɛɡləʒəns] *n.* 疏忽

3. **bitter** [ˋbɪtɚ] *a.* 痛苦的；苦的

   例: Roy had numerous bitter experiences when he lived in Africa.

   （羅伊住在非洲時有許多慘痛的經驗。）

   ＊numerous [ˋnjumərəs] *a.* 許多的（= many）

   I like dark chocolate that tastes bitter but is still full of flavor.

   （我喜歡那種吃起來苦苦的仍卻充滿風味的黑巧克力。）

All Good Things Must Come to an End

Index | Links | about | comments | Photo

July 26

While we were on the bus to the airport, Chuck and I started **reminiscing** about his whole trip here. We **cracked up** about the time he **spilled** his fish balls all over his new shirt. We **laughed** about him **overpaying** for **souvenirs** for his mother. We even **chuckled** about our fight. After he **checked in**, I told him I'd miss him. He said this was the best trip ever, but all good things must come to an end.

About me

Tom

Calendar

◄   *July*   ►

Sun	Mon	Tue	Wed	Thu	Fri	Sat
		1	2	3	4	5
6	7	8	9	10	11	12
13	14	15	16	17	18	19
20	21	22	23	24	25	26
27	28	29	30	31		

Blog Archive

► July (26)
► June
► May
► April
► March
► February
► January
► December
► November
► October
► September
► August

天下無不散的筵席

July 26

　　查克和我在往機場的巴士上開始回想他在這裡的旅程。我們說到他打翻魚丸，灑得他新襯衫到處都是時笑到快崩潰。還笑他幫媽媽買的紀念品買貴了。我們甚至還對吵架的事感到好笑。他辦理登機後，我跟他說我會想念他。他說這是他最棒的旅程，不過天下無不散的筵席。

About me

Tom

Calendar

◄　　　*July*　　　►

Sun	Mon	Tue	Wed	Thu	Fri	Sat
		1	2	3	4	5
6	7	8	9	10	11	12
13	14	15	16	17	18	19
20	21	22	23	24	25	26
27	28	29	30	31		

Blog Archive

▸ July (26)
▸ June
▸ May
▸ April
▸ March
▸ February
▸ January
▸ December
▸ November
▸ October
▸ September
▸ August

Tom at Blog 於 July 07.26. PM 11:55 發表 | 回覆 (0) | 引用 (0) | 收藏 (0) | 轉寄給朋友 | 檢舉

親朋好友聚會的時候，常會一『笑』不可收拾，就如同網誌中的主角們，像是被點到笑穴一樣，說什麼都覺得好笑。網誌裡用到了幾個關於『笑』的說法，以下為您一一道來：

crack up　　捧腹大笑，笑到崩潰

crack sb up　　（讓某人）捧腹大笑

例: Mark made faces that really cracked me up.

（馬克扮的鬼臉讓我笑死了。）

　　＊make faces　　扮鬼臉

laugh [læf] *vi.* 笑

laugh at...　　嘲笑……

例: Everyone laughed at Adam's idea of becoming a famous singer.

（每個人都嘲笑亞當想成為歌星的想法。）

chuckle [ˈtʃʌkḷ] *vi.* 輕聲地笑；暗自發笑

例: The girls started to chuckle when they saw a man wearing pink pants.

（那些女孩看到一個穿粉紅長褲的男人時，開始偷笑了起來。）

不管是中文還是英文，『笑』都是有分程度的。除了上述幾種，我們可能還會『微笑』（smile [smaɪl]）、『露齒而笑』（grin [grɪn]）、『傻笑、咯咯地笑』（giggle [ˈgɪgḷ]）、『冷笑』（sneer [snɪr]）和『爆笑』（burst into laughter = burst out laughing）。不管是哪一種笑，記得天天笑口常開，好運自然會跟著來！

例: When Bob saw his brother with his zipper down, he burst out laughing.

（鮑伯看到他弟弟拉鏈沒拉時，爆笑了出來。）

　　＊zipper [ˈzɪpɚ] *n.* 拉鍊

字 詞 幫幫忙！

1. All good things must come to an end.
天下無不散的筵席 / 花無百日紅。

come to an end　　結束

例: Fred and Ricky's business partnership came to an end last month.
（佛瑞德和瑞奇在生意上的合作關係於上個月結束了。）
＊partnership [`partnɚˌʃɪp] *n.* 合作關係

2. **reminisce** [ˌrɛmə`nɪs] *vi.* 回想
reminisce about...　　回想……
例: May always reminisces about her high school sweetheart when she hears this song.
（小梅聽到這首歌時總會想起她高中時的情人。）

3. **spill** [spɪl] *vt.* 潑，灑；使溢出
三態為：spill, spilled / spilt [spɪlt], spilled / spilt。
例: The little kid spilled a glass of juice on his mother's white skirt.
（那個小朋友把一杯果汁灑到他媽媽的白裙子上。）

4. **overpay** [ˌovɚ`pe] *vi.* 多付錢
例: Kent was furious when he found out he overpaid for his new laptop.
（肯特發現他的新筆電買貴了時非常生氣。）
＊furious [`fjurɪəs] *a.* 憤怒的
laptop [`læpˌtɑp] *n.* 筆記型電腦（= laptop computer）
desktop [`dɛskˌtɑp] *n.* 桌上型電腦（= desktop computer）

5. **souvenir** [`suvəˌnɪr] *n.* 紀念品
例: Anita brought back some souvenirs for us from her trip to Paris.
（艾妮塔從她的巴黎之行帶回了一些紀念品給我們。）

6. **check in**　　辦理登機 / 住房手續
例: You'd better check in at least one hour before the plane takes off.
（你最好在飛機起飛前至少一小時先辦理登機。）
＊take off　　（飛機）起飛
After checking in at the hotel, Emily came to meet us right away.
（艾蜜莉在飯店登記入住後，就立刻來和我們會合。）

Unit 8

The Unexpected Always Happens

Index | Links | about | comments | Photo

July 27

Today, I was waiting at the bus stop when an **elderly** man stepped into the road, causing a bus to **come to a screeching halt**. Then, the bus wouldn't start up again. What's even worse, the bus **blocked** the street, so other buses couldn't get by. When I got to work late, I explained to my boss that it was the old man's **fault** and not mine. So I guess you could say that I <u>**threw**</u> the elderly man <u>**under the bus**</u>!

About me

Tom

Calendar

◄　　　　*July*　　　　►

Sun	Mon	Tue	Wed	Thu	Fri	Sat
		1	2	3	4	5
6	7	8	9	10	11	12
13	14	15	16	17	18	19
20	21	22	23	24	25	26
27	28	29	30	31		

Blog Archive

► July (27)
► June
► May
► April
► March
► February
► January
► December
► November
► October
► September
► August

Tom at Blog 於 July 07.27. PM 5:55 發表 | 回覆 (0) | 引用 (0) | 收藏 (0) | 轉寄給朋友 | 檢舉

天有不測風雲

July 27

　　今天我在公車站牌等車時,有一個老先生走到馬路上,使得公車緊急煞車。接著公車就無法再發動。更糟的是,公車堵住街道,所以其他公車無法通過。我到公司時已經遲到了,我向老闆解釋這一切都是老先生的錯,跟我無關。所以我想你可以說我讓這位老先生作了我的代罪羔羊。

Tom at Blog 於 July 07.27. PM 5:55 發表｜回覆 (0)｜引用 (0)｜收藏 (0)｜轉寄給朋友｜檢舉

網誌中的場景雖然是在公車站，但文中所說的 throw sb under the bus 可不是真的把人推到公車底下，而是指為了保護自己而犧牲或出賣別人，也就是『使某人成為代罪羔羊』或『讓某人揹黑鍋』。然而這樣的行為，倒是把別人一腳踢到公車下成為替死鬼沒什麼兩樣。

throw sb under the bus　　使某人成為代罪羔羊，讓某人揹黑鍋

例: The party <u>threw</u> its leader <u>under the bus</u> for losing the election.

= The party <u>blamed</u> its leader for losing the election.

（該政黨把這次選舉失利推在黨主席身上。）

　　＊blame [blem] *vt.* 責備，指責

　　　blame sb for sth　　因某事責備某人

表『替死鬼』的的說法則為：

scapegoat [`skep,ɡot] *n.* 代罪羔羊，替死鬼

例: The celebrity was made a scapegoat in the murder trial.

（那位名人在這樁謀殺案的審判中成了代罪羔羊。）

　　＊suspect [`sʌspɛkt] *n.* 嫌犯

1.　elderly [`ɛldə·lɪ] *a.* 年長的

　　the elderly　　年長者

= elderly people

　　例: Nancy is such a good girl that she always gives her seat to the elderly on the bus.

　　　（南西是個好女孩，她搭公車時總會把自己的座位讓給老人家。）

2.　come to a screeching halt　　緊急煞車

= screech to a halt

　　screech [skritʃ] *vi.* 發出尖銳刺耳聲

　　halt [hɔlt] *n.* 停止

注意:

come to a screeching halt 或 screech to a halt 是指車輛因緊急煞車突然停下來（常伴有刺耳的輪胎摩擦聲）；而 grind to a halt 是指車輛等慢慢停下來；skid to a halt 則是指車輛因天雨或下雪打滑至一邊停下。

＊grind [graɪnd] *vi.* 研磨，磨碎（三態為：grind, ground [graʊnd], ground）

skid [skɪd] *vi.* 滑行

例: The train screeched to a halt and left several passengers injured.

（火車突然緊急煞車，造成數名乘客受傷。）

The taxi ground to a halt to pick the passenger up.

（那輛計程車慢慢停下來好讓乘客上車。）

＊pick sb up / pick up sb　　搭載某人

The car skidded to a halt on the icy road.

（那輛轎車在結冰的路上打滑而停下來。）

3. **block** [blɑk] *vt.* 阻擋，堵塞

例: The tall man in front of me is blocking my view.

（在我前方的高大男子擋住了我的視線。）

4. **fault** [fɔlt] *n.* 錯誤，過錯

be at fault　　有過錯；應當負責

= be in the wrong

find fault with...　　對……吹毛求疵，挑剔……

例: No one was at fault in the accident.

（這次意外誰都沒有錯。）

David is hard to get along with because he always finds fault with others.

（大衛很難相處，因為他老是挑剔他人。）

Martha was fed up with her husband finding fault with her cooking.

（瑪莎受夠了她老公總是對她煮的菜嫌東嫌西。）

＊be fed up with...　　受夠了／厭煩……

Lost in the City

Index | *Links* | *about* | *comments* | *Photo*

July 28

I **was supposed to** meet Heidi at a restaurant in a part of town I **was** not **familiar with**. I knew I **was lost** right after leaving the MRT, but I tried to <u>**keep my head**</u> and **asked** a **vendor for directions**. He told me I should go left. Then, after walking for 10 minutes, I asked another vendor. She **added fuel to the fire** and told me I missed the place because it was right by the MRT. **It turned out that** I was late by about a half hour.

About me

Tom

Calendar

◀ *July* ▶

Sun	Mon	Tue	Wed	Thu	Fri	Sat
		1	2	3	4	5
6	7	8	9	10	11	12
13	14	15	16	17	18	19
20	21	22	23	24	25	26
27	28	29	30	31		

Blog Archive

- ► July (28)
- ► June
- ► May
- ► April
- ► March
- ► February
- ► January
- ► December
- ► November
- ► October
- ► September
- ► August

Tom at Blog 於 July 07.28. PM 09:02 發表 | 回覆 (0) | 引用 (0) | 收藏 (0) | 轉寄給朋友 | 檢舉

July 28

　　我和海蒂要在一間餐廳碰面，那間餐廳位在城裡一處我不熟悉的地方。一離開捷運站後，我就知道自己迷路了，不過我設法保持鎮靜，向小販問路。他告訴我應該要向左走。然後走了 10 分鐘後，我又問了另一位小販。她告訴我說我已錯過那個地方，因為它就在捷運站旁而已，她的這席話簡直就是火上加油。結果我遲到了快半個小時。

Tom at Blog 於 July 07.28. PM 09:02 發表 | 回覆 (0) | 引用 (0) | 收藏 (0) | 轉寄給朋友 | 檢舉

迷路時最怕因為慌張而亂了陣腳，所謂『路長在嘴上』，如果真的不認得路，就應該像網誌作者一樣 keep one's head（保持鎮靜），然後向他人問路即可。『保持鎮靜』的說法除了 keep one's head，還可等於下列片語：

keep one's head 保持冷靜，保持鎮靜

= keep one's cool

= remain / stay calm

＊calm [kɑm] *a.* 鎮靜的

例: Sam tried to keep his cool and answer the questions from the company's manager during the interview.

（山姆在面試時，設法保持鎮靜回答公司經理的問題。）

＊interview [ˈɪntəˌvju] *n.* 面試

When Luke was stuck in the elevator, he told himself to stay calm and wait to be rescued.

（路克被困在電梯時，他告訴自己要保持冷靜等待救援。）

＊elevator [ˈɛləˌvetə] *n.* 電梯

rescue [ˈrɛskju] *vt.* 救援

不過要是像作者一樣，遇到搞不清楚狀況的人亂指路，結果繞了一大圈還找不到目的地，還是很有可能因此 lose one's head（失去冷靜）！

lose one's head 失去冷靜，失去理智

= lose one's cool

= lose one's poise

＊poise [pɔɪz] *n.* 鎮靜

例: Marvin almost lost his head when he found out that his girlfriend was dating his good friend.

（馬文發現他女友和他的好友約會時，差點就失去理智。）

1. **lost** [lost] *a.* 迷路的

be / get lost 迷路

例: I don't know which way to go — I'm lost.
（我不知道要走哪條路 —— 我迷路了。）

2. **be supposed to V** 應該……（語氣比 should 委婉些）

例: Jenny was supposed to meet me at eight o'clock, but she didn't show up.
（珍妮應該要在 8 點和我碰面，但她卻沒有出現。）

3. **be familiar with...** 熟悉……

be familiar to sb 對某人而言很熟悉

familiar [fəˈmɪljɚ] *a.* 熟悉的

例: The new worker isn't familiar with the company rules.
（那位新來的員工不熟悉公司的規定。）

The story of *Snow White* is familiar to most children in Taiwan.
（《白雪公主》的故事對大多數台灣的孩子而言都很熟悉。）

4. **ask sb for directions** 向某人問路

directions [dəˈrɛkʃənz] *n.* 行路的指引（恆用複數）

例: Paul pulled over his car and asked a police officer for directions.
（保羅把車開到路邊，向一位警察問路。）

＊pull over... 把……開到路邊

5. **vendor** [ˈvɛndɚ] *n.* 攤販

a street vendor 路邊小販

6. **add fuel to the fire** 火上加油

fuel [ˈfjuəl] *n.* 燃料

例: Andy's remark added fuel to the fire and caused a lot of trouble.
（安迪的言論火上加油，引起了很多麻煩。）

7. **It turns out + that** 子句 結果（竟然）……

例: It turned out that Kent was the one who stole the watch.
（結果肯特居然是那個偷錶的人。）

Catch-22

July 29

As I was walking down the street **the other day**, I **spotted** a NT$1,000 bill on the ground. At first, I thought I had just **lucked out**. But then, as I looked at the bill, I felt it was a Catch-22. If I picked it up, I would be happy, but someone would have lost some cash. **On the other hand**, if I left it there, I'd be **upset** because maybe the real owner wouldn't find it before someone else took it.

About me

Tom

Calendar

◄   *July*   ►

Sun	Mon	Tue	Wed	Thu	Fri	Sat
		1	2	3	4	5
6	7	8	9	10	11	12
13	14	15	16	17	18	19
20	21	22	23	24	25	26
27	28	29	30	31		

Blog Archive

- ► July (29)
- ► June
- ► May
- ► April
- ► March
- ► February
- ► January
- ► December
- ► November
- ► October
- ► September
- ► August

Tom at Blog 於 July 07.29. PM 10:30 發表 | 回覆 (0) | 引用 (0) | 收藏 (0) | 轉寄給朋友 | 檢舉

進退兩難

July 29

　　前幾天我走在路上，發現地上有一張千元台幣大鈔。起先我覺得自己真走運。可是後來當我走上前看著鈔票，發現自己陷入兩難的情況。我若撿了錢會很開心，但就會有人損失一筆錢。話又說回來，我若把錢留在那裡就會很懊惱，因為或許在真正的失主找到之前，別人已經把它撿走了。

About me

Tom

Calendar

◄　　　　*July*　　　　►

Sun	Mon	Tue	Wed	Thu	Fri	Sat
			1	2	3	4	5
6	7	8	9	10	11	12
13	14	15	16	17	18	19
20	21	22	23	24	25	26
27	28	29	30	31		

Blog Archive

▸ July (29)
▸ June
▸ May
▸ April
▸ March
▸ February
▸ January
▸ December
▸ November
▸ October
▸ September
▸ August

Tom at Blog 於 July 07.29. PM 10:30 發表 | 回覆 (0) | 引用 (0) | 收藏 (0) | 轉寄給朋友 | 檢舉

網誌標題出現的 Catch-22 是其來有自的。美國作家赫勒（Joseph Heller）於 1961 年發表的小說中，主角是二次大戰中美國空軍轟炸機飛行員，在目睹身邊多位戰友死亡後決定退役，為此他必須假裝自己得了精神病。但這違反第二十二條軍規。該條軍規規定：精神病者可以退役，但必須由本人提出申請。而懂得提出申請的人一定不會是精神病者。這本小說被譽為美國最偉大的作品之一。此後 Catch-22 也成了美式英語中『自相矛盾、進退維谷』的代稱。

例: The man's Catch-22 was that he was in love with his best friend's wife. If he told her, he would lose them both.

（這名男子因為愛上死黨的老婆，所以面臨進退兩難的局面。如果他跟她表白，那他兩者都會失去。）

此外，還可以用 be (caught) in a dilemma 來表示『處在進退兩難 / 左右為難的情況中』。

be (caught) in a dilemma　　處在進退兩難 / 左右為難的情況中
dilemma [dəˋlɛmə] n. 進退兩難；困境

例: Tom was caught in a dilemma — should he hire his sister or his best friend?

（湯姆陷於左右為難的處境 —— 他該雇用自己的妹妹還是最好的朋友？）

1. **the other day**　　前些時候（用於過去式）
   some other day　　改天（用於未來式）
   例: Olivia told me that she was followed by a weird guy the other day.

   （奧莉維亞跟我說她前幾天被一個奇怪的男子跟蹤。）

   ＊weird [wɪrd] a. 怪異的

   I'm sorry, but I can't go to the movies with you tonight. Let's go some other day.

   （很抱歉今晚不能和你去看電影。咱們改天再去吧。）

2. **spot** [spɑt] *vt.* 無意間見到，發現 & *n.* 地點

   on the spot 　　當場

   例: I spotted John walking into the building.

   （我看見阿強走進這棟大樓。）

   The boy was caught stealing a toy on the spot.

   （這男孩偷玩具時當場被逮個正著。）

3. **luck out** 　　走運

   例: Ryan really lucked out. He invested at just the right time and made a lot of money.

   （萊恩真走運。適時投資讓他大賺一筆。）

   ＊invest [ɪnˋvɛst] *vi.* 投資

4. **on the other hand** 　　另一方面來說；話又說回來

   注意:

   on the other hand 常與 on one hand 並用，形成下列用法：

   on (the) one hand...on the other (hand)...

   一方面……另一方面……

   例: This job does pay a lot of money. But on the other hand, it also involves a lot of stress.

   （這份工作的薪水不少；但話說回來，它的壓力也很大。）

   I don't know if you should date John. On one hand, he is a nice guy. On the other, he's ugly.

   （我不知道妳該不該跟阿強約會。一方面他是個好好先生，另一方面他卻長相欠佳。）

5. **upset** [ʌpˋsɛt] *a.* 生氣的，苦惱的；難過的，不舒服的

   例: I was upset when I realized my girlfriend had lied to me.

   （發現女友對我說謊時，我很不爽。）

   Walter was suffering from an upset stomach because he had the flu.

   （華特因為得了流行性感冒所以腸胃不適。）

   ＊suffer from... 　　受……之苦；罹患……（疾病）

What's That Smell

Index | Links | about | comments | Photo

July 30

As I got on my **scooter**, I stepped in **a pile of** dog **poop**. I was **furious** at my neighbor for letting his dog poop next to my scooter and **having the nerve** not **to** clean it up. I **wiped** my shoe on the grass to **get rid of** it and thought I was OK. However, the moment I walked into my office, the secretary yelled, "Who's **stinking up** the place? It smells like a dirty **diaper**!"

About me

Tom

Calendar

◄   *July*   ►

Sun	Mon	Tue	Wed	Thu	Fri	Sat
		1	2	3	4	5
6	7	8	9	10	11	12
13	14	15	16	17	18	19
20	21	22	23	24	25	26
27	28	29	30	31		

Blog Archive

▸ July (30)
▸ June
▸ May
▸ April
▸ March
▸ February
▸ January
▸ December
▸ November
▸ October
▸ September
▸ August

Tom at Blog 於 July 07.30. PM 05:45 發表 | 回覆 (0) | 引用 (0) | 收藏 (0) | 轉寄給朋友 | 檢舉

什麼味道這麼臭？

July 30

　　就在我騎上機車之際，我踩到一坨狗屎。我被我的鄰居氣死了，他居然讓自家的狗在我的機車旁大便，卻沒有膽把它清乾淨。我在草坪上用草把鞋子上的狗屎清掉，然後我就以為沒事了。然而，我一走進辦公室，秘書就大叫：『是誰把這裡搞得這麼臭？聞起來像是沾了大便的尿布。』

About me

Tom

Calendar

◄　　　*July*　　　►

Sun	Mon	Tue	Wed	Thu	Fri	Sat
		1	2	3	4	5
6	7	8	9	10	11	12
13	14	15	16	17	18	19
20	21	22	23	24	25	26
27	28	29	30	31		

Blog Archive

▸ July (30)
▸ June
▸ May
▸ April
▸ March
▸ February
▸ January
▸ December
▸ November
▸ October
▸ September
▸ August

Tom at Blog 於 July 07.30. PM 05:45 發表 | 回覆 (0) | 引用 (0) | 收藏 (0) | 轉寄給朋友 | 檢舉

網誌中出現的 nerve [nɝv] 原指『神經』，為可數名詞，有下列用法：

get on one's nerves 　使某人心煩，使某人心神不寧

例: My mom's nagging really gets on my nerves.

（老媽的嘮叨實在搞得我心煩。）

　＊nagging [ˋnægɪŋ] *n.* 嘮叨

nerve 亦可作不可數名詞，表『勇氣』，即等於 courage [ˋkɝɪdʒ]，網誌中所提的 have the nerve to V 就是『有勇氣做……』之意。

have the nerve to V 　有勇氣做……
= have the courage to V
= have the guts to V

　＊guts [gʌts] *n.* 勇氣（恆為複數）

例: I don't have the nerve to tell Marry that I want to break up with her.

（我沒有勇氣告訴瑪莉我想和她分手。）

　＊break up with sb 　和某人分手

如果要表『鼓起勇氣』，則可用下列句構：

get up one's nerve to V 　某人鼓起勇氣做……
= pluck up one's courage to V

　＊pluck [plʌk] *vt.* 鼓（勇氣）；拔（雞毛）

例: Paul got up his nerve to ask Eva to dance with him.

= 　Paul plucked up his courage to ask Eva to dance with him.

（保羅鼓起勇氣邀伊娃與他共舞。）

字詞幫幫忙！

1. **scooter** [ˋskutɚ] *n.* 小機車（俗稱『小綿羊』）
   motorcycle [ˋmotɚ͵saɪkl̩] *n.* 摩托車

2. **a pile of...** 　一堆……
   pile [paɪl] *n.* 堆
   例: I had a big pile of paperwork to do after my long vacation.
   （度完長假後我有一大堆的文書要處理。）

3. **poop** [pup] *n.* 排泄物 & *vi.* 排便（口語，是 shit 的文雅說法）
   dog poop   狗屎

4. **furious** [ˈfjʊrɪəs] *a.* 憤怒的
   be furious at / with sb   對某人生氣
   = be angry with sb
   = be mad at sb
   be furious at sth   對某事感到憤怒
   = be angry at sth
   例: Jerry was furious at / with himself for failing the test.
   （傑瑞很氣自己沒考及格。）

   Ted was furious at his son's bad manners.
   （泰德對他兒子的沒禮貌感到很生氣。）
   ＊manners [ˈmænəz] *n.* 禮貌（恆為複數）

5. **wipe** [waɪp] *vt.* 擦去，擦拭
   例: The waitress wiped the table with a wash cloth.
   （這名女服務生用一塊抹布擦桌子。）

6. **get rid of...**   擺脫……，除去……
   例: Harry got rid of some old furniture before he moved into
   his new apartment.
   （哈利在搬進新公寓前丟掉了一些舊傢俱。）
   ＊furniture [ˈfɜnɪtʃə] *n.* 傢俱（集合名詞，不可數）

7. **stink up...**   使……充滿臭味
   stink [stɪŋk] *vt.* 使充滿臭味 & *vi.* 發臭
   stinky [ˈstɪŋkɪ] *a.* 發臭的
   例: The stinky tofu is stinking up the whole room.
   （臭豆腐把整個房間搞得臭氣沖天。）
   ＊stinky tofu   臭豆腐
   Would you throw away these old shoes? They stink!
   （你能不能丟掉這些舊鞋子？它們臭死了！）

8. **diaper** [ˈdaɪpə] *n.* 尿布

Speaking ill

Index | Links | about | comments | Photo

July 31

Today my manager took me into his office and told me I was lazy. I **bristled with rage** but just put my head down and walked away. Later in the day, I went to **take a leak** and saw Jim in the bathroom. I told him what had happened and really <u>**talked bad about**</u> my manager. Just then, I heard a **toilet flush** and the manager came out. He told me that I should **watch my mouth** and not speak ill of others.

About me

Tom

Calendar

◄   *July*   ►

Sun	Mon	Tue	Wed	Thu	Fri	Sat
		1	2	3	4	5
6	7	8	9	10	11	12
13	14	15	16	17	18	19
20	21	22	23	24	25	26
27	28	29	30	31		

Blog Archive

- ▸ July (31)
- ▸ June
- ▸ May
- ▸ April
- ▸ March
- ▸ February
- ▸ January
- ▸ December
- ▸ November
- ▸ October
- ▸ September
- ▸ August

Tom at Blog 於 July 07.31. PM 03:28 發表 | 回覆 (0) | 引用 (0) | 收藏 (0) | 轉寄給朋友 | 檢舉

說人壞話

July 31

今天經理把我帶進他的辦公室，跟我說我很懶惰。我很憤怒，但只是頭低低地離開。那天稍後我去撇小條，看到吉姆在洗手間裡。我告訴他發生的事，並狠狠地說了一頓關於經理的壞話。就在那時，我聽到馬桶的沖水聲，接著經理走出來。他說我說話應該要當心點，不要說別人的壞話。

About me

Tom

Calendar

◄   *July*   ►

Sun	Mon	Tue	Wed	Thu	Fri	Sat
		1	2	3	4	5
6	7	8	9	10	11	12
13	14	15	16	17	18	19
20	21	22	23	24	25	26
27	28	29	30	**31**		

Blog Archive

▸ July (31)
▸ June
▸ May
▸ April
▸ March
▸ February
▸ January
▸ December
▸ November
▸ October
▸ September
▸ August

Tom at Blog 於 July 07.31. PM 03:28 發表 | 回覆 (0) | 引用 (0) | 收藏 (0) | 轉寄給朋友 | 檢舉

網誌作者說了經理的壞話，結果不小心被本人聽到，真的是糗大了。那麼說人壞話、詆毀某人的英文該怎樣說呢？就是 speak ill of sb。這裡的 ill [ɪl] 當副詞，表『不友善地；惡劣地』。如果想要強調背著某人說他的壞話，就在 speak ill of sb 後加上 behind one's back，變成 speak ill of sb behind one's back 就可以了。以下為『說壞話、道是非』的綜合整理：

speak ill of sb　　說某人壞話
= talk bad about sb

speak ill of sb behind his / her back
在背後說某人壞話（back 需配合單複數變化使用）

talk behind sb's back　　背著某人說他閒話（back 需配合單複數變化使用）

bad-mouth [ˈbædˌmaʊθ] *vt.* 說⋯⋯壞話

例: I heard John speaking ill of you behind your back yesterday.
（我昨天聽到約翰背著你說你的壞話。）

Tina is the kind of person who loves to talk about others behind their backs.
（蒂娜是那種喜歡在背後說人閒話的人。）

Kelly told Max that he'd better stop bad-mouthing her.
（凱莉跟麥克斯說他最好停止說她壞話。）

字 詞幫幫忙！

1. **bristle with rage / anger**　　火冒三丈

   bristle [ˈbrɪsl] *vi.* 發怒

   bristle 原為名詞，表『豬鬃』或動物背上的『短毛』。動物發火時，背上的短毛就會豎立起來，因此 bristle 作動詞用時，可引申為『發怒』之意，常與 with rage / anger 搭配使用。

   rage [redʒ] *n.* 憤怒

例: Walter bristled with rage as he saw the damage to his
new car.
（華特看到自己新車受到的損壞時，氣得火冒三丈。）

2. **take a leak**　　撒小條，小便（俚語，限男性使用，為較粗魯的說法）
leak [lik] *n. & vi.* 滲漏，漏（水、油、瓦斯等）
go for / have / take a pee　　上小號（口語用法）
＊pee [pi] *n. & vi.* 小便（口語）
例: Frank said he needed to take a leak before leaving, so
we had to wait for him.
（法蘭克說在離開前他得先去小個便，所以我們必須等他。）
Gas that is leaking can easily cause an explosion.
（漏氣的瓦斯很容易引起爆炸。）
＊explosion [ɪkˋsploʒən] *n.* 爆炸

3. **toilet** [ˋtɔɪlɪt] *n.* 馬桶；化妝室，廁所（英）

4. **flush** [flʌʃ] *n. & vt.* 沖水；沖洗
flush the toilet　　沖馬桶
例: Don't forget to flush the toilet after you finish using it.
（上完廁所後別忘了沖馬桶。）
I flushed the dirt out of my eye with some water.
（我用些水沖掉眼睛裡的灰塵。）
＊dirt [dɝt] *n.* 泥土；灰塵

5. **watch one's mouth**　　說話當心點（用於告訴某人要小心說話）
watch one's back　　防範背後；小心，謹慎
例: Watch your mouth, Darren. What you just said was really
rude.
（說話當心點，戴倫。你剛說的話非常無禮。）
You'd better watch your back. I heard James wants to
fight you.
（你最好小心點，我聽說詹姆士想找你打架。）

Don't Panic!

Index | *Links* | *about* | *comments* | *Photo*

August 01

The **elevator** stopped suddenly between floors, and the lights **went out**. All the people inside it with me were **terrified** and started **pounding** on the door. One woman really **freaked out**. She said she **was scared of** small spaces and then started yelling **at the top of her lungs**. After five minutes, the man on the other side of me asked her if she could **zip** it. She **ignored** him and screamed until we were **rescued**.

About me

Tom

Calendar

◄   *August*   ►

Sun	Mon	Tue	Wed	Thu	Fri	Sat
					1	2
3	4	5	6	7	8	9
10	11	12	13	14	15	16
17	18	19	20	21	22	23
24	25	26	27	28	29	30
31						

Blog Archive

► August (1)
► July
► June
► May
► April
► March
► February
► January
► December
► November
► October
► September

Tom at Blog 於 August 08.01. PM 04:37 發表 | 回覆 (0) | 引用 (0) | 收藏 (0) | 轉寄給朋友 | 檢舉

別驚慌

August 01

　　電梯在兩層樓的中間突然停下來，電燈也熄了。包括我在內，電梯裡所有人都嚇壞了，並且開始敲打電梯門。一位女士真的嚇壞了。她說自己害怕狹小的空間，隨後便放聲大叫。5 分鐘後，在我另外一邊的先生問她是否可以閉上嘴巴。她不理他，繼續叫到我們被救出去為止。

About me

Tom

Calendar

◄　　*August*　　►

Sun	Mon	Tue	Wed	Thu	Fri	Sat
					1	2
3	4	5	6	7	8	9
10	11	12	13	14	15	16
17	18	19	20	21	22	23
24	25	26	27	28	29	30
31						

Blog Archive

- ► August (1)
- ► July
- ► June
- ► May
- ► April
- ► March
- ► February
- ► January
- ► December
- ► November
- ► October
- ► September

Tom at Blog 於 August 08.01. PM 04:37 發表 | 回覆 (0) | 引用 (0) | 收藏 (0) | 轉寄給朋友 | 檢舉

freak [frik] 原為名詞，表『怪人』之意。但 freak 作動詞時則表『害怕』，與 out 搭配使用，表『（使）嚇得要死』的意思。以下介紹關於『嚇得要死』的相關用法：

freak out	嚇得要死
freak sb out	把某人嚇得要死，嚇壞某人
scare sb to death	把某人嚇得要死
be scared to death	被嚇得要死
scare sb out of his / her wits	某人被嚇得魂不附體
be scared out of his / her wits	被嚇得魂不附體

＊wit [wɪt] *n.* 理智

例: The sight of a large snake in her bathtub freaked Gina out.

（看到浴缸裡有隻大蛇把吉娜給嚇壞了。）

＊bathtub [ˋbæθˏtʌb] *n.* 浴缸

If I see that movie, I know I'll be scared out of my wits.

（我知道如果我看那部電影，一定會被嚇得魂都沒了。）

字詞幫幫忙！

1. **panic** [ˋpænɪk] *vi.* 驚慌，慌張 & *n.* 驚恐

   本字過去式及過去分詞形為 panicked；現在分詞及動名詞形為 panicking。

   in (a) panic　　驚慌失措的

   例: Tanya panicked at the sound of the fire alarm.

   （譚雅聽到火警鈴聲大作時非常驚慌。）

   ＊alarm [əˋlɑrm] *n.* 警報器

   We were all in panic when the 921 earthquake struck.

   （921 地震發生時，我們全都驚慌失措。）

2. **elevator** [ˋɛləˏvetɚ] *n.* 電梯

   escalator [ˋɛskəˏletɚ] *n.* 電扶梯

3. go out　（燈、火）熄滅

例: We were watching TV when the light suddenly went out.
（我們在看電視時電燈突然熄了。）

4. terrified [ˈtɛrəˌfaɪd] *a.* 感到害怕 / 恐懼的

5. pound [paʊnd] *vi.* & *vt.* 猛力敲打；猛擊

例: My brother pounded on the door with his fists because he was angry.

= My brother pounded his fists on the door because he was angry.
（我弟弟因為生氣而用雙拳猛捶房門。）

＊fist [fɪst] *n.* 拳頭

6. be scared of...　害怕……

= be afraid of...
= be frightened of...
= be terrified of...

例: Karen is scared of her father's temper.
（凱倫很怕她爸爸發脾氣。）

7. at the top of one's lungs　用某人最大音量

lung [lʌŋ] *n.* 肺

例: I yelled at the top of my lungs, but Frank still didn't hear me.
（我使盡全力地喊，但法蘭克還是沒聽到我的聲音。）

8. zip [zɪp] *vt.* 閉上（嘴巴）；拉開 / 拉上拉鍊

zipper [ˈzɪpɚ] *n.* 拉鍊

zip your lip　別開口

例: You'd better zip your lip or the teacher will yell at you.
（你最好別開口，否則老師要對你大吼了。）

9. ignore [ɪgˈnɔr] *vt.* 忽視；不理睬

例: When people I don't know talk to me on the street, I just ignore them.
（有陌生人在街上和我說話時，我一概置之不理。）

10. rescue [ˈrɛskju] *vt.* 援救

Where Is My Head

Index | Links | about | comments | Photo

August 02

I usually leave work as soon as the clock **strikes** six so that I can go home and exercise in the park near my apartment. The problem today was that when I got home, I realized I had **locked** my keys in my apartment. I went down to my **landlord's** place on the fifth floor and asked him for his **spare** keys. He told me, **"If your head weren't attached to your body, you might forget it."**

About me

Tom

Calendar

◄   *August*   ►

Sun	Mon	Tue	Wed	Thu	Fri	Sat
					1	2
3	4	5	6	7	8	9
10	11	12	13	14	15	16
17	18	19	20	21	22	23
24	25	26	27	28	29	30
31						

Blog Archive

- ► August (2)
- ► July
- ► June
- ► May
- ► April
- ► March
- ► February
- ► January
- ► December
- ► November
- ► October
- ► September

Tom at Blog 於 August 08.02. PM 09:56 發表 | 回覆 (0) | 引用 (0) | 收藏 (0) | 轉寄給朋友 | 檢舉

我的腦袋呢？

August 02

　　通常 6 點一到，我就會準時下班，這樣我才能回家去公寓附近的公園運動。但今天有個問題就是：我到家時發現自己竟然把鑰匙留在家裡了。我跑下去 5 樓找房東，跟他拿備用鑰匙。他說：『要不是你的頭黏在你的身體上，你可能連頭也會忘記帶。』

About me

Tom

Calendar

◄　　*August*　　►

Sun	Mon	Tue	Wed	Thu	Fri	Sat
					1	2
3	4	5	6	7	8	9
10	11	12	13	14	15	16
17	18	19	20	21	22	23
24	25	26	27	28	29	30
31						

Blog Archive

▸ August (2)
▸ July
▸ June
▸ May
▸ April
▸ March
▸ February
▸ January
▸ December
▸ November
▸ October
▸ September

Tom at Blog 於 August 08.02. PM 09:56 發表│回覆 (0)│引用 (0)│收藏 (0)│轉寄給朋友│檢舉

attach 表『繫住、固定、使附著』，而在網誌中，房東跟作者開玩笑說："If your head weren't attached to your body, you might forget it."（要不是你的頭黏在你的身體上，你可能連頭也會忘記帶。）這種表達方式雖非固定用法，但卻是外國人常用來表示某人粗心健忘的玩笑話。

attach [əˋtætʃ] *vt.* 繫住；固定；使附著（與介詞 to 並用）
be attached to...　　 固定在 / 附著在……上
attach A to B　　　 將 A 繫在 / 固定在 B 上
例: There is a trailer attached to this truck.
　　（這輛卡車後面連結著一輛拖車。）
　　＊trailer [ˋtrelɚ] *n.* 拖車
　　Jerry attached the speakers to his laptop.
　　（傑瑞將喇叭接到他的筆記型電腦。）

除了上述說法，還可用 forgetful 表『健忘的』，或 absent-minded 表『心不在焉的』。

forgetful [fɚˋgɛtfəl] *a.* 健忘的
be forgetful of...　　 忘記……；對……很健忘
absent-minded [ˏæbsn̩tˋmaɪndɪd] *a.* 健忘的；心不在焉的
例: Ben has to rely on notes a lot because he is rather forgetful.
　　（小班必須常依賴筆記，因為他相當健忘。）
　　Gary was often forgetful of his wife's birthday.
= 　Gary often forgets his wife's birthday.
　　（蓋瑞常常忘記太太的生日。）
　　My absent-minded husband has left our son in the car three times this month.
　　（我那神經很大條的丈夫這個月曾 3 度把兒子留在車子裡。）

1. **strike** [straɪk] *vt.* 敲鐘，報時
　　三態為：strike, struck [strʌk], struck。

strike + 數字 （鐘）敲響……時間

strike the hour 整點報時

例: Cinderella has to leave the party when the clock strikes twelve.

（灰姑娘必須在 12 點鐘聲響起時離開舞會。）

When the clock struck the hour, the train approached the station.

（火車在整點的時候進站。）

＊approach [ə`protʃ] *vt.* 接近，靠近

2. **lock** [lɑk] *vt.* 鎖上 & *n.* 鎖

unlock [ʌn`lɑk] *vt.* 開鎖

例: Rosa used a combination lock for her suitcase.

（羅莎用密碼鎖來鎖她的行李箱。）

＊a combination lock 密碼鎖

combination [ˌkɑmbə`neʃən] *n.* （密碼鎖的）號碼組合

Kent had a hard time unlocking his car door.

（肯特很難打開他的車門鎖。）

3. **landlord** [`lænd͵lɔrd] *n.* 房東

landlady [`lænd͵ledɪ] *n.* 女房東

4. **spare** [spɛr] *a.* 備用的 & *vt.* 騰出

a spare key 備用鑰匙

a spare tire 備胎

例: You should make sure that your car has a spare tire in case of emergency.

（你務必要在車上放備用輪胎以免有緊急狀況發生。）

＊emergency [ɪ`mɝdʒənsɪ] *n.* 緊急情況

Excuse me. Do you have a few minutes to spare?

（不好意思。請問可以挪出幾分鐘給我嗎？）

Unit 15

A Pain in the Neck

Index | Links | about | comments | Photo

Usually, I try to blog about the good things and experiences in my daily life, but not today. My **supervisor** tried to **play a dirty trick on** me today. He told me that he wanted to **increase** my **responsibilities** and send me **on a** two-day **business trip**. But I **heard it through the grapevine** that he just didn't want to go himself because the customer is a real pain in the neck.

Tom

Calendar

Sun	Mon	Tue	Wed	Thu	Fri	Sat
					1	2
3	4	5	6	7	8	9
10	11	12	13	14	15	16
17	18	19	20	21	22	23
24	25	26	27	28	29	30
31						

Blog Archive

▸ August (3)
▸ July
▸ June
▸ May
▸ April
▸ March
▸ February
▸ January
▸ December
▸ November
▸ October
▸ September

Tom at Blog 於 August 08.03. PM 06:18 發表 | 回覆 (0) | 引用 (0) | 收藏 (0) | 轉寄給朋友 | 檢舉

燙手山芋

August 03

通常我會想在部落格上寫一些生活中發生的好事和經歷，不過今天例外。今天我上司想對我耍卑鄙的手段。他告訴我他想要加重我的職責，讓我去出差兩天。但是根據我聽到的小道消息是他自己不想去，因為這個顧客很難搞。

About me

Tom

Calendar

◄　　*August*　　►

Sun	Mon	Tue	Wed	Thu	Fri	Sat
					1	2
3	4	5	6	7	8	9
10	11	12	13	14	15	16
17	18	19	20	21	22	23
24	25	26	27	28	29	30
31						

Blog Archive

- ▸ August (3)
- ▸ July
- ▸ June
- ▸ May
- ▸ April
- ▸ March
- ▸ February
- ▸ January
- ▸ December
- ▸ November
- ▸ October
- ▸ September

Tom at Blog 於 August 08.03. PM 06:18 發表 | 回覆 (0) | 引用 (0) | 收藏 (0) | 轉寄給朋友 | 檢舉

誰都不想遇到難搞的顧客，因為遇到這種事感覺就像被蚊蟲叮到一樣，疼痛難耐卻又揮之不去，所以英文裡才會出現 a pain in the neck 這樣的說法。pain [pen] 表『疼痛、痛苦』，neck [nɛk] 是『脖子』，形容人或事物像是脖子上的疼痛，就表示『令人頭痛 / 很討厭的人或事』。也可以說成 a pain in the ass（ass [æs] 指屁股），但這是較粗俗的說法。

例: Jack is a real pain in the neck because he likes to find fault with others.

（傑克真討人厭，因為他喜歡對人吹毛求疵。）

＊find fault with...　　挑剔……，對……吹毛求疵

fault [fɔlt] *n.* 缺點，毛病

要形容這種討人厭的人或事物，英文裡還有 a thorn in one's flesh。thorn [θɔrn] 表『刺』，flesh [flɛʃ] 表『肉』，本俚語字面上的意思為『肉中刺』，用來形容讓人不快或痛苦的人或事物，就如同中文常說的『眼中釘』。

a thorn in one's flesh　　某人的眼中釘

= a thorn in one's side

例: Mary considers Andy a thorn in her side because he knows so many secrets about her.

（瑪莉覺得安迪就像是她的眼中釘，因為他知道太多有關她的秘密。）

grapevine [ˈgrep͵vaɪn] 表『葡萄藤』，**hear it through the grapevine** 意思就是指『順著葡萄藤而聽到某事』，想像一下彎彎曲曲、藤蔓錯綜複雜的葡萄藤就像八卦網一樣，所以才引申為『從小道消息得知某事』。辦公室待久了總是令人感到無聊，適度的八卦可以增進同事情誼，生活也多了一些交集。如果哪天我們想和同事聊八卦，就可以用 "I heard it through the grapevine that..."（我從小道消息聽說……）來做開場白。

例: I heard it through the grapevine that the company is going to lay off 50 percent of the staff.

= My sources told me that the company is going to lay off 50 percent of the staff.

= A little bird told me that the company is going to lay off 50 percent of the staff.

（我聽說公司將裁員百分之五十。）

＊ source [sɔrs] *n.* 來源

1. supervisor [ˈsupəˌvaɪzə] *n.* 上司
例: Kyle's supervisor was not happy with his work performance.
（凱爾的上司對他的工作表現不滿意。）

2. play a dirty trick on sb　　對某人耍卑劣的詭計
play a trick on sb　　對某人惡作劇／開玩笑
trick [trɪk] *n.* 惡作劇；詭計
例: Mike reminded me to watch out for Kevin because he enjoys playing dirty tricks on others.
（麥克提醒我要提防凱文，因為他很愛對別人耍卑劣的手段。）
＊watch out for...　　留意……
Mary played a trick on her sleeping brother by throwing a water balloon at him.
（瑪莉把水球丟到她正在睡覺的弟弟身上來捉弄他。）

3. increase [ɪnˈkris] *vt.* 增加
decrease [dɪˈkris] *vt.* 減少

4. responsibility [rɪˌspɑnsəˈbɪlətɪ] *n.* 責任
take responsibility for...　　負責……
例: You must take responsibility for the mistake you've made and not just blame others.
（你必須為自己犯的錯負責，而不要只是怪罪他人。）

5. on a business trip　　出差中
注意:
凡表『探險』、『旅遊』、『旅程』等名詞，以及表持續性或時間性的任務或動作時，通常介詞用 on 來表示，如：on duty（執勤、值班）、on an expedition（在探險）、on a hike（在健行）、on leave（休假中）、on a mission（執行任務）、on a picnic（在野餐）、on tour（巡迴演出中）、on a trip（在旅行）等。
例: Jack is on a business trip and won't come back until this Friday.
（傑克去出差，要到這星期五才會回來。）
The band is on tour in Japan right now.
（那支樂團目前正在日本巡迴演出。）

Unit 16

The Traffic Jam Blues

Index | *Links* | *about* | *comments* | *Photo*

August 04

I woke up at five o'clock in the morning today. I thought I had **plenty of** time to pack my bags and get to the airport. What I didn't expect was the traffic. It was a **nightmare**! I didn't arrive at the airport until an hour before my flight was supposed to leave. **To make matters worse**, I **lost my way** in the airport and couldn't find the counter. Luckily, I made it to the gate with five minutes to **spare**.

About me

Tom

Calendar

◄　　　August　　　►

Sun	Mon	Tue	Wed	Thu	Fri	Sat
					1	2
3	4	5	6	7	8	9
10	11	12	13	14	15	16
17	18	19	20	21	22	23
24	25	26	27	28	29	30
31						

Blog Archive

▸ August (4)
▸ July
▸ June
▸ May
▸ April
▸ March
▸ February
▸ January
▸ December
▸ November
▸ October
▸ September

Tom at Blog 於 August 08.04. PM 03:55 發表 | 回覆 (0) | 引用 (0) | 收藏 (0) | 轉寄給朋友 | 檢舉

塞車讓人好鬱卒

August 04

　　我今早 5 點就起床。原以為有充分的時間打包行李和去機場。沒料到的是交通狀況。那真是場惡夢！直到我班機預訂起飛的一小時前我才抵達機場。更糟的是，我在機場裡迷了路，找不到櫃檯。幸好我到達登機門時還剩 5 分鐘。

About me

Tom

Calendar

◄　　　August　　　►

Sun	Mon	Tue	Wed	Thu	Fri	Sat
					1	2
3	4	5	6	7	8	9
10	11	12	13	14	15	16
17	18	19	20	21	22	23
24	25	26	27	28	29	30
31						

Blog Archive

▸ August (4)
▸ July
▸ June
▸ May
▸ April
▸ March
▸ February
▸ January
▸ December
▸ November
▸ October
▸ September

Tom at Blog 於 August 08.04. PM 03:55 發表 | 回覆 (0) | 引用 (0) | 收藏 (0) | 轉寄給朋友 | 檢舉

塞車是許多居住在大城市居民的惡夢。若是在趕時間時碰到塞車，那更是讓人欲哭無淚。那麼『塞車』的英文該怎麼說呢？就是出現在網誌標題的 traffic jam，是可數名詞，也等於 snarl-up。以下就為您介紹各式表『塞車』的英文說法：

traffic jam [ˈtræfɪk ˌdʒæm] *n.* 塞車，交通阻塞（可數名詞，單數時之前應置不定冠詞 a）

= snarl-up [ˈsnɑrlˌʌp] *n.*

　＊jam [dʒæm] *n.* 堵塞，擁擠 & *vt.* 使擁塞

　traffic congestion　　交通阻塞現象（不可數）

　＊congestion [kənˈdʒɛstʃən] *n.* 阻塞（不可數）

　heavy traffic　　繁忙的交通（不可數）

　be / get caught in a traffic jam　　被困在車陣中

= be / get stuck in a traffic jam

　＊be caught in...　　被困在……中

= be stuck in...

　Traffic is jammed.　　塞車了。

例: The reason why Tina was late is that she was caught in a traffic jam.

　　（蒂娜遲到的原因是因為她被困在車陣中。）

　　The bus was delayed for 30 minutes due to the heavy traffic.

　　（這班公車因為繁忙的交通狀況而延誤了半小時。）

　　＊delay [dɪˈle] *vt.* 延誤，耽擱

而通常塞車的情形多發生在上下班交通尖峰時刻，英文就是 rush hour(s)。

例: Traffic is heavy during rush hours.

　　（上下班尖峰時刻，交通流量都很大。）

字 詞 幫幫忙！

1. blues [bluz] *n.* 憂鬱（恆為複數）

　　blue [blu] *a.* 憂鬱的；藍色的

the Monday blues 　　 星期一上班憂鬱症

feel blue 　　 感到憂鬱

例: Betty has been feeling very blue lately. I'm worried about her.

（貝蒂最近一直非常憂鬱。我很擔心她。）

2. **plenty of +** 不可數名詞 / 複數名詞 　　 充分的 / 不少的……

例: Steven won the lottery and now has plenty of money.

（史蒂芬中了樂透，現在很有錢。）

*lottery [ˈlɑtərɪ] *n.* 彩券

Doctors recommend drinking plenty of water if you have a cold.

（醫生建議若患感冒，要補充大量水分。）

3. **nightmare** [ˈnaɪtˌmɛr] *n.* 惡夢，夢魘

例: The little kid woke up from a nightmare, crying for his parents.

（這個小孩從惡夢中驚醒，哭著要找爸媽。）

4. **To make matters worse, S + V** 　　 更糟的是，……

= Even worse, S + V

例: Edward was lost in the mountains. To make matters worse, he had forgotten to bring his cell phone.

（艾德華在山裡迷路。更糟的是，他忘了帶手機。）

5. **lose one's way** 　　 迷路

= get lost

例: The boys lost their way in the woods.

（這些男孩在森林中迷了路。）

6. **spare** [spɛr] *vt.* 剩下；挪出，騰出

例: We had two hours to spare, so we looked around in a gift shop.

（我們還剩下兩個小時，所以就到禮品店逛逛。）

The beggar asked passersby to spare him some change.

（那名乞丐請過路人給他一些零錢。）

*passersby [ˈpæsəˌzˌbaɪ] *n.* 路人（複數形）

passerby [ˈpæsəˌbaɪ] *n.* 路人（單數形）

The Cheapest of the Cheap

Index | *Links* | *about* | *comments* | *Photo*

August 05

My company has never **been known for luxury** business trips, and what happened to me on my trip <u>**sucked**</u>. The hotel I was staying at was really <u>**crappy**</u>. When I saw my room after I checked in, I almost called my boss and quit. It was **extremely** small and didn't even have a window. **Additionally**, there were cigarette **burns** all over the **rug**. When I asked for a different room, they told me there were no **vacancies** left.

About me

Tom

Calendar

◄   August   ►

Sun	Mon	Tue	Wed	Thu	Fri	Sat
					1	2
3	4	5	6	7	8	9
10	11	12	13	14	15	16
17	18	19	20	21	22	23
24	25	26	27	28	29	30
31						

Blog Archive

- ► August (5)
- ► July
- ► June
- ► May
- ► April
- ► March
- ► February
- ► January
- ► December
- ► November
- ► October
- ► September

Tom at Blog 於 August 08.05. PM 07:31 發表 | 回覆 (0) | 引用 (0) | 收藏 (0) | 轉寄給朋友 | 檢舉

爛透了

August 05

　　我的公司向來就不是以豪華的出差待遇聞名，這次出差發生在我身上的事實在糟透了。我投宿的飯店真的有夠爛。當我登記住房後看到房間時，我差一點打電話給我老闆跟他辭職。房間小不拉磯，甚至連個窗戶都沒有。此外，小地毯上到處都是香煙燒過的痕跡。當我要求換另外一間房時，他們告訴我沒有空房了。

Tom at Blog 於 August 08.05. PM 07:31 發表｜回覆 (0)｜引用 (0)｜收藏 (0)｜轉寄給朋友｜檢舉

網誌中的動詞 suck [sʌk] 原本表『吸、吮』，但在俚語中則可作『爛、差勁、糟糕』。而形容事物『糟糕的、差勁的』，除了最常用的形容詞 terrible [ˈtɛrəbl]、horrible [ˈhɔrəbl]、awful [ˈɔfl] 外，還可以像網誌中用 crappy [ˈkræpɪ]。crappy 來自於名詞 crap [kræp] 這個字，為不可數名詞，表『廢物、垃圾』之意。

例: To be honest, this movie really sucks.
（坦白說，這部電影真是糟透了。）

I don't like my new hairstyle. The barber did a crappy job.
（我不喜歡我的新髮型。那個理髮師的手藝真是爛透了。）

These cheaply-made cameras are all crap; they break the first time you use them.
（這些廉價相機都是垃圾；它們只要用一次就壞了。）

1. be known for sth   因某事物而聞名
be known as + 身分 / 稱號   以……身分出名；被稱為……
例: Raymond is known for his unusual voice.
（雷蒙以他特殊的嗓音聞名。）

Sean is known as a very talented writer.
（眾人皆知尚恩是一個很有才華的作家。）
＊talented [ˈtæləntɪd] a. 有才華的

2. luxury [ˈlʌkʃərɪ] a. 豪華的（本字作形容詞用時，始終置於名詞前）
& n. 奢侈品（可數）；奢侈（不可數）
luxurious [lʌgˈʒurɪəs] a. 奢侈的
a luxury hotel   豪華飯店
a luxury suite   豪華套房
a luxury car   豪華轎車
例: Mary keeps buying luxury items. I think she is too wasteful.
（瑪麗狂買奢侈品。我認為她太浪費了。）
＊wasteful [ˈwestfəl] a. 浪費的

We had to give up all luxuries during the financial crisis.
（發生財務危機時，我們必須放棄所有的奢侈品。）

Mr. & Mrs. Wang are used to living in luxury.
（王先生夫婦習慣過著奢侈的生活。）

Most people would like to live in luxurious homes.
（大部分人都想住豪宅。）

3. **extremely** [ɪkˈstrimlɪ] *adv.* 非常地

   例: If you never take a chance, your life will be extremely boring.
   （如果你從不冒險，生命就會平淡無奇。）
   ＊take a chance 　冒險一試

4. **additionally** [əˈdɪʃənəlɪ] *adv.* 此外

= in addition

   例: The rent for my apartment is cheap. Additionally, the location is perfect.
   （我的公寓租金便宜。此外，地點更是棒透了。）
   ＊location [loˈkeʃən] *n.* 地點，位置

5. **burn** [bɝn] *n.* 燒痕 & *vt.* 燃燒

   例: Mary was so angry at John that she burned up all his letters.
   （瑪莉非常氣阿強，所以燒掉所有他寄來的信。）

6. **rug** [rʌg] *n.* 小地毯（尤指放在壁爐前客廳地板上的方毯）
   carpet [ˈkɑrpɪt] *n.* 地毯（指覆蓋全部地板的地毯）

7. **vacancy** [ˈvekənsɪ] *n.* 空房；空缺
   vacant [ˈvekənt] *a.* 空著的；空缺的
   a job vacancy 　職缺

= a job opening

   例: There are still some vacancies at the hotel.
   （旅館尚有一些空房。）

   I think Sam should be suitable for the job vacancy.
= I think Sam should be suitable for the vacant position.
   （我認為山姆應該會適合這個職缺。）

   The house won't be vacant until the end of the month.
   （房子要到月底才會空出來。）

Unit 18

Under the Gun

Index | Links | about | comments | Photo

August 06

I'm **sweating** heavily as I write this. My supervisor didn't give me the full information on the **presentation**, and now he won't **answer his phone** or email. I feel like I'm under the gun because I don't want to do a terrible job for our company. I'm totally **at a loss** but don't really know how to get myself out of this situation. Is there anyone out there who can **get me off the hook**?

About me

Tom

Calendar

◄ August ►

Sun	Mon	Tue	Wed	Thu	Fri	Sat
					1	2
3	4	5	6	7	8	9
10	11	12	13	14	15	16
17	18	19	20	21	22	23
24	25	26	27	28	29	30
31						

Blog Archive

▸ August (6)
▸ July
▸ June
▸ May
▸ April
▸ March
▸ February
▸ January
▸ December
▸ November
▸ October
▸ September

Tom at Blog 於 August 08.06. PM 02:07 發表 | 回覆 (0) | 引用 (0) | 收藏 (0) | 轉寄給朋友 | 檢舉

壓力有夠大

August 06

當我在寫這篇網誌時，正在頻頻冒汗。我的上司非但沒給我報告的完整資訊，他現在也不接我的電話或回email。我不想把公司的業務搞砸，所以壓力超大。我完全不知道該怎麼辦，也不知該如何才能全身而退。到底有沒有人可以讓我脫離這個困境？

About me

Tom

Calendar

◄　　　*August*　　　►

Sun	Mon	Tue	Wed	Thu	Fri	Sat
					1	2
3	4	5	6	7	8	9
10	11	12	13	14	15	16
17	18	19	20	21	22	23
24	25	26	27	28	29	30
31						

Blog Archive

▸ August (6)
▸ July
▸ June
▸ May
▸ April
▸ March
▸ February
▸ January
▸ December
▸ November
▸ October
▸ September

Tom at Blog 於 August 08.06. PM 02:07 發表 | 回覆 (0) | 引用 (0) | 收藏 (0) | 轉寄給朋友 | 檢舉

71

網誌中的男主角所面臨到的簡直就是叫天天不靈、叫地地不應的困境，這時他承受著莫大的壓力，就像是被人用槍（gun [gʌn]）指著一樣，因此英文中才有 be under the gun 一說，來表示某人必須在限定的時間內解決一個問題或完成一項任務，因而承受極大的壓力，就好像有人拿著槍逼著他把事情做完一樣，因此 be under the gun 就用來表示『承受極大的壓力』。

例: Working for a newspaper, Jenny is often under the gun to meet deadlines.

（珍妮在報社上班，常常都得承受截稿的壓力。）

＊deadline [ˈdɛdˌlaɪn] n. 截止期限

表『承受壓力』的說法尚有下列：

be under (a lot of) pressure　　承受（很大的）壓力

pressure [ˈprɛʃɚ] n. 壓力

be stressed out　　壓力過大的

＊stress [strɛs] vt. 使有壓力 & n. 壓力

例: Raising three children by himself, Hal is under a lot of stress.

（哈爾獨立扶養 3 個小孩，因此備感壓力。）

還記得彼得潘（Peter Pan）裡的虎克船長嗎？他的名字之所以叫做虎克（Hook）就是因為他左手的招牌金鉤子，而鉤子的英文便是hook [hʊk]。此外，hook 也可表釣魚的『釣鉤』。試想如果一個人被釣鉤給鉤住了無法逃脫，這時必然期盼有人前來解救，好讓他 off the hook（脫離釣鉤），因此 get sb off the hook 就是『使某人脫困』之意。

例: Kevin got me off the hook by switching his shift with me so that I could go see my son's school play.

（凱文答應和我換班使我脫離困境，好讓我能去看兒子的學校公演。）

＊switch [swɪtʃ] vt. 交換

shift [ʃɪft] n. 輪班

有關 hook 的另一個慣用語為 by hook or (by) crook，表『不擇手段』或『千方百計地』來達到目的。crook [krʊk] 同 hook 表『鉤子』之意，此慣用語的辭源不明，但其中一種說法為：古代的英國莊園園主們只允許佃戶用一種牧羊人的曲柄杖（shepherd's crook），或一把綁在木棒上的彎刀（被稱為 hook）來打下樹枝作為取暖的材料之用，佃戶們便想盡辦法用 hook 或 crook 來砍下樹枝，於是就有了 by hook or (by) crook 這麼一說。

例: Alex will try to get promoted by hook or crook.
（艾力克斯會不擇手段獲得升遷。）
＊promote [prə'mot] vt. 升職

1. **sweat** [swɛt] vi. 流汗 & n. 汗水
   sweat heavily　　汗流浹背，揮汗如雨
   = sweat a lot
   = sweat like a pig
   例: Randy sweats like a pig while driving because his car's air-conditioner is broken.
   （由於車子的冷氣壞了，所以藍迪開車時汗如雨下。）
   ＊air-conditioner ['ɛr,kəndɪʃənə] n. 空調系統；冷氣機

2. **presentation** [,prɛzən'teʃən] n.（口頭）報告；說明
   例: At the end of the school semester, everyone in the class has to give a presentation on the novel.
   （學期末的時候，班上的每個人都必須針對這本小說做口頭報告。）

3. **answer sb's / the phone**　　接（某人的）來電
   answer sb's / the email　　回（某人的）電子郵件
   例: I called Amy last night, but no one answered the phone.
   （我昨晚打給艾咪，但沒人接電話。）

4. **be at a loss**　　困惑，不知所措
   loss [lɔs] n. 迷失
   例: Richard was at a loss when he was diagnosed with cancer.
   （理查被診斷出罹患癌症時，他不知所措。）
   ＊diagnose ['daɪəg,noz] vt. 診斷
   Tom was at a loss for words when he bumped into his ex-wife.
   （湯姆碰到前妻時不知道該說什麼才好。）
   ＊bump into sb　　偶然遇見某人
   = run into sb

Unit 19

It's Over!

Index | *Links* | *about* | *comments* | *Photo*

August 07

I did get to talk to my supervisor before the presentation, and he gave me some **pointers**. The presentation <u>**went off without a hitch**</u>, and I'm 90 percent sure that I have **sealed** the deal. During the meeting, I was **distracted** by the secretary who was **taking notes**. **Afterwards**, I asked her if she wanted to go out for some drinks to **celebrate**. I'm going to **pick** her **up** right now. Thank goodness this day is almost over.

About me

Tom

Calendar

◄   August   ►

Sun	Mon	Tue	Wed	Thu	Fri	Sat
					1	2
3	4	5	6	7	8	9
10	11	12	13	14	15	16
17	18	19	20	21	22	23
24	25	26	27	28	29	30
31						

Blog Archive

- ▸ August (7)
- ▸ July
- ▸ June
- ▸ May
- ▸ April
- ▸ March
- ▸ February
- ▸ January
- ▸ December
- ▸ November
- ▸ October
- ▸ September

Tom at Blog 於 August 08.07. PM 06:43 發表 | 回覆 (0) | 引用 (0) | 收藏 (0) | 轉寄給朋友 | 檢舉

會議結束啦！

August 07

在說明會前，我和主管說到了話，他也給了我一些指示。說明會進行得很順利，而我有九成把握能敲定這筆交易。在開會時，我被那位做筆記的秘書分了心。會議後，我問她是否想出去喝點東西慶祝。我現在正要去接她。謝天謝地，今天終於快結束了。

About me

Tom

Calendar

◄   *August*   ►

Sun	Mon	Tue	Wed	Thu	Fri	Sat
					1	2
3	4	5	6	7	8	9
10	11	12	13	14	15	16
17	18	19	20	21	22	23
24	25	26	27	28	29	30
31						

Blog Archive

▸ August (7)
▸ July
▸ June
▸ May
▸ April
▸ March
▸ February
▸ January
▸ December
▸ November
▸ October
▸ September

Tom at Blog 於 August 08.07. PM 06:43 發表 | 回覆 (0) | 引用 (0) | 收藏 (0) | 轉寄給朋友 | 檢舉

這麼說就對了！

讓人頭大的說明會終於結束，尤其是會議又進展得很順利，一筆大生意眼看就要成交，是該好好慶祝一番！網誌中提到會議進行得很順利使用到 go off without a hitch，hitch [hɪtʃ] 表『障礙、故障』，因此 go off without a hitch 意指事情毫無障礙、順利地進行。

go off without a hitch 進行得很順利

= go off well

= go (off) smoothly

＊smoothly [ˋsmuðlɪ] *adv.* 順利地

例: The dancers practiced day and night to make sure their performance would go off without a hitch.

（這些舞者日以繼夜地練習，以確保表演能順利進行。）

So far, the plan has been going smoothly.

（到目前為止，這項計劃一直進行得很順利。）

 字詞幫幫忙！

1. **pointer** [ˋpɔɪntɚ] *n.* 指示，提示（= hint）

   give sb some pointers 給予某人一些指示／提示

   例: The gym teacher gave us some pointers on shooting basketballs.

   （體育老師給我們一些投籃的指示。）

2. **seal** [sil] *vt.* 確認；封住，密封

   seal the deal 敲定一筆交易

   例: Kent got promoted right after he sealed the deal with a big client.

   （肯特在和大客戶敲定那筆交易後馬上就被升遷了。）

   ＊promote [prəˋmot] *vt.* 晉升

   Gary sealed the letter with glue.

   （蓋瑞用膠水把信封黏住。）

   ＊glue [glu] *n.* 膠水

3. **distract** [dɪˋstrækt] *vt.* 使分心

   distract sb from N/V-ing　　使某人從……分心

   例: A beautiful woman distracted the construction workers
   from their work.

   （一位美女使建築工人分心而無法專心工作。）

   * construction [kənˋstrʌkʃən] *n.* 建築，建造

   The baby's cries distracted the mother from cooking dinner.

   （寶寶的哭聲使她媽媽無法專心煮晚餐。）

4. **take notes**　　做筆記（notes 恆用複數）

   比較:

   take note of...　　注意……

   = take notice of...

   = take heed of...

   * heed [hid] *n.* 留心，注意

   例: Tom never takes notes in class.

   （湯姆上課時從來不抄筆記。）

   Kathy didn't take note of what the teacher said and
   missed the point of the whole lecture.

   （凱西沒注意聽老師說話，因此漏掉了整堂課的重點。）

5. **afterwards** [ˋæftɚwɚdz] *adv.* 之後（= afterward）

   例: Eileen and I went out for dinner. Afterwards, we went to
   the movies.

   （艾琳和我外出吃晚飯。之後便去看電影。）

6. **celebrate** [ˋsɛləˏbret] *vt.* 慶祝

   例: There were around 20 people in Annie's house to
   celebrate her birthday yesterday.

   （昨天安妮家裡大約有 20 個人幫她慶生。）

7. **pick sb up / pick up sb**　　接某人

   例: Jim has to leave earlier today because he is going to pick
   up his wife at the airport.

   （吉姆今天得提早離開，因為他要去機場接他太太。）

Unit 20

The Hair of the Dog

Index | *Links* | *about* | *comments* | *Photo*

August 08

I really need to **work on** being **on time** to airports. Holly the hot secretary and I **hit it off**. We had a great dinner, and the conversation was **fantastic**. She even **dropped a hint** that she was interested in seeing me again. But because I drank so much, I didn't hear the **wake-up call** this morning. I **barely** made it to the airport and now the **flight attendant** is bringing me a cocktail, some "hair of the dog" to help me **cure** my <u>hangover</u>.

About me

Tom

Calendar

◄   August   ►

Sun	Mon	Tue	Wed	Thu	Fri	Sat
					1	2
3	4	5	6	7	8	9
10	11	12	13	14	15	16
17	18	19	20	21	22	23
24	25	26	27	28	29	30
31						

Blog Archive

► August (8)
► July
► June
► May
► April
► March
► February
► January
► December
► November
► October
► September

Tom at Blog 於 August 08.08. PM 01:15 發表 | 回覆 (0) | 引用 (0) | 收藏 (0) | 轉寄給朋友 | 檢舉

再來一杯好解酒

August 08

　　對於準時到達機場這件事，我真的需要多加努力。那位火辣秘書荷莉和我一拍即合。我們吃了頓很棒的晚餐，也聊得很開心。她甚至暗示她有興趣再和我見面。可是因為我喝太多了，我根本沒聽到早上叫我起床的電話鈴聲。我抵達機場時差點就來不及，而現在空服員正給我一杯雞尾酒，就是用來幫助解我宿醉的酒。

About me

Tom

Calendar

◄　　　*August*　　　►

Sun	Mon	Tue	Wed	Thu	Fri	Sat
					1	2
3	4	5	6	7	8	9
10	11	12	13	14	15	16
17	18	19	20	21	22	23
24	25	26	27	28	29	30
31						

Blog Archive

▸ August (8)
▸ July
▸ June
▸ May
▸ April
▸ March
▸ February
▸ January
▸ December
▸ November
▸ October
▸ September

Tom at Blog 於 August 08.08. PM 01:15 發表 | 回覆 (0) | 引用 (0) | 收藏 (0) | 轉寄給朋友 | 檢舉

a / the / some hair of the dog 這句俚語完整的說法其實是 a / the / some hair of the dog that bit you。它的典故出自以前的某個傳說：如果不小心被狗咬傷，只要從咬傷人的那條狗身上取下一些狗毛塗抹在傷口上，就可以治癒。這句話經過演變後，被用來比喻『一個人酩酊大醉之後，隔天早上用來解宿醉（hangover [ˈhæŋˌovɚ]）的一杯酒』。也就是以毒攻毒，以酒解酒的意思。

例：　Brian:　You were so drunk last night.

　　　Daniel:　Yeah, my head aches so much right now. I think some "hair of the dog" would probably make me feel better.

（布萊恩：你昨天真是醉得一塌糊塗。）

（丹尼爾：是啊，我現在頭超痛的。我想再來杯解宿醉的酒能讓我感覺好些。）

Justin had a terrible hangover the day after his birthday party.

（在自己生日派對的隔天，賈斯汀宿醉得很嚴重。）

字 詞幫幫忙！

1. **work on...**　　致力於……

   例: How long have you been working on this project?

   （你花了多少時間在做這個企劃案？）

2. **on time**　　　準時

   in time　　　及時

   例: Thanks to Albert's help, I was able to finish the work on time.

   （多虧艾伯特的幫助，我能準時把工作做完。）

   ＊thanks to...　　多虧／由於……

   We got to the train station just in time to catch the last train home.

   （我們到達火車站，剛好及時趕上回家的最後一班火車。）

3. **hit if off (with sb)**　　（和某人）一拍即合／合得來

   例: I knew you would hit it off with my friend Henry.

   （我就知道妳和我朋友亨利會合得來。）

4. fantastic [fæn'tæstɪk] *a.* 極好的，很棒的

例: That dress looks fantastic on Catherine.
（那件洋裝穿在凱瑟琳身上超好看的。）

5. drop a hint　　作出暗示

hint [hɪnt] *n.* 暗示

例: Teresa dropped a hint about what she wanted for her birthday.
（泰瑞莎暗示她生日想要的禮物。）

6. a wake-up call　　叫人起床的電話（不限於在什麼時間）

a morning call　　（特指）在早上叫人起床的電話

wake up sb / wake sb up　　叫醒某人

例: Phil asked the staff in the hotel to give him a wake-up call at 7:30 p.m.
（菲爾要飯店的員工在晚上 7 點半時打電話叫他起床。）

I have an early meeting tomorrow. Could you please give me a morning call at 6:00?
（我明天有個早會要開。可不可以請你早上 6 點打電話叫我起床？）

7. barely ['bɛrlɪ] *adv.* 幾乎不；勉強

例: David spoke with such a heavy accent that I barely understood him.
（大衛說話的口音很重，我幾乎聽不懂他在說什麼。）

＊accent ['æksənt] *n.* 口音

Martin's income is barely enough for him to support his family.
（馬丁的收入僅勉強夠他養家活口而已。）

8. flight attendant ['flaɪt əˌtɛndənt] *n.* 空服員

9. cure [kjʊr] *vt.* 治癒，治療 & *n.* 治療；療法

cure sb of + 疾病　　治癒某人的某疾病

例: This medicine will cure you of your cough.
（這種藥會治好你的咳嗽。）

Scientists have yet to find a cure for the common cold.
（科學家還沒找到治癒一般感冒的方法。）

Promise of a Raise

Index | *Links* | *about* | *comments* | *Photo*

August 09

When I walked into my boss's office, he told me that he'd just **hung up with** the company I'd gone to meet. They'd accepted our offer, and he was very pleased. My boss **promised** to give me a raise as a **reward**, but he had promised that a few times before! Finally, I told him I wouldn't mind going back there **as long as** they **upgraded** my hotel. **That way**, I'd be able to date Holly, the company's hot secretary.

About me

Tom

Calendar

◄ *August* ►

Sun	Mon	Tue	Wed	Thu	Fri	Sat
					1	2
3	4	5	6	7	8	9
10	11	12	13	14	15	16
17	18	19	20	21	22	23
24	25	26	27	28	29	30
31						

Blog Archive

► August (9)
► July
► June
► May
► April
► March
► February
► January
► December
► November
► October
► September

允諾加薪

August 09

　　我走進老闆的辦公室，他告訴我說他剛剛和我之前拜會的公司通完電話。他們接受我們的條件，所以老闆很高興。他承諾要幫我加薪以作為獎勵，不過之前他已經講過好幾次同樣的話了！最後，我告訴他只要把我的飯店升等，我並不介意再次出差。那樣，我就能夠跟荷莉——對方公司的辣妹秘書——約會了。

About me

Tom

Calendar

◄　　*August*　　►

Sun	Mon	Tue	Wed	Thu	Fri	Sat
					1	2
3	4	5	6	7	8	9
10	11	12	13	14	15	16
17	18	19	20	21	22	23
24	25	26	27	28	29	30
31						

Blog Archive

▸ August (9)
▸ July
▸ June
▸ May
▸ April
▸ March
▸ February
▸ January
▸ December
▸ November
▸ October
▸ September

Tom at Blog 於 August 08.09. PM 02:45 發表 | 回覆 (0) | 引用 (0) | 收藏 (0) | 轉寄給朋友 | 檢舉

本網誌標題中的 promise 就是『承諾；答應；保證』的意思，作名詞用。此外，promise 亦可當及物動詞，仍表『承諾；答應；保證』之意。

promise [`prɑmɪs] *n.* & *vt.* 承諾；答應；保證

promise (sb) to V　　承諾／答應（某人）做……

promise (sb) + that 子句　　承諾／答應（某人）……

例: Before you promise to do it, you'd better think it over.

（你在答應做那件事之前最好考慮清楚。）

Sherry promised me that she would keep the secret for me.

（雪莉向我承諾會幫我保守這個秘密。）

以下補充幾個與『承諾』或『發誓』有關的字詞及用法：

vow [vaʊ] *n.* 誓言 & *vt.* 發誓

vow to V　　發誓要（做）……

vow + that 子句　　發誓……

例: Keith vowed to quit smoking cold turkey.

（凱斯發誓要一次就把菸戒成功。）

　　＊cold turkey　　一勞永逸地（視作副詞）

　　swear [swɛr] *vt.* 發誓

三態為：swear, swore [swɔr], sworn [swɔrn]。

swear to V　　發誓要（做）……

swear + that 子句　　發誓……

例: Nick swore that he didn't kill his wife.

（尼克發誓他沒殺死他太太。）

1. raise [rez] *n.* 加薪

give sb a raise　　幫某人加薪

get a pay / salary cut　　被減薪

例: Our boss gave us a raise the other day.

（前幾天我們老闆幫大家加薪了。）

Tom got a pay cut because of the economic recession.
（湯姆因為不景氣而被減薪。）

＊economic recession　　經濟蕭條 / 不景氣

2. **hang up with sb**　　　　和某人講完電話

hang up on sb　　　　　（對方尚未講完就）掛斷某人的電話

例: I just hung up with the doctor. He told me my test results were fine.
（我剛和醫生通完電話。他告訴我說我的檢查結果正常。）

Helen hung up on her boyfriend yesterday because they were fighting.
（海倫昨天掛她男友電話，因為他們吵架了。）

3. **reward** [rɪˋwɔrd] *n.* 獎勵；報酬 & *vt.* 獎勵；報答

as a reward　　作為獎勵 / 報酬

reward sb with sth　　用某物獎賞某人

例: My mother bought my sister a Barbie doll as a reward for being good.
（媽媽買了一個芭比娃娃給我妹妹，以獎勵她乖乖聽話。）

The boss rewarded David with a day off for doing a great job.
（老闆因大衛工作表現優異而放他一天假以作為獎勵。）

4. **as long as...**　　只要……

= so long as...

例: As long as you do your best, your parents will be proud of you.
（只要你盡力而為，你的父母就會以你為榮。）

5. **upgrade** [ˌʌpˋgred] *vt.* 使升級，提升

例: We upgraded our computer hardware to improve our efficiency.
（我們將電腦硬體升級以提高效率。）

＊efficiency [ɪˋfɪʃənsɪ] *n.* 效率

6. **That way, S + V**　　那樣一來，……

This way, S + V　　這樣一來，……

例: Let's go to a coffee shop. This way, we can do our homework while we have coffee.
（咱們去咖啡店吧。這樣我們就可以邊喝咖啡邊寫作業。）

Feeling under the Weather

Index | Links | about | comments | Photo

August 10

I woke up this morning sweating **profusely**. I walked into the bathroom and **looked at myself in the mirror**. My face was all red, and I knew that I had a <u>fever</u>. Within a few minutes, I was **freezing cold** and needed to put on some more clothes. I called my boss and told him I was too sick to come to work, but he **insisted** that I **show up** because I had important work to finish.

About me

Tom

Calendar

◄ August ►

Sun	Mon	Tue	Wed	Thu	Fri	Sat
					1	2
3	4	5	6	7	8	9
10	11	12	13	14	15	16
17	18	19	20	21	22	23
24	25	26	27	28	29	30
31						

Blog Archive

- ► August (10)
- ► July
- ► June
- ► May
- ► April
- ► March
- ► February
- ► January
- ► December
- ► November
- ► October
- ► September

Tom at Blog 於 August 08.10. PM 01:32 發表 | 回覆 (0) | 引用 (0) | 收藏 (0) | 轉寄給朋友 | 檢舉

身體不適

Index | *Links* | *about* | *comments* | *Photo*

August 10

　　我今天早上滿身大汗地醒來。我走進浴室裡照鏡子。我滿臉通紅，於是我知道自己發燒了。不到幾分鐘我就覺得冷得要死，需要多穿上幾件衣服。我打電話給老闆，告訴他我病得太嚴重無法去上班，但他堅持我進公司，因為我有重要的工作待完成。

About me

Tom

Calendar

◄　　*August*　　►

Sun	Mon	Tue	Wed	Thu	Fri	Sat
					1	2
3	4	5	6	7	8	9
10	11	12	13	14	15	16
17	18	19	20	21	22	23
24	25	26	27	28	29	30
31						

Blog Archive

▸ August (10)
▸ July
▸ June
▸ May
▸ April
▸ March
▸ February
▸ January
▸ December
▸ November
▸ October
▸ September

Tom at Blog 於 August 08.10. PM 01:32 發表 | 回覆 (0) | 引用 (0) | 收藏 (0) | 轉寄給朋友 | 檢舉

網誌作者因為發燒（have a fever，fever [ˈfivɚ] n. 發燒）所以全身無力又發冷，而最有可能引起作者這些症狀的就屬 cold [kold]（感冒）或 flu [flu]（流行性感冒，為 influenza [ˌɪnfluˈɛnzə] 的縮寫）。catch (a) cold 表示『得了感冒』，have the flu 表示『得了流感』（flu 之前一定要置 the）。除了發燒以外，其他有關身體不適的症狀（symptom [ˈsɪmptəm]）英文該怎麼說呢？以下就為您做簡單的介紹：

have a sore throat　　　　喉嚨痛

have a runny nose　　　　　流鼻涕

＊不可寫成：have a running nose（有一隻正在跑步的鼻子）

sneeze [sniz] vi. 打噴嚏 & n. 噴嚏

cough [kɔf] vi. & n. 咳嗽

headache [ˈhɛdˌek] n. 頭痛

stomachache [ˈstʌməkˌek] n. 腹痛

diarrhea [ˌdaɪəˈriə] n. 腹瀉

dizzy [ˈdɪzɪ] a. 頭暈目眩的

例: Because I caught a cold a few days ago, I have a runny nose and sore throat.

（因為我前幾天感冒了，所以我流鼻涕又喉嚨痛。）

Brian said he felt dizzy and had a serious stomachache.

（布萊恩說他頭暈目眩，肚子又痛得厲害。）

字 詞幫幫忙！

1. **feel / be under the weather**　　身體感到不適（尤指感冒）

例: Bill felt under the weather soon after he came back from work.

（比爾下班回來不久就感到身體不舒服。）

2. **profusely** [prəˈfjuslɪ] adv. 大量地

sweat profusely　　大量流汗

= sweat heavily

例: The side effect of this medicine is that I sweat profusely after taking it.

（這種藥的副作用就是我服用後會大量流汗。）

＊ side effect [ˈsaɪd ɪˌfɛkt] n. 副作用

3. **look at oneself in the mirror**　　某人照鏡子

mirror [ˈmɪrɚ] *n.* 鏡子

注意:

因為我們照鏡子時會往『鏡中』照去，故英文中表『照鏡子』會說
look in the mirror 或 look into the mirror，而不可說 look at the
mirror。

4. **freezing cold**　　極冷的，冷得受不了

注意:

此處的 freezing [ˈfrizɪŋ] 作副詞用，修飾形容詞 cold（冷的），
freezing cold 表『冷得快要結凍似的』；也可以用 biting [ˈbaɪtɪŋ] 來
修飾 cold，biting cold 表『冷得好像皮膚被咬而感到刺痛般的冷』。
freezing 及 biting 均為現在分詞作副詞，有 very（很）的意味，修飾其
後的形容詞。其他常見的此類用法尚有：scorching / boiling hot（極熱
的，熱得好像要燒焦似的）、hopping mad（氣瘋了，氣得好像要跳腳
似的）等。

例: I don't want to go outside because it's freezing cold today.
（我不想出去，因為今天外面超冷的。）

例: I don't think it's a good idea to play baseball on such a
scorching hot day.
（我覺得這麼大熱天打棒球實在不是個好主意。）

5. **insist** [ɪnˈsɪst] *vt.* & *vi.* 堅持

insist + that 子句　　　堅持……

insist on + N/V-ing　　　堅持……

例: Mary insisted that Paul (should) apologize to her.
（瑪莉堅持保羅應該向她道歉。）

The teacher insisted on having weekly spelling tests.
（這位老師堅持要有拼字週考。）

6. **show up**　　出現，出席

= turn up

例: Wendy promised she would show up at my birthday
party, but she wasn't there.
（溫蒂承諾她會在我的生日派對上露臉，但她並沒有出現。）

No Bluff

August 11

Besides being **sick** at the office all day, my boss **treated** me really badly. He said he thought he had **called my bluff** by making me come in to work. When he found out that I was actually ill, he felt bad, but he still made me **stay late** to make some sales calls to America. I felt **even** worse when I left, and I knew I was really sick of one thing—working for this guy.

About me

Tom

Calendar

◄   August   ►

Sun	Mon	Tue	Wed	Thu	Fri	Sat
					1	2
3	4	5	6	7	8	9
10	**11**	12	13	14	15	16
17	18	19	20	21	22	23
24	25	26	27	28	29	30
31						

Blog Archive

▸ August (11)
▸ July
▸ June
▸ May
▸ April
▸ March
▸ February
▸ January
▸ December
▸ November
▸ October
▸ September

Tom at Blog 於 August 08.11. PM 07:56 發表｜回覆 (0)｜引用 (0)｜收藏 (0)｜轉寄給朋友｜檢舉

我沒有裝病

August 11

　　除了整天在辦公室病懨懨的以外，我的老闆對我真的很糟。他說他以為叫我來上班，就能拆穿我的西洋鏡。但他發現我是真的生病時，雖然有點歉疚，卻仍要我留到很晚打業務電話到美國。我下班時覺得病的更嚴重了，我知道我真的受夠了一件事──替這個傢伙做事。

Tom at Blog 於 August 08.11. PM 07:56 發表 | 回覆 (0) | 引用 (0) | 收藏 (0) | 轉寄給朋友 | 檢舉

bluff 無論作名詞或動詞用時，均有『欺騙』、『嚇唬』、『虛張聲勢』之意，而網誌中的 call one's bluff 則表『揭露某人虛張聲勢的做法』。這個俚語來自撲克牌遊戲，有時當你拿到一手爛牌卻企圖讓別人認為你的牌好極了，但這時別人卻不相信你，對你進行挑戰，這就是 call your bluff（拆穿你的西洋鏡）。

bluff [blʌf] *n.* & *vt.* 欺騙；嚇唬；虛張聲勢
call one's bluff　　揭露某人虛張聲勢的做法，揭穿某人
bluff sb into V-ing　　虛張聲勢騙某人做……

例: The teacher called his student's bluff when he phoned his parents and asked if the family dog really ate their son's homework.
（這位老師拆穿學生的西洋鏡，因為他打電話到學生家裡，問對方父母是否家裡的狗真把他們兒子的作業吃掉了。）

I bluffed Kathy into thinking I was a famous photographer.
（我唬弄凱西，讓她以為我是知名攝影師。）
＊photographer [fəˈtɑɡrəfɚ] *n.* 攝影師

字詞幫幫忙！

1. besides + N/V-ing　除了……之外
= in addition to + N/V-ing
Besides, S + V　此外，……
= In addition, S + V

例: Besides the latest hits, this radio station plays golden oldies.
（這個廣播電台除了播放最新的熱門歌曲外，還播放經典老歌。）
＊oldie [ˈoldɪ] *n.* 老歌（複數形為 oldies）

Our company sells new and used cars. In addition, we have a car rental service.
（我們公司賣新車和中古車。除此之外，我們還有租車服務。）
＊rental [ˈrɛntl̩] *a.* 出租的

2. sick [sɪk] *a.* 生病的；厭煩的
be sick of...　厭倦……，對……感到厭煩

= be tired of...

= be fed up with...

例: I'm sick of getting up early every morning.
（我厭煩每天都要這麼早起。）

I'm fed up with listening to Annie's constant complaining.
（安妮牢騷發個不停，聽得我煩死了。）

* constant [`kɑnstənt] *a.* 不斷的

complain [kəm`plen] *vi.* 抱怨

3. **treat** [trit] *vt.* 對待；請客

treat sb to sth　　招待某人某事

例: No matter how angry you get, you can never treat your friends like that.
（不管多麼生氣，你也不能那樣對待朋友。）

On my birthday, my best friend treated me to a movie.
（生日時，我最要好的朋友請我去看電影。）

4. **stay late**　　待到很晚

stay up late + V-ing　　熬夜做……

= sit up late + V-ing

例: You can come to work early rather than stay late if you'd like.
（如果你想的話，可以早點來上班就不用留到很晚。）

Now that the final exams are over, you don't have to stay up late studying every night.
（既然期末考考完了，你就不用每晚熬夜讀書了。）

5. **even +** 比較級形容詞／副詞　　更加……

注意:

可用來修飾比較級形容詞或副詞的計有下列六個:

far, much, still, even, a lot, a great deal

例: Smoking doesn't do anyone any good. I've heard that second-hand smoke may be even more harmful than actually smoking.
（抽菸對任何人都沒有好處。我聽說二手菸甚至比吸菸更有害。）

* harmful [`hɑrmfəl] *a.* 有害的

Amy is much more diligent in her studies than she was last year.
（艾咪比去年用功多了。）

* diligent [`dɪlədʒənt] *a.* 勤勉的

Bad Things Come in Threes

August 12

They say that **misfortunes never come singly**. If that's the **case**, people should avoid me because besides being sick, I'm blogging now from the hospital. On the way to work, a car came **out of nowhere** and hit me. I**'m alive and well**, **obviously**, but I have a **bum** leg now, and the doctor is checking to see if I need **surgery**.

About me

Tom

Calendar

◄　　　August　　　►

Sun	Mon	Tue	Wed	Thu	Fri	Sat
					1	2
3	4	5	6	7	8	9
10	11	12	13	14	15	16
17	18	19	20	21	22	23
24	25	26	27	28	29	30
31						

Blog Archive

► August (12)
► July
► June
► May
► April
► March
► February
► January
► December
► November
► October
► September

Tom at Blog 於 August 08.12. PM 02:17 發表 | 回覆 (0) | 引用 (0) | 收藏 (0) | 轉寄給朋友 | 檢舉

禍不單行

August 12

　　人家說禍不單行。如果真是那樣的話，大家應該要離我遠一點，因為除了生病外，我現在正在醫院裡寫這篇網誌。上班途中，一輛不知從哪冒出來的汽車撞上我。顯然我現在還活得好好的，但是我腿可瘸了，而且醫生正在檢查我是否需要動手術。

About me

Tom

Calendar

◄　　*August*　　►

Sun	Mon	Tue	Wed	Thu	Fri	Sat
					1	2
3	4	5	6	7	8	9
10	11	12	13	14	15	16
17	18	19	20	21	22	23
24	25	26	27	28	29	30
31						

Blog Archive

▸ August (12)
▸ July
▸ June
▸ May
▸ April
▸ March
▸ February
▸ January
▸ December
▸ November
▸ October
▸ September

Tom at Blog 於 August 08.12. PM 02:17 發表 | 回覆 (0) | 引用 (0) | 收藏 (0) | 轉寄給朋友 | 檢舉

95

中國人相信壞事總會接踵而來，因此有『禍不單行』一說，外國人對此也有類似的迷信，而且還認為災難要來一次就會來 3 個，因此才有標題 bad things come in threes 的說法。

例: After he was fired, Larry went broke, and got divorced, which really proves that bad things come in threes.

（賴瑞被炒魷魚後，接著又破產還離婚，這還真證明了禍不單行啊。）

英文中還有更貼近中文『禍不單行』的說法，如網誌中所提：

Misfortunes never come singly. 禍不單行。

misfortune [mɪsˋfɔrtʃən] *n.* 不幸，災禍

singly [ˋsɪŋglɪ] *adv.* 個別地，單獨地

例: Lucy was sent to the emergency room due to a car accident. However, misfortunes never come singly, and she was robbed on her way home from the hospital.

（露西因為出車禍而進急診室。但禍不單行的是，她出院回家的路上又遭到搶劫。）

＊the emergency room 急診室

It never rains but it pours. 禍不單行。

＊pour [pɔr] *vi.* 下大雨；傾倒

注意:

此處的 but 等於 if not（若非），but it pours 等於 if it doesn't pour。整句話按字面翻譯為『老天若不下傾盆大雨，就絕不下雨』，換言之，『老天若下雨，就一定下傾盆大雨』，引申為『禍不來則已，若來則是接踵而來』，也就是中文所謂的『屋漏偏逢連夜雨』、『禍不單行』之意。

例: Not only did I get on the wrong bus, but I lost my cell phone on it as well. I can only say that it never rains but it pours!

（我不只上錯公車還在上頭搞丟了手機。我只能說這真是屋漏偏逢連夜雨！）

字 詞 幫幫忙！

1. **case** [kes] *n.* 狀況，情形

   If it / this / that is the case, S + V 如果情形是這樣 / 那樣的話，……

例: The weather report says that there may be a typhoon coming this weekend. If that is the case, we will cancel our plans to go camping.

（氣象報告說這個週末可能會有颱風。如果是那樣的話，我們將取消露營的計劃。）

2. out of nowhere　　不知從哪冒出來的，突然出現

= from nowhere

in the middle of nowhere　　在荒郊野外

例: A dog jumped out from nowhere and bit Marcus.

（一隻不知從哪跳出來的狗咬了馬克斯一口。）

We got lost in the middle of nowhere.

（我們在荒郊野外迷了路。）

3. be alive and well　　健康（愉快）的

be alive and kicking　　精神飽滿；生氣勃勃

例: Last time I saw Jimmy, he was alive and well.

（上次我看到吉米時，他過得挺好的。）

David: How's your grandma? I heard she just turned 80.

Daisy: She's alive and kicking. She still goes jogging every morning.

（大衛：妳祖母好嗎？聽說她剛過 80 歲。）

（黛西：她生龍活虎，每天早上還去慢跑呢。）

4. obviously [ˋɑbvɪəslɪ] *adv.* 明顯地，顯而易見地

例: Molly didn't hear from that guy after their first date. Obviously, he wasn't interested in her.

（莫莉和那男生第一次約會後就沒有他的消息。很顯然地，那男的對她沒興趣。）

5. bum [bʌm] *a.* 瘸的，殘疾的（= disabled [dɪsˋebl̩d]）

6. surgery [ˋsɝdʒərɪ] *n.* 手術（不可數）

operation [͵ɑpəˋreʃən] *n.* 手術（可數）

perform surgery on...　　替……動手術／開刀

= perform an operation on...

My Foot Is Killing Me

Index | *Links* | *about* | *comments* | *Photo*

August 13

   After all was said and done, the doctor told me I should have surgery to put some **pins** in my **ankle**. However, I have to wait for two days because there are **currently** no beds **available** in the hospital. The real problem is that my boss won't allow me to **take** any more **sick leave**. Instead, I'll have to **take personal leave** while I'm **hospitalized**.

About me

Tom

Calendar

◄			August			►
Sun	Mon	Tue	Wed	Thu	Fri	Sat
					1	2
3	4	5	6	7	8	9
10	11	12	**13**	14	15	16
17	18	19	20	21	22	23
24	25	26	27	28	29	30
31						

Blog Archive

- ► August (13)
- ► July
- ► June
- ► May
- ► April
- ► March
- ► February
- ► January
- ► December
- ► November
- ► October
- ► September

Tom at Blog 於 August 08.13. PM 03:18 發表 | 回覆 (0) | 引用 (0) | 收藏 (0) | 轉寄給朋友 | 檢舉

痛死人的腳

August 13

　　總而言之，醫生告訴我，我得開刀在腳踝打鋼釘。但由於醫院裡目前沒有空床位，所以我必須等兩天。真正的問題是我老闆不會允許我再請病假。所以我住院時，反而得請事假。

About me

Tom

Calendar

◄　　　*August*　　　►

Sun	Mon	Tue	Wed	Thu	Fri	Sat
					1	2
3	4	5	6	7	8	9
10	11	12	13	14	15	16
17	18	19	20	21	22	23
24	25	26	27	28	29	30
31						

Blog Archive

▸ August (13)
▸ July
▸ June
▸ May
▸ April
▸ March
▸ February
▸ January
▸ December
▸ November
▸ October
▸ September

Tom at Blog 於 August 08.13. PM 03:18 發表│回覆 (0)│引用 (0)│收藏 (0)│轉寄給朋友│檢舉

腳踝打鋼釘？光聽就讓人感到寒毛直豎！網誌作者的腳肯定是傷得不輕，才會需要這種手術。難怪他的網誌標題是 My Foot Is Killing Me，這裡的 be killing sb 並不是真的要致人於死，而是一種誇張的說法，相當於中文說的『痛死人了』。因此『人的身體器官 + be killing sb』指的就是『身體該處痛得不得了』。

例: I have been sitting in the office all day, and my back is killing me! I really need to get a massage after work.

（我在辦公室坐了一整天，我的背快痛死了。下班後我真的需要去按摩一下。）

＊massage [məˋsɑʒ] *n.* 按摩

Kent called and said his head was killing him, so he wouldn't go to the movies with us.

（肯特打電話來說他頭痛得要命，所以不和我們去看電影了。）

要是碰到讓人恨得牙癢癢而不舒服的情形，同樣也可以用『某事物 + be killing sb』來表示『……讓某人很受不了』。

例: Patty felt that working for her boss was killing her, so she quit and started her own business.

（派蒂覺得為她老闆工作生不如死，所以便辭去工作自己創業。）

另外，kill sb 還可以用來表『讓某人笑到肚子痛』。

例: Turn this movie off. It's really killing me. I can't stop laughing.

（把這部電影關掉。我快笑死了，停都停不住。）

1. **After all is said and done, S + V**　　話說到底 / 總之，……

= When all is said and done, S + V

例: After all was said and done, Ed and Amy decided to get married whether their parents approved or not.

（總之，艾德和艾咪決定不管他們的父母同不同意都要結婚。）

2. **pin** [pɪn] *n.* 釘；大頭針

   be on pins and needles　　如坐針氈，坐立不安

   ＊needle [ˋnidl̩] *n.* 縫衣針

   例: Before the announcement of the winner was made, the participants had been on pins and needles.

   （在宣布優勝者之前，參賽者如坐針氈。）

   ＊announcement [əˋnaʊnsmənt] *n.* 宣布

   　participant [pɑrˋtɪsəpənt] *n.* 參賽者

3. **ankle** [ˋæŋkl̩] *n.* 踝，足踝

4. **currently** [ˋkɝəntlɪ] *adv.* 目前

5. **available** [əˋveləbl̩] *a.* 可得到的；可利用的；有空的（= free，以人作主詞）

   例: Are there any seats available on the afternoon flight?

   （下午的班機還有沒有空位？）

   Are you available now?

   =　Are you free now?

   =　Do you have time now?

   （你現在有空嗎？）

6. **take sick leave**　　請病假

   take personal leave　　請事假

   take + 一段時間 + off　　請（一段時間的）假

   例: If you take sick leave, you must bring a doctor's note.

   （你若請病假，需要把醫生診斷證明帶來。）

   Jack has been taking personal leave for five days, but no one knows where he has gone.

   （傑克已請了 5 天事假，但沒人知道他去了哪裡。）

   Sarah took three days off in order to travel to Thailand.

   （莎拉請 3 天假到泰國旅遊。）

7. **hospitalize** [ˋhɑspɪtə͵laɪz] *vt.* 使住院（常用被動語態）

   例: Larry was hospitalized after his car accident.

   （賴瑞因車禍而住院。）

Unit 26

Successful Surgery

Index | Links | about | comments | Photo

August 14

After five days in the **hospital**, I finally got released. I still have to **wear a cast** for two months, so I probably won't **be out and about** any time soon. But **at least** I'm able to **get around** by myself on **crutches**. Monday will be my first day back at work in a week, and I **wonder** if I will still have a job.

About me

Tom

Calendar

◄   August   ►

Sun	Mon	Tue	Wed	Thu	Fri	Sat
					1	2
3	4	5	6	7	8	9
10	11	12	13	14	15	16
17	18	19	20	21	22	23
24	25	26	27	28	29	30
31						

Blog Archive

- ► August (14)
- ► July
- ► June
- ► May
- ► April
- ► March
- ► February
- ► January
- ► December
- ► November
- ► October
- ► September

Tom at Blog 於 August 08.14. PM 02:54 發表 | 回覆 (0) | 引用 (0) | 收藏 (0) | 轉寄給朋友 | 檢舉

手術順利

August 14

住院住了 5 天後，我終於出院了。但我還是得打兩個月的石膏，所以暫時沒辦法隨心所欲地出門活動。但起碼我還可以自己拄著拐杖到處走動。星期一將是我請假一個禮拜後回到公司的第一天，不知道我的工作丟了沒。

About me

Tom

Calendar

◄ *August* ►

Sun	Mon	Tue	Wed	Thu	Fri	Sat
					1	2
3	4	5	6	7	8	9
10	11	12	13	14	15	16
17	18	19	20	21	22	23
24	25	26	27	28	29	30
31						

Blog Archive

▸ August (14)
▸ July
▸ June
▸ May
▸ April
▸ March
▸ February
▸ January
▸ December
▸ November
▸ October
▸ September

Tom at Blog 於 August 08.14. PM 02:54 發表 | 回覆 (0) | 引用 (0) | 收藏 (0) | 轉寄給朋友 | 檢舉

平時骨頭的保健可輕忽不得，除了多補充鈣質，平時運動走路也要小心，否則像網誌作者發生意外，不但得動手術，還得忍受上石膏的不方便、拄拐杖甚或坐輪椅的煎熬。通常骨折的護理方式不外乎是上石膏或戴夾板，以下是一些與骨折護理相關的用法：

wear a cast　　　　打石膏
＊cast [kæst] *n.*（固定骨折用的）石膏（= plaster cast [`plæstɚ ˌkæst]）
wear a splint　　　　戴夾板
＊splint [splɪnt] *n.*（固定斷骨的）夾板
put a pin in...　　　　在……打入鋼釘
put a brace on...　　　在……裝支架／護具
＊brace [bres] *n.* 支架

例: John broke his leg and had to wear a cast.
　（約翰摔斷了腿，所以必須打石膏。）
The doctor suggested putting pins in Mrs. Anderson's fractured hip.
　（醫生建議為安德森太太骨折的臀骨裝上鋼釘。）
＊fracture [`fræktʃɚ] *vt.* 使骨折；使斷裂

在國外，病人通常會讓親朋好友在石膏或夾板上留下簽名，並在拆掉石膏後留下當作紀念品（souvenir [ˌsuvəˋnɪr]）。而拆掉石膏、移除夾板的說法如下：

get the cast (cut) off　　拆石膏
remove a cast / splint　　移除石膏／夾板
＊remove [rɪˋmuv] *vt.* 移除
例: After getting the cast cut off, Zack kept it as a souvenir.
　（拆掉石膏後，柴克把它留下當作紀念。）
John struggled to walk for two days after the doctor removed his cast.
　（醫生拆掉他的石膏後，約翰有 2 天走路很吃力。）

字詞幫幫忙！

1. hospital [`hɑspɪtl] *n.* 醫院
　be admitted to (the) hospital　　被准許住院
　be released from (the) hospital　　出院

*admit [əd`mɪt] *vt.* 接納

*release [rɪ`lis] *vt.* 釋放

例: John was admitted to the hospital because he had a stroke.
（約翰因為中風而入院。）

*stroke [strok] *n.* 中風

Claire is recovering well, and she should be released from the hospital soon.
（克萊兒恢復的情形良好，應該很快就可以出院了。）

2. be / get out and about　外出走動

例: You should get out and about more often. Don't just sit inside all day.
（你該多出去活動活動。不要成天坐在室內。）

3. at least　至少

例: If you can't tell me the answer, at least give me a hint.
（如果你不能告訴我答案，至少給我個提示。）

*hint [hɪnt] *n.* 暗示

Cathy practiced the piano for at least three hours a day before her concert.
（凱西在她的演奏會前每天至少練習 3 小時的鋼琴。）

4. get around　四處走動

例: It is not easy to get around in a big city without a car.
（在大城市中沒有車子到哪裡都不方便。）

5. crutch [krʌtʃ] *n.*（支在腋下的）丁形拐杖

on crutches　用拐杖

例: It's quite inconvenient for patients on crutches to go to the bathroom.
（拄拐杖的病患如廁挺不方便的。）

7. wonder [`wʌndɚ] *vt.* 納悶，想知道

注意:

wonder 之後通常以 if / whether 或疑問詞（what, when, where, why, how 等）引導的名詞子句作受詞。

例: I was wondering if you'd come to my birthday party.
（我想知道你是否會來我的生日派對。）

I wonder what Tommy said to make his mother so angry.
（我想知道湯米到底說了什麼讓他媽媽那麼生氣。）

Back to Work

August 15

As soon as I got to work, I saw a huge **pile** of **files** on my desk. After trying to **catch up with** my work, I felt **as though** I **was mad as a hatter**. It wasn't easy to do things like getting a drink of water or going to the bathroom because of my cast. By noon, I really wanted to go home. This job is **leaving a** really **bad taste in my mouth**.

About me

Tom

Calendar

◄ August ►

Sun	Mon	Tue	Wed	Thu	Fri	Sat
					1	2
3	4	5	6	7	8	9
10	11	12	13	14	15	16
17	18	19	20	21	22	23
24	25	26	27	28	29	30
31						

Blog Archive

- ► August (15)
- ► July
- ► June
- ► May
- ► April
- ► March
- ► February
- ► January
- ► December
- ► November
- ► October
- ► September

Tom at Blog 於 August 08.15. PM 02:03 發表｜回覆 (0)｜引用 (0)｜收藏 (0)｜轉寄給朋友｜檢舉

回到工作崗位

August 15

　　我一回去上班就看到桌上疊了一大堆檔案。在設法趕工作進度後，我覺得自己彷彿快抓狂了。因為我打了石膏，像是拿杯水喝或是上廁所都很不方便。到了中午，我真的很想回家去。這份工作真是讓我厭惡極了。

About me

Tom

Calendar

◀　　　August　　　▶

Sun	Mon	Tue	Wed	Thu	Fri	Sat
					1	2
3	4	5	6	7	8	9
10	11	12	13	14	15	16
17	18	19	20	21	22	23
24	25	26	27	28	29	30
31						

Blog Archive

▸ August (15)
▸ July
▸ June
▸ May
▸ April
▸ March
▸ February
▸ January
▸ December
▸ November
▸ October
▸ September

Tom at Blog 於 August 08.15. PM 02:03 發表｜回覆 (0)｜引用 (0)｜收藏 (0)｜轉寄給朋友｜檢舉

還記得《愛麗絲夢遊仙境》中，有個歇斯底里的瘋帽匠（The Mad Hatter）嗎？網誌裡主角就是用這個角色來形容自己受了傷，卻還要瘋狂趕工作進度而接近瘋狂狀態。

其實瘋帽匠這個角色是其來有自的：過去西方人在做氈帽的過程中要用到汞來處理動物的毛，使其容易黏結成氈，才能製作出氈帽。而帽匠在製作過程中，往往會吸進過多的汞而造成慢性中毒，導致言行舉止異常，因此英文裡才有『瘋得像個帽匠』（be as mad as a hatter）一詞，用來形容一個人『發瘋的、精神錯亂的』。

例: David was (as) mad as a hatter after he lost his job and his wife on the same day.

（大衛在同一天失去工作和太太後就精神錯亂了。）

taste [test] 原意為『味道』，網誌中提及的 leave a bad taste in one's mouth 字面上的意思是『在某人嘴裡留下不好的味道』，引申為某件事或某個人『讓某人覺得不悅／厭惡』或是『讓某人留下不好的印象』。

例: Working with Neil really left a bad taste in my mouth because he was very irresponsible and selfish.

（和尼爾工作真讓我覺得厭惡，因為他既不負責任又自私。）

＊irresponsible [ˌɪrɪˈspɑnsəbl̩] a. 不負責任的

Sherry left a bad taste in our mouths because of her arrogant attitude.

= Sherry made a bad impression on us because of her arrogant attitude.

（由於雪莉高傲的態度，所以給我們留下了不好的印象。）

＊make a bad / good impression on sb　給某人留下壞／好印象

impression [ɪmˈprɛʃən] n. 印象

arrogant [ˈærəgənt] a. 傲慢的

1. As soon as + S + V, S + V　　一……就……

= The moment + S + V, S + V

= The instant + S + V, S + V

例: As soon as I get home, I'll give you a call.
（我一回家就會打電話給你。）

2. pile [paɪl] *n.* 一堆 & *vi.* 堆積

a pile of...　　一堆的……

pile up　　堆積，累積

例: We always have a large pile of garbage to take out on Monday evenings.
（每逢星期一晚上，我們都有一堆垃圾要拿出去倒。）

The bills started to pile up on my desk after I lost my job.
（丟了工作之後，我桌上的帳單開始堆積如山。）

3. file [faɪl] *n.* 檔案

keep...on file　　將……建檔

例: The secretary kept the records of today's meeting on file.
（那位秘書將今天的會議紀錄建檔。）

4. catch up with...　　迎頭趕上……

keep up with...　　跟上……；與……並駕齊驅

例: The bus is driving off, but I think we can catch up with it if we run.
（公車快要開走了，但我想如果我們用跑的話就可以趕上它。）

Peter works so fast that no one in the office can keep up with him.
（彼得工作之快，辦公室裡沒有一個人跟得上他。）

5. as though + S + V　　彷彿 / 好像……

= as if + S + V

例: Rick yelled at me for no reason as though I had made a huge mistake.
（瑞克莫名其妙對我大吼，好像我犯了什麼滔天大罪。）

Keeping Quiet

Index | Links | about | comments | Photo

August 16

Finally, my boss called me into his office to ask me how I was. I told him that my ankle was OK, but I felt the **workload** was **a little bit** too heavy for my first day back. He was **shocked** and told me that's because I had taken too much time off work recently. I had to **bite my lip**. If I didn't keep quiet, I would **end up** telling him my true feeling about the job. That might get me fired.

About me

Tom

Calendar

◀   *August*   ▶

Sun	Mon	Tue	Wed	Thu	Fri	Sat
					1	2
3	4	5	6	7	8	9
10	11	12	13	14	15	16
17	18	19	20	21	22	23
24	25	26	27	28	29	30
31						

Blog Archive

▸ August (16)
▸ July
▸ June
▸ May
▸ April
▸ March
▸ February
▸ January
▸ December
▸ November
▸ October
▸ September

Tom at Blog 於 August 08.16. PM 03:15 發表 | 回覆 (0) | 引用 (0) | 收藏 (0) | 轉寄給朋友 | 檢舉

保持沉默

August 16

老闆終於把我叫進他的辦公室，詢問我現在如何。我說我的腳踝還好，但是覺得我回來第一天的工作量有一點太重。他很震驚，然後跟我說那是因為我最近請太多假的緣故。我必須咬緊嘴唇忍住不生氣。如果我不保持沉默的話，到頭來我一定會告訴他我對這份工作真正的感受，而這或許會讓我丟掉飯碗。

About me

Tom

Calendar

◄ *August* ►

Sun	Mon	Tue	Wed	Thu	Fri	Sat
					1	2
3	4	5	6	7	8	9
10	11	12	13	14	15	16
17	18	19	20	21	22	23
24	25	26	27	28	29	30
31						

Blog Archive

- ► August (16)
- ► July
- ► June
- ► May
- ► April
- ► March
- ► February
- ► January
- ► December
- ► November
- ► October
- ► September

Tom at Blog 於 August 08.16. PM 03:15 發表 | 回覆 (0) | 引用 (0) | 收藏 (0) | 轉寄給朋友 | 檢舉

111

網誌作者向老闆提到工作過多，卻被說是因為請假過多才造成的，因此作者氣得牙癢癢地，可是卻又不能多說什麼。網誌裡用了 bite one's lip 來形容他的感覺，bite [baɪt] 就是『咬』，lip [lɪp] 就是嘴唇。當你為了忍耐怒氣，或是壓抑自己的情緒時，是不是下意識地就會咬著自己的嘴唇呢？

bite one's lip （為忍住憤怒或克制不滿情緒等而）咬緊嘴唇，忍氣吞聲

＊bite 動詞三態為：bite, bit [bɪt], bitten ['bɪtn̩]。

例: Nick bit his lip when he was treated unfairly.

（尼克遭受到不公平對待時忍氣吞聲。）

除了 bite one's lip 之外，以下再介紹其他有關 lip 的常用說法：

button one's lip（採單數 lip） 閉上嘴巴，停止說話

= zip one's lips（採複數 lips）

＊button ['bʌtn̩] vt. 扣上（鈕扣）

zip [zɪp] vt. 拉上（拉鍊）

例: Why don't you button your lip? I'm tired of listening to your complaints.

（你為什麼不閉上嘴巴？我聽你抱怨聽得煩死了。）

＊complaint [kəm'plent] n. 抱怨

curl one's lips 撇嘴（表示不屑、輕蔑、厭惡等）

＊curl [kɝl] vt. 使彎曲；捲曲

例: After listening to Jack's plan, Lisa just curled her lips and said it was impractical.

（聽了傑克的計劃後，麗莎撇撇嘴，說這太不實際。）

＊impractical [ɪm'præktɪkl̩] a. 不切實際的

read one's lips 讀唇語

例: I couldn't hear Jenny, but I could read her lips.

（我聽不到珍妮說什麼，但我可以讀她的唇語。）

字詞幫幫忙！

1. **workload** [`wɜk,lod] *n.* 工作量

   例: The heavy workload made John work overtime every day.

   （沉重的工作量使得約翰每天加班。）

2. **a little (bit)...**　　有點……

   例: Jeff acted a little bit weird today. What's the matter with him?

   （傑夫今天行為舉止有點怪。他怎麼了？）

   ＊weird [wɪrd] *a.* 怪異的

3. **shocked** [ʃɑkt] *a.* 感到震驚的

   shocking [`ʃɑkɪŋ] *a.* 令人震驚的

   例: Everyone was shocked when Jane married a man she knew for only a week.

   （當阿珍嫁給一個她才認識一星期的人時，大家都非常震驚。）

   It's shocking that John committed suicide. He looked like a very happy man.

   （約翰自殺的事讓人很震驚。他看起來像是個很快樂的人。）

   ＊commit suicide　　自殺

   　commit [kə`mɪt] *vt.* 犯（罪）

   　suicide [`suə,saɪd] *n.* 自殺

4. **end up +** 現在分詞 / 介詞片語　　到頭來 / 結果 / 最後……

   例: Kelly married a rich man, but she ended up divorcing him and becoming a single mother.

   （凱莉嫁給一位有錢人，但她最後跟他離婚，成了一位單親媽媽。）

   ＊divorce [də`vɔrs] *vt.* 與……離婚

   The thief was caught and ended up in jail.

   （這名小偷被捕，最後進了監獄。）

Unfair Office Practices

August 17

Change is happening at my office right now. It seems like my company is going to cut some "unnecessary **spending**," **according to** what my boss said. I'm worried that I'm one of those who will be fired. I don't believe I **deserve** it because I've been here for years. Also, I think that I've been **working my fingers to the bone** for this company.

About me

Tom

Calendar

◄   *August*   ►

Sun	Mon	Tue	Wed	Thu	Fri	Sat
					1	2
3	4	5	6	7	8	9
10	11	12	13	14	15	16
17	18	19	20	21	22	23
24	25	26	27	28	29	30
31						

Blog Archive

- ► August (17)
- ► July
- ► June
- ► May
- ► April
- ► March
- ► February
- ► January
- ► December
- ► November
- ► October
- ► September

Tom at Blog 於 August 08.17. PM 01:54 發表 | 回覆 (0) | 引用 (0) | 收藏 (0) | 轉寄給朋友 | 檢舉

公司不公平的作為

Index | Links | about | comments | Photo

August 17

　　辦公室裡現在豬羊變色。根據老闆說的,看樣子公司將要削減一些『不必要的支出』。我很擔心成為將來被解僱的其中一人。但是我不認為自己應該被解僱,因為我在這裡工作了這麼多年。此外,我認為自己盡心盡力,像拼命三郎一樣為公司賣命。

Tom

Calendar

◄　　　*August*　　　►

Sun	Mon	Tue	Wed	Thu	Fri	Sat
					1	2
3	4	5	6	7	8	9
10	11	12	13	14	15	16
17	18	19	20	21	22	23
24	25	26	27	28	29	30
31						

Blog Archive

▸ August (17)
▸ July
▸ June
▸ May
▸ April
▸ March
▸ February
▸ January
▸ December
▸ November
▸ October
▸ September

Tom at Blog 於 August 08.17. PM 01:54 發表 | 回覆 (0) | 引用 (0) | 收藏 (0) | 轉寄給朋友 | 檢舉

網誌作者使用 I've been working my fingers to the bone 來形容自己像拼命三郎一樣為公司賣命，為什麼呢？finger [ˈfɪŋɡɚ] 指『手指』，bone [bon] 是『骨頭』，因此 work one's fingers to the bone 字面上意思是『工作到手指的骨頭都看得見』，不難想像工作有多努力認真，所以 work one's fingers to the bone 便引申為『拼命工作、工作勤奮』之意。

例: Gina worked her fingers to the bone to finish the project on time.
（吉娜拼了命為了要準時完成那項企劃案。）

此外，**work one's butt off** 也是『非常努力工作』之意。butt [bʌt] 是『屁股』，本俚語按字面意思是『工作到連屁股都磨掉了』，當然也是指『工作很拚命 / 努力』。

例: Eric works his butt off running his restaurant.
（艾瑞克非常努力經營他的餐廳。）

1. unfair [ʌnˈfɛr] *a.* 不公平的；不公正的
   fair [fɛr] *a.* 公平的；公正的
   例: It is unfair to ask your little sister to do all the chores. She is only eight years old.
   （要你的小妹做所有的雜務很不公平。她只有 8 歲耶。）
   ＊chore [tʃɔr] *n.* 雜務
     do chores　　做雜事
   The judge's decision was fair to both sides.
   （法官的判決對雙方都公平。）

2. practice [ˈpræktɪs] *n.* 實施，實行
   put...into practice　　將……付諸實現
   例: I won't believe you unless you can put what you have said into practice.
   （除非你把說的話付諸實行我才會相信你。）

3. spending [ˈspɛndɪŋ] *n.* 開銷，花費

例: Because of her crazy spending, Amy ended up in debt a couple of years ago.

（由於愛咪花錢花得很兇，幾年前她就開始負債了。）

＊debt [dɛt] *n.* 債務，負債

4. according to... 　　根據……

例: According to our supervisor, we will have five days off in September.

（根據我們的上司說，我們 9 月將有 5 天假期。）

＊supervisor [ˈsupɚˌvaɪzɚ] *n.* 上司

5. deserve [dɪˈzɝv] *vt.* 應得，值得

＊deserve 其後可接名詞或不定詞片語作受詞。

Sb deserves it. 　　這是某人應得的。

deserve + N/to V 　　應得／值得……

例: Why don't you take a day off? You deserve it.

（你何不休一天假？那是你應得的。）

The hardworking employee deserves a promotion.

（那個勤奮的員工獲得升遷是應該的。）

＊employee [ˌɛmplɔɪˈi] *n.* 僱員，職員

promotion [prəˈmoʃən] *n.* 升遷

Those who make more money deserve to pay higher taxes.

（錢賺得較多的人理當付較多的稅。）

deserve 也常用在貶意的用法上，表『活該、自作自受』的意思，通常使用過去式。

例: Gary: I can't believe I was suspended from school.

Lucy: You deserved it. The teacher caught you cheating on the test.

= You asked for it. The teacher caught you cheating on the test.

= (It) Served you right. The teacher caught you cheating on the test.

（蓋瑞：我真不敢相信我遭到學校的停課處分。）

（露西：你活該。誰叫老師抓到你考試作弊。）

＊suspend [səˈspɛnd] *vt.* 使停學

Sweating Bullets

Index | *Links* | *about* | *comments* | *Photo*

August 18

While I was enjoying a coffee this afternoon, I watched our boss talk to Sam. **All of a sudden**, Sam **burst into tears** and then **rushed out of** his office. It was quite **embarrassing** because he **slammed** the door and then went over to his desk and started **packing up** his **belongings**. Everyone in the office was **stunned**, and I was sweating bullets because I knew I was next.

About me

Tom

Calendar

◄   *August*   ►

Sun	Mon	Tue	Wed	Thu	Fri	Sat
					1	2
3	4	5	6	7	8	9
10	11	12	13	14	15	16
17	18	19	20	21	22	23
24	25	26	27	28	29	30
31						

Blog Archive

▸ August (18)
▸ July
▸ June
▸ May
▸ April
▸ March
▸ February
▸ January
▸ December
▸ November
▸ October
▸ September

憂心忡忡

August 18

　　今天下午正當我在喝咖啡時，我看到我們老闆在跟山姆講話。突然間，山姆哭了起來並衝出他的辦公室。他甩上門後便走到他的辦公桌開始收拾個人物品，場面簡直尷尬極了。辦公室裡所有人都看傻了，而我也開始坐立難安了起來，因為我知道下一個就是我。

About me

Tom

Calendar

◄　　　*August*　　　►

Sun	Mon	Tue	Wed	Thu	Fri	Sat
					1	2
3	4	5	6	7	8	9
10	11	12	13	14	15	16
17	18	19	20	21	22	23
24	25	26	27	28	29	30
31						

Blog Archive

▸ August (18)
▸ July
▸ June
▸ May
▸ April
▸ March
▸ February
▸ January
▸ December
▸ November
▸ October
▸ September

Tom at Blog 於 August 08.18. PM 05:32 發表│回覆 (0)│引用 (0)│收藏 (0)│轉寄給朋友│檢舉

標題 sweat [swɛt] 作動詞表『流汗、出汗』，而 bullet [ˋbulɪt] 則是『子彈』。sweat bullets 字面上表『揮汗如子彈』，也就是『大量出汗』之意。試想當一個人極度焦慮的時候，常常會冒出如子彈大的汗珠，故此用法引申為一個人『非常擔心、十分著急』之意，就如同網誌作者『挫著等』的意思一樣。

表『汗如雨下』時，除了 sweat bullets 外，尚有下列說法：

sweat buckets　　大量出汗，汗如雨下

= sweat like a pig

= sweat heavily

= sweat a lot

　＊bucket [ˋbʌkɪt] *n.* 水桶

例: Marcus was soon sweating buckets after shooting some hoops in the sun.

（馬克思在豔陽下射籃了幾次後便汗流浹背。）

　　＊shoot hoops　　（籃球）投籃

　　　hoop [hup] *n.*（籃球）籃框

sweat 作名詞時，有下列俚語用法：

No sweat.　　沒問題。小意思。

= No problem.

例: Helen: Could you help me put the luggage in the trunk?

　　Berry: No sweat!

（海倫：可以麻煩你幫我把行李放進後車廂嗎？）

（貝瑞：沒問題！）

🔍 字詞幫幫忙！

1. all of a sudden　　　　突然地

= suddenly [ˋsʌdn̩lɪ] *adv.*

2. burst into tears　　　　突然大哭起來

= burst out crying

burst into laughter　　突然大笑起來

= burst out laughing

例: The little girl burst out crying when the nurse gave her a shot in her arm.
（護士在那名小女孩手臂上打針時，她放聲大哭了起來。）

Johnny's funny face made Carol burst into laughter.
（強尼做的鬼臉讓卡蘿大笑了出來。）

3. rush out of...　　衝出……

4. embarrassing [ɪmˋbærəsɪŋ] *a.* 令人尷尬的，令人困窘的

embarrassed [ɪmˋbærəst] *a.* 感到尷尬的，感到困窘的

例: It was quite embarrassing for me to attend my ex-girlfriend's wedding.
（去參加我前女友的婚禮實在挺尷尬的。）

Jack felt embarrassed when he slipped on stage.
（傑克在台上滑倒時感覺超糗的。）

5. slam [slæm] *vt.* 猛地關上

例: Mike's mom kept telling him not to slam the refrigerator door.
（麥克的媽媽一再叫他關冰箱門不要用甩的。）

6. pack up...　　把……打包／裝箱

例: Jerry didn't pack up his bags until the night before his trip to France.
（傑瑞直到要去法國的前一晚才打包他的行李。）

7. belongings [bəˋlɔŋɪŋz] *n.* 所有物；攜帶物品（恆為複數）

personal belongings　　個人隨身攜帶物品

例: All of our personal belongings were scanned before we boarded the flight.
（我們所有的個人隨身攜帶物品在登機前都經過掃瞄。）

＊scan [skæn] *vt.* 掃瞄

8. stun [stʌn] *vt.* 使大吃一驚，使目瞪口呆

例: Phillip's strange dance moves stunned his girlfriend.
（菲力普奇怪的舞步讓他的女友看得目瞪口呆。）

The Axe

August 19

As soon as I walked into my boss's office, I could tell that I was going to **get the axe**. The **tension** in the air was so **thick** that I felt like I could cut it with a knife. He **sat** me **down** and said that I failed an **internal review**, but he wouldn't show me the results. I **was pissed off**, but I didn't **make a scene** like Sam.

About me

Tom

Calendar

◄   August   ►

Sun	Mon	Tue	Wed	Thu	Fri	Sat
					1	2
3	4	5	6	7	8	9
10	11	12	13	14	15	16
17	18	19	20	21	22	23
24	25	26	27	28	29	30
31						

Blog Archive

- ► August (19)
- ► July
- ► June
- ► May
- ► April
- ► March
- ► February
- ► January
- ► December
- ► November
- ► October
- ► September

Tom at Blog 於 August 08.19. PM 03:37 發表 | 回覆 (0) | 引用 (0) | 收藏 (0) | 轉寄給朋友 | 檢舉

回家吃自己

Index | Links | about | comments | Photo

August 19

一走進老闆的辦公室，我看得出我就要被炒魷魚了。
空氣裡的緊張氣氛沉重到我覺得可以用刀子把它切開。他
讓我坐下，然後說我沒通過內部審查，但是他不肯讓我看
結果。我氣炸了，可是我沒像山姆那樣丟人現眼。

About me

Tom

Calendar

◄　　　　August　　　　►

Sun	Mon	Tue	Wed	Thu	Fri	Sat
					1	2
3	4	5	6	7	8	9
10	11	12	13	14	15	16
17	18	19	20	21	22	23
24	25	26	27	28	29	30
31						

Blog Archive

▸ August (19)
▸ July
▸ June
▸ May
▸ April
▸ March
▸ February
▸ January
▸ December
▸ November
▸ October
▸ September

Tom at Blog 於 August 08.19. PM 03:37 發表 | 回覆 (0) | 引用 (0) | 收藏 (0) | 轉寄給朋友 | 檢舉

123

標題中的 axe [æks] 是指『斧頭』，試想一下，在辦公室裡得到一把斧頭，感覺是不是就像中文裡說的『被砍頭』，準備回家吃自己呢？因此 get the axe 就是『被解僱』的意思。

例: Marvin got the axe because he was caught stealing money from the cash register.

（馬文被炒魷魚，因為他被抓到偷收銀機的錢。）

＊cash register　　收銀機

英文裡這類被公司炒魷魚或開除的說法還不少，除了最常見的 get fired 之外，還有以下數種常見的說法：

get the boot

boot [but] 是『靴子』，get the boot 字面上的意思為『得到靴子』，也就是被人踢了一腳，叫你走路的意思，因此引申為『被炒魷魚』。

get the sack
= get sacked

sack [sæk] 原指『麻袋』，get the sack 字面上的意思是『得到麻袋』。從前雇主開除員工後，都會給他們一個麻袋以便收拾自己的物品捲舖蓋走路，所以本俚語後來就引申為『被開除』之意。sack 也可作動詞用，表『開除（某人）』。

例: If you don't want to get the boot, you'd better clock in on time each day.

= If you don't want to get the sack, you'd better clock in on time each day.

= If you don't want to get sacked, you'd better clock in on time each day.

（如果你不想捲舖蓋走路，最好每天準時打卡上班。）

＊clock in / out　　上班 / 下班打卡

 字詞幫幫忙！

1. **tension** [ˈtɛnʃən] *n.* 緊繃；緊張

   例: There was a lot of tension between the two countries after the terrorist attack.

   （恐怖攻擊行動發生後，兩國之間的關係很緊張。）

Massage helps relieve tension in the shoulders and back.
（按摩有助於減輕肩膀和背部的肌肉緊繃。）
＊relieve [rɪˋliv] *vt.* 緩和（痛苦、情緒等）

2. **thick** [θɪk] *a.* 厚重的
thin [θɪn] *a.* 稀薄的

3. **sit sb down**　　使某人坐下
比較:
seat sb　　安排某人坐下
＊seat [sit] *vt.* 使就座
例: The teacher tried to sit the noisy student down.
　　（那位老師試圖要讓那吵鬧的學生坐下。）
　　The waitress seated me by the window.
　　（服務生把我安排在窗邊坐下。）

4. **internal** [ɪnˋtɜn!] *a.* 內部的
external [ɪkˋstɜnəl] *a.* 外部的

5. **review** [rɪˋvju] *n.* 審查；評論

6. **be pissed off**　　感到很生氣（粗俗用語）
piss sb off　　惹某人生氣（粗俗用語）
piss [pɪs] *vt.* 使生氣 & *vi.* 小便（粗俗用語）
例: Mike was pissed off when he knew that he didn't get the promotion.
　　（麥克得知自己未獲得升遷時簡直氣炸了。）
　　It really pissed me off when my scooter broke down on the way to work.
　　（我的機車在上班途中拋錨，真是把我氣炸了。）

7. **make a scene**　　當眾大吵大鬧（以致丟人現眼或出醜）；出洋相
scene [sin] *n.* （在公開場合）吵鬧
例: Mary was mad at her boyfriend and made a scene by slapping him on the street.
　　（瑪莉對她男友很火大，在街上當眾打了他一巴掌丟人現眼。）

Unit 32

Hopping Mad

Index | *Links* | *about* | *comments* | *Photo*

August 20

I wasn't so upset when I left work, but by the time I got home, I was hopping mad. The more I thought about it, the more **stark raving mad** I became. My boss had always treated me **poorly**, but I felt **disrespected** by his **lame** excuse. I believe he fired me for no reason, and I'm going to **the Department of Labor** to **file** a **complaint**.

About me

Tom

Calendar

◄ August ►

Sun	Mon	Tue	Wed	Thu	Fri	Sat
					1	2
3	4	5	6	7	8	9
10	11	12	13	14	15	16
17	18	19	20	21	22	23
24	25	26	27	28	29	30
31						

Blog Archive

► August (20)
► July
► June
► May
► April
► March
► February
► January
► December
► November
► October
► September

Tom at Blog 於 August 08.20. PM 07:14 發表 | 回覆 (0) | 引用 (0) | 收藏 (0) | 轉寄給朋友 | 檢舉

126

氣到跳腳

Index | Links | about | comments | Photo

August 20

　　我離職時並沒有很生氣，但回到家後我卻氣到跳腳。我越想越火大。我老闆對我總是很糟，但他的爛理由卻讓我覺得很不受尊重。我認為他沒來由的就開除我，我要去勞工局申訴才是。

About me

Tom

Calendar

◄　　　*August*　　　►

Sun	Mon	Tue	Wed	Thu	Fri	Sat
					1	2
3	4	5	6	7	8	9
10	11	12	13	14	15	16
17	18	19	20	21	22	23
24	25	26	27	28	29	30
31						

Blog Archive

▶ August (20)
▶ July
▶ June
▶ May
▶ April
▶ March
▶ February
▶ January
▶ December
▶ November
▶ October
▶ September

Tom at Blog 於 August 08.20. PM 07:14 發表 | 回覆 (0) | 引用 (0) | 收藏 (0) | 轉寄給朋友 | 檢舉

網誌主角無故被老闆解僱，所以感到很不爽。網誌的標題 hopping mad 就是用來形容人『氣到跳腳』、『火大到不行』。 hopping [ˋhɑpɪŋ] 出自動詞 hop，指『跳躍』之意，在此處當副詞，用來修飾形容詞 mad （生氣的）。而網誌裡用的 stark raving mad 和 hopping mad 一樣，也是『非常火大』的意思。以下就介紹英文中有關『生氣』的說法：

hopping mad 氣到跳腳

stark raving mad 火冒三丈，非常火大

= **stark staring mad**

＊stark [stɑrk] *adv.* 完全，全然（口語，等於 entirely，只用於上列片語中）

raving [ˋrevɪŋ] *adv.* 瘋瘋癲癲地

staring [ˋstɛrɪŋ] *adv.* 完全（口語，亦等於 entirely，只用於上列片語中）

fly into a rage 勃然大怒

＊rage [redʒ] *n.* 盛怒，狂怒

例: Linda was hopping mad about the mistake that Jeff made on the document.

（琳達對於傑夫文件裡犯的錯誤氣到跳腳。）

The superstar was stark raving mad when she was told that her concert had been canceled.

（當這名巨星得知她的演唱會被取消時，簡直火冒三丈。）

My parents flew into a rage when they found out I was kicked out of school.

（我父母發現我被退學時勃然大怒。）

 字 詞幫幫忙！

1. **poorly** [ˋpʊrlɪ] *adv.* 糟糕地，不好地

2. **disrespected** [ˏdɪsrɪˋspɛktɪd] *a.* 沒有受到尊重的
   disrespect [ˏdɪsrɪˋspɛkt] *vt.* 對……不敬 / 無禮
   例: I felt disrespected when Tracy turned her back while I was talking to her.
   （我跟崔西講話時，她卻背對我，讓我感到不受尊重。）

You shouldn't disrespect your parents and talk to them like this.
（你不應該對父母不敬，這樣對他們說話。）

3. lame [lem] *a.* 跛腳的；無說服力的
   a lame excuse　　一個薄弱／沒說服力的藉口

4. the Department of Labor　　勞工局
   labor [`lebɚ] *n.* 勞工

5. file [faɪl] *vt.* & *vi* 提出（申請、申訴等）
   file for...　　（向法院）申請……
   例: The locals filed a lawsuit against the construction company over noise pollution.
   （當地百姓對該建築公司提出噪音污染的訴訟。）
   ＊lawsuit [`lɔˏsut] *n.* 訴訟
   　 construction [kənˋstrʌkʃən] *n.* 建造，建設
   After a major argument with her husband, Mrs. Lee filed for a divorce.
   （李太太與先生大吵一架後，向法院申請離婚。）

6. complaint [kəmˋplent] *n.* 控告；抱怨
   complain [kəmˋplen] *vi.* 抱怨
   complain of...　　訴說……（病痛）
   complain about...　　抱怨……
   例: I'm tired of listening to your complaints. If you don't like your job, why don't you quit?
   （我很厭倦聽你抱怨。如果你不喜歡你的工作，為什麼不辭職呢？）
   Bob has been complaining of a headache, but he refuses to see a doctor.
   （鮑伯一直訴說頭痛，但他不願去看醫生。）
   Anna complained about the inconvenience caused by the construction of the subway.
   （安娜抱怨地鐵施工帶來的不便。）
   ＊inconvenience [ˏɪnkənˋvinjəns] *n.* 不方便

Forget about It

August 21

I spent two or three hours at the Department of Labor today, and it was **in vain**. The woman I talked to told me my boss **was free to** do whatever he wanted. **After all**, it was his company, and I failed the review. She **advised** me that it should **be out of the question** for me to win a **case** against him. **Eventually**, I **gave up** and **headed** home. Now, I'm going to **polish up** my **resume** and find a new job.

About me

Tom

Calendar

◄   August   ►

Sun	Mon	Tue	Wed	Thu	Fri	Sat
					1	2
3	4	5	6	7	8	9
10	11	12	13	14	15	16
17	18	19	20	21	22	23
24	25	26	27	28	29	30
31						

Blog Archive

- ► August (21)
- ► July
- ► June
- ► May
- ► April
- ► March
- ► February
- ► January
- ► December
- ► November
- ► October
- ► September

Tom at Blog 於 August 08.21. PM 06:58 發表 | 回覆 (0) | 引用 (0) | 收藏 (0) | 轉寄給朋友 | 檢舉

算了吧

Index | *Links* | *about* | *comments* | *Photo*

August 21

　　我今天在勞工局花了兩三個小時，卻徒勞無功。和我說話的那位女士告訴我說，我老闆想怎麼做就怎麼做。畢竟，那是他的公司，而且我的考核沒過。她勸告我說，我告老闆的官司應該不可能會贏。最後我放棄了，便打道回府。現在我要潤飾我的履歷找新工作了。

About me

Tom

Calendar

◀　　*August*　　▶

Sun	Mon	Tue	Wed	Thu	Fri	Sat
					1	2
3	4	5	6	7	8	9
10	11	12	13	14	15	16
17	18	19	20	21	22	23
24	25	26	27	28	29	30
31						

Blog Archive

▸ August (21)
▸ July
▸ June
▸ May
▸ April
▸ March
▸ February
▸ January
▸ December
▸ November
▸ October
▸ September

Tom at Blog 於 August 08.21. PM 06:58 發表 | 回覆 (0) | 引用 (0) | 收藏 (0) | 轉寄給朋友 | 檢舉

做任何事情最怕費盡心機，努力了老半天，到頭來卻白忙一場、徒勞無功，就像網誌中所用到的 in vain。vain [ven] 原是形容詞，表『虛榮的』，但 vain 亦可作名詞，恆與 in 並用，形成 in vain 的用法，就是『徒勞無功、白費工夫』之意。

in vain　　徒勞無功，白費工夫

= to no avail
= to no purpose
= without result
　＊avail [əˋvel] *n.* 效用

例: We tried to persuade George to quit smoking, but (it was) in vain.

= We tried in vain to persuade George to quit smoking.

（我們設法說服喬治戒菸，但是沒有用。）

Helen looked for her puppy in the park for hours, but to no avail.

（海倫在公園裡找她的小狗找了好幾個小時，但是徒勞無功。）

1. be free to V　　隨意 / 任意（做）……

例: You are free to order anything you want. It's on me.
（你可以隨意點任何你想吃的東西，我請客。）

2. After all, S + V　　畢竟 / 終究，……

例: Don't expect too much of Billy. After all, he is only a child.
（別對比利期望太大。畢竟，他還只是個孩子。）

3. advise [ədˋvaɪz] *vt.* 勸告，建議

advise + that 子句　　勸告 / 建議……

注意:

advise 之後接 that 子句作受詞時，為意志動詞，故 that 子句中須使用助動詞 should，但 should 常予以省略，而直接接原形動詞。

例: I advised that John (should) save money for a rainy day.
（我建議約翰應該要存錢以備不時之需。）

4. **be out of the question**　不可能

= be impossible

例: Tom: Can I borrow the car, Dad?

　　Dad: No. It's out of the question.

（湯姆：我能借用你的車子嗎，老爸？）

（老爸：不行。門兒都沒有。）

5. **case** [kes] *n.* 官司，案件

win / lose a case　　打贏官司 / 輸掉官司

例: The famous lawyer never lost a case.

（那位名律師從沒打輸過一場官司。）

6. **eventually** [ɪˋvɛntʃʊəlɪ] *adv.* 最後，終於

例: At first, Tina was suspicious, but I eventually earned her trust.

（起初蒂娜對我心存懷疑，但我最後贏得了她的信任。）

＊suspicious [səˋspɪʃəs] *a.* 猜疑的

7. **give up (...)**　　放棄（……）

例: Anna plans to give up her job and take care of her children full-time.

（安娜計劃放棄她的工作專心照顧孩子。）

8. **head +** 地方副詞（**home, there, here** 等）　前往某地

head to + 地方名詞　　前往某地

= head for + 地方名詞

例: I'm heading for Tokyo this afternoon.

（我今天下午就要前往東京。）

9. **polish (up)...**　　潤飾 / 改善……

polish [ˋpɑlɪʃ] *vi.* & *vt.* 潤飾；擦亮

例: I have to polish up this report before I turn it in.

（繳交這份報告前，我必須再潤飾一下。）

Before the guests arrived, Kathy polished all of the silverware in the kitchen.

（客人到達前，凱西將廚房裡所有的銀器都擦得亮晶晶。）

10. **resume** [ˌrɛzjʊˋme] *n.* 履歷表

The First Interview

Index | *Links* | *about* | *comments* | *Photo*

August 22

I've sent out about 25 emails over the past week and finally got my first interview. When I went down to the office, I **screwed** it **up big time**. First of all, I was half an hour late because I didn't know the **exact directions**. Then, when I got there, I was all **sweaty** because I had been looking for the office so long. Finally, the interviewer and I just didn't **click**. I guess I will have to **try my luck** elsewhere.

About me

Tom

Calendar

◄　　August　　►

Sun	Mon	Tue	Wed	Thu	Fri	Sat
					1	2
3	4	5	6	7	8	9
10	11	12	13	14	15	16
17	18	19	20	21	22	23
24	25	26	27	28	29	30
31						

Blog Archive

▸ August (22)
▸ July
▸ June
▸ May
▸ April
▸ March
▸ February
▸ January
▸ December
▸ November
▸ October
▸ September

Tom at Blog 於 August 08.22. PM 08:23 發表 | 回覆 (0) | 引用 (0) | 收藏 (0) | 轉寄給朋友 | 檢舉

面試第一回合

August 22

　　過去一個星期我寄出了大約 **25** 封的電子郵件，最後終於獲得第一次面試機會。我去到對方公司時徹底把它搞砸了。首先，我遲到了半個鐘頭，因為我不知道確切的位置。接著當我總算到了那裡後，卻因找辦公室找了老半天而滿身大汗。最後，我和面試官似乎就是不對盤，看來我得到別的地方碰碰運氣囉。

About me

Tom

Calendar

◀　　*August*　　▶

Sun	Mon	Tue	Wed	Thu	Fri	Sat
					1	2
3	4	5	6	7	8	9
10	11	12	13	14	15	16
17	18	19	20	21	22	23
24	25	26	27	28	29	30
31						

Blog Archive

▸ August (22)
▸ July
▸ June
▸ May
▸ April
▸ March
▸ February
▸ January
▸ December
▸ November
▸ October
▸ September

Tom at Blog 於 August 08.22. PM 08:23 發表｜回覆 (0)｜引用 (0)｜收藏 (0)｜轉寄給朋友｜檢舉

網誌中的 click [klɪk] 是動詞，原表『（使）發出卡嗒聲』，諸如筆敲桌面、鞋跟踏地或將門關緊的聲音都可以用 click 這個字來表示。

例: The man sitting next to me kept clicking his pen, which was annoying.

（坐我旁邊的那個男的不斷按他的筆而發出卡嗒聲，真令人心煩。）

此外，click 作名詞時可表『（點滑鼠時發出的）卡嗒聲』，因此 click 作動詞也有『按滑鼠點擊』之意，與介詞 on 並用。我們常在網頁上看到 click here 就是表『點擊此處』。

click on...　　用電腦滑鼠點擊……

例: Just click on the icon and the file will open.

（只要用滑鼠在圖像上點一下，檔案就會開啟。）

＊icon [ˋaɪkɑn] *n.* （電腦）圖像

但若用在人與人之間，click 的意思可又大不同了。當我們說 A and B click 或 A clicks with B，其實是表『A 和 B 一拍即合／一見如故』。類似的說法如下：

hit it off (with sb)　　（和某人）一拍即合／一見如故

get along (with sb)　　（和某人）處得來

例: My mother and my girlfriend seemed to click after I introduced them to each other.

（我介紹我媽和女友互相認識後，她們似乎一拍即合。）

Amanda hit it off with her new co-worker as soon as they met.

（亞曼達和她的新同事一見面就很投緣。）

Richard and his older brother just can't get along, so they seldom see each other.

（李察和他哥哥就是處不來，因此他們鮮少往來。）

字詞幫幫忙！

1. **interview** [ˋɪntɚ͵vju] *n.* 面試，面談

2. screw...up / screw up... 把……搞糟 / 弄糟

= mess...up / mess up...

例: The boss warned Becker that if he screwed up the project, he could say goodbye to his promotion.
（老闆警告貝克如果他搞砸這個專案的話，就得跟升遷說拜拜了。）

3. big time 十分，極度（作副詞用）

= to an extreme degree

＊extreme [ɪkˋstrim] *a.* 極度的

例: Benny lent me some money to tide me over until I get paid, so I owed him big time.
（班尼在我發薪水前借給我一些錢讓我度過難關，所以我欠他一份大人情。）

＊tide sb over 幫某人度過難關

4. exact [ɪgˋzækt] *a.* 精準的，準確的

5. directions [dəˋrɛkʃənz] *n.*（行路的）指引（恆為複數）

direction [dəˋrɛkʃən] *n.* 方向

a sense of direction 方向感

例: Susan got lost in the night market, so she asked a vendor to give her directions.
（蘇珊在夜市裡迷路，所以她請小販為她指路。）

Bob is a man without a sense of direction, so he never drives without bringing a GPS with him.
（鮑伯是個沒方向感的人，所以他開車一定會帶著『全球衛星定位系統』。）

6. sweaty [ˋswɛtɪ] *a.* 滿身是汗的

7. try one's luck 碰碰某人的運氣

例: Ralph wanted to try his luck at the casino, but he ended up losing his shirt.
（羅夫想在賭場試試手氣，結果卻輸得精光。）

＊casino [kəˋsino] *n.* 賭場

lose one's shirt 某人失去一切

Unit 35

Down-and-Out

Index | *Links* | *about* | *comments* | *Photo*

August 23

It's been a couple of weeks, and I still don't have any **leads** on jobs. Right now, I'd **give my right arm to** have some **income** coming in. My rent is **due**, and I'm hungry. I haven't **been so down-and-out** in a long time. I guess I should take a **part-time** job just to **pay my bills**.

About me

Tom

Calendar

◄   August   ►

Sun	Mon	Tue	Wed	Thu	Fri	Sat
					1	2
3	4	5	6	7	8	9
10	11	12	13	14	15	16
17	18	19	20	21	22	23
24	25	26	27	28	29	30
31						

Blog Archive

▸ August (23)
▸ July
▸ June
▸ May
▸ April
▸ March
▸ February
▸ January
▸ December
▸ November
▸ October
▸ September

Tom at Blog 於 August 08.23. PM 10:34 發表 | 回覆 (0) | 引用 (0) | 收藏 (0) | 轉寄給朋友 | 檢舉

窮困潦倒的日子

August 23

　　幾個星期過去了，我的工作還是沒著落。現在我願意不惜任何代價好讓自己有收入進來。我的房租到期了，而且又餓著肚子。我已經很久沒這麼落魄了。我想我該去找個兼職工作好支付我的帳單。

Tom at Blog 於 August 08.23. PM 10:34 發表 | 回覆 (0) | 引用 (0) | 收藏 (0) | 轉寄給朋友 | 檢舉

雖說錢不是萬能，但沒錢還真是萬萬不能！所以失業後一直找不到工作的網誌作者面臨餓肚子和繳房租的時刻，才會說出 "I'd give my right arm to get some income coming in." 這樣的話。give one's right arm 字面上是『給出某人的右手臂』，由於大多數人都是右撇子，所以我們得依賴右手做很多事，因此當你說出願意『給出右手臂』時，就表示你願意『不惜任何代價去做某件事』，這便是『有錢能使鬼推磨』的最佳寫照啊！

give one's right arm to V 　　不惜任何代價做……

= give one's eyeteeth to V

　　＊eyetooth [ˈaɪˌtuθ] *n.* 犬齒（複數為 eyeteeth [ˈaɪˌtiθ]）

= canine tooth [ˈkenaɪn ˌtuθ]（複數為 canine teeth）

　例: Thousands of people would give their right arm to get a job at this multinational company.

　　（數以千計的人願意不惜一切代價到這間跨國公司上班。）

　　＊multinational [ˌmʌltaɪˈnæʃənḷ] *a.* 跨國的

另外，以下的用法則有『竭盡全力／不遺餘力（做）……』的意思：

do one's best / utmost to V 　　竭盡全力／不遺餘力（做）……

= do one's level best to V

= try one's best to V

= make every effort to V

= spare no effort to V

= go all out to V

= go out of one's way to V

= leave no stone unturned to V

　　＊unturned [ʌnˈtɜnd] *a.* 未翻轉的

　例: Mr. Chen made every effort to give his family a good life.

　　（陳先生竭盡全力給他的家人過好日子。）

　　Ted always goes out of his way to please his boss and hopefully get a promotion.

　　（泰德總是使出渾身解數討好上司，希望因此獲得升遷。）

　　The police left no stone unturned in their search for the missing child.

　　（警方不遺餘力搜尋那個失蹤的孩子。）

字詞幫幫忙！

1. be down-and-out

窮困潦倒的，落魄的（指一個人沒有工作、沒有錢又無人幫忙的困境）

例: Jack has been down-and-out since he went bankrupt last year.

（傑克自從去年破產後，就變得窮困潦倒。）

*bankrupt [ˋbæŋkrʌpt] *a.* 破產的

go bankrupt　破產（此處 go 表『變成』，相當 become 之意。）

2. lead [lid] *n.* 線索（可數，常用複數）

例: Mandy is very depressed because she still doesn't have any leads on her missing dog.

（曼蒂非常沮喪，因為她走失的狗狗現在一點下落都沒有。）

3. income [ˋɪnˏkʌm] *n.* 收入

a high / low income　高收入 / 低收入

= a large / small income

例: People with high incomes usually have to pay more taxes.

（高收入的人通常都得多繳稅。）

4. due [dju] *a.* 到期的

例: I need to cash this check later because my rent is due today.

（我等一下得去兌換這張支票，因為我的租金今天到期。）

5. part-time [ˋpɑrtˏtaɪm] *a.* & *adv.* 兼職的 / 地

full-time [ˋfʊlˏtaɪm] *a.* & *adv.* 全職的 / 地

例: When I was in college, I had a part-time job at a fast-food restaurant.

（我唸大學時曾在速食店打過工。）

Nancy works part-time / full-time as a cram school teacher.

（南西在補習班當兼職 / 全職老師。）

6. pay one's bills　付某人的帳單

例: Terry's salary is hardly enough for him to pay his bills, let alone buy a car.

（泰瑞的薪水要付帳單都快不夠了，更別說是要買車了。）

*let alone...

更別提……（有連接詞作用，此處連接兩個原形動詞片語 pay his bills 及 buy a car）

Unit 36

Waiting Tables

Index | *Links* | *about* | *comments* | *Photo*

August 24

I was **searching** through the want **ads** recently, and I found a job that could **be right up my alley**. It was for a waiter at a **fancy** restaurant. I've never waited tables, but I'm a quick learner. I **aced** the interview, and I'll start work tomorrow. I'm excited that I'll have some income, but I'm nervous because I don't want to **mess up** people's **orders**.

About me

Tom

Calendar

◄   *August*   ►

Sun	Mon	Tue	Wed	Thu	Fri	Sat
					1	2
3	4	5	6	7	8	9
10	11	12	13	14	15	16
17	18	19	20	21	22	23
24	25	26	27	28	29	30
31						

Blog Archive

▸ August (24)
▸ July
▸ June
▸ May
▸ April
▸ March
▸ February
▸ January
▸ December
▸ November
▸ October
▸ September

Tom at Blog 於 August 08.24. PM 05:18 發表 | 回覆 (0) | 引用 (0) | 收藏 (0) | 轉寄給朋友 | 檢舉

服務生初體驗

August 24

　　我最近都在徵人廣告上找工作，結果我找到一個可能會適合我的差事，那就是在一家高級餐廳當服務生，我從來沒端過盤子，但我學得很快。我順利通過了面試，明天我就要開始上工了。我很興奮會有收入，但我還蠻緊張的，因為我不想搞砸別人點的菜。

About me

Tom

Calendar

◀　　*August*　　▶

Sun	Mon	Tue	Wed	Thu	Fri	Sat
					1	2
3	4	5	6	7	8	9
10	11	12	13	14	15	16
17	18	19	20	21	22	23
24	25	26	27	28	29	30
31						

Blog Archive

► August (24)
► July
► June
► May
► April
► March
► February
► January
► December
► November
► October
► September

Tom at Blog 於 August 08.24. PM 05:18 發表 | 回覆 (0) | 引用 (0) | 收藏 (0) | 轉寄給朋友 | 檢舉

143

alley [`ælɪ] 原指『小巷、巷道』，一般都在大馬路的後面，但 be (right) up one's alley 或 be (right) down one's alley 的意思是『很適合某人的興趣或才能』、『（正）合某人的口味／胃口』（right 在此為強調用法，表『正是』），若是將一個人的興趣或專長的領域比喻為一條窄巷，那麼這個片語便十分容易理解了。

例: Basketball is right up Eddie's alley.

（籃球這種運動完全適合艾迪。）

A suite with a view of the coast is right down Sean's alley.

（這間有海景的套房正合尚恩的胃口。）

下列用法則表『不是某人所好、不對某人的胃口』：

be not one's cup of tea　　不是某人所好，不對某人的胃口（僅用於否定句中）

例: Bill: Would you like to go see that new action movie with me?

Lily: No, thanks. That type of film isn't exactly my cup of tea.

（比爾：妳要和我去看那部新的動作片嗎？）

（莉莉：不，謝了。那種類型的電影不合我的胃口。）

字詞幫幫忙！

1. **wait tables**　　（在餐館）端盤子，服務顧客

   wait on sb　　服侍（某人）進餐

   例: Nicholas worked his way through college by waiting tables.

   （尼可拉斯靠在餐廳端盤子唸完大學。）

   Amy has waited on all kinds of customers, and the worst ones were the ones that didn't tip.

   （艾咪服侍過各種客人，而最糟的就是那些不給小費的客人。）

2. **search** [sɜtʃ] *vi.* & *vt.* 搜尋

   search for...　　搜尋……

   例: Police have been searching for the missing child for nearly two weeks.

   （警方尋找那名失蹤兒童已近兩個星期。）

Mike searched every possible place for his car keys.
（麥克在每個可能的地方找他車鑰匙。）

3. **ad** [æd] *n.* 廣告（為 advertisement [ˌædvɚ'taɪzmənt / 'ædɚˌtaɪzmənt] 的縮寫）

want ads　　徵人廣告

place / put an ad / advertisement　　刊登廣告

例: My company will place an advertisement in the newspaper for a secretary next week.
（我的公司下星期將在報上刊登徵聘秘書的廣告。）

4. **fancy** ['fænsɪ] *a.* 昂貴的，豪華的

例: Terry treated his parents to a fancy vacation.
（泰瑞招待他爸媽去渡一個豪華的假期。）

5. **ace** [es] *vt.* 在……方面表現出色；（考試）考得好

ace the interview　　順利通過面試

ace the test　　考試考得很好

例: Berry aced all of his final exams in his last semester of high school.
（在他高中的最後一個學期，貝瑞所有期末考科目都考得很好。）

6. **mess up... / mess...up**　　把……搞砸 / 弄糟

例: My husband messed up the kitchen while preparing dinner.
（我老公煮晚餐時把廚房搞得一團糟。）

7. **order** ['ɔrdɚ] *n.* 點菜；訂購

take one's order　　記下客人點的菜

place an / one's order　　（某人）訂貨，下訂單

例: It took forever for the waiter to come to take our order.
（我們等了很久，服務生才過來幫我們點菜。）

The product will be delivered in one week after you place your order online.
（在網路上下單後，商品會在一週內送達。）

A Forgetful First Day

Index | Links | about | comments | Photo

August 25

I used to think I **was cool as a cucumber**, but I've realized that I'm a **total screw-up**. I thought waiting tables would **be a piece of cake**, but **in reality**, it's not as simple as I **imagined**. I forgot people's orders, and two or three times, I had to give the **customers** free food because they waited so long for their order. The restaurant said they are going to take that money out of my **paycheck**.

About me

Tom

Calendar

◄   *August*   ►

Sun	Mon	Tue	Wed	Thu	Fri	Sat
					1	2
3	4	5	6	7	8	9
10	11	12	13	14	15	16
17	18	19	20	21	22	23
24	25	26	27	28	29	30
31						

Blog Archive

▸ August (25)
▸ July
▸ June
▸ May
▸ April
▸ March
▸ February
▸ January
▸ December
▸ November
▸ October
▸ September

Tom at Blog 於 August 08.25. PM 09:39 發表 | 回覆 (0) | 引用 (0) | 收藏 (0) | 轉寄給朋友 | 檢舉

August 25

　　我以前都覺得自己臨危不亂，但我現在才了解自己真是個笨手笨腳的人。我以為招呼顧客會是再簡單不過的事，但事實上卻不如我想像中的簡單。我忘記顧客點的餐，還有兩三次，我得因為顧客等餐等太久而免費招待食物。餐廳說他們會從我的薪水裡扣除這些費用。

About me

Tom

Calendar

◄　　　August　　　►

Sun	Mon	Tue	Wed	Thu	Fri	Sat
					1	2
3	4	5	6	7	8	9
10	11	12	13	14	15	16
17	18	19	20	21	22	23
24	25	26	27	28	29	30
31						

Blog Archive

▸ August (25)
▸ July
▸ June
▸ May
▸ April
▸ March
▸ February
▸ January
▸ December
▸ November
▸ October
▸ September

Tom at Blog 於 August 08.25. PM 09:39 發表｜回覆 (0)｜引用 (0)｜收藏 (0)｜轉寄給朋友｜檢舉

由於 cucumber [ˈkjukəmbɚ]（黃瓜）這種植物充滿了水分，所以瓜內的溫度會比外部的溫度低上好幾度。因此歐美人士總喜歡在吃勁辣食物時，用 cucumber 作為小菜，以其涼爽的口感來抑制辣度。這也就是為什麼會有 be (as) cool as a cucumber 的說法。cool [kul] 一般當形容詞時，意為『涼爽的』，但在形容人的情緒時，亦可解釋為『冷靜的、沉著的』，所以上述俚語字面上的意思是『如黃瓜一般涼爽』，引申為某人『臨危不亂、十分冷靜』。

例: Anna is always (as) cool as a cucumber, so I believe she will do well in the interview.

（安娜總是臨危不亂，所以我相信她的面試會表現很好。）

當我們覺得事情很容易就可以做好時，往往會說做那件事簡單地像吃飯、喝水一樣，而英文裡類似的說法便是『像吃塊蛋糕一樣簡單』：

It's a piece of cake.　　這件事簡單得很。這真是易如反掌。

= It's as easy as a pie.

= It's a cinch.

　＊cinch [sɪntʃ] *n.* 極容易的事情，輕鬆的工作

例: It's a piece of cake for Mark to strike up a conversation with pretty girls.

（和正妹打開話匣子對馬克而言是件輕而易舉的事。）

　＊strike up a conversation with sb　與某人打開話匣子

Preparing a meal is as easy as pie for Tina. She used to be a chef in a restaurant.

（對蒂娜來說，煮一頓飯根本沒什麼。她以前是餐廳的主廚。）

1. **forgetful** [fɚˈɡɛtfəl] *a.* 健忘的

unforgettable [ˌʌnfɚˈɡɛtəbḷ] *a.* 難忘的

例: Jim is a forgetful person. He often leaves his wallet and keys at home when he's out.

（吉姆是個健忘的人。他出門時常把皮夾和鑰匙忘在家裡。）

The trip to Paris was an unforgettable experience for me.
（那趟巴黎之旅對我而言是次難忘的經驗。）

2. **total** [`totl] *a.* 完全的，十足的

例: This party is a total failure. Neither the food nor the music is satisfying.
（這場派對真是糟透了。食物和音樂沒一樣令人滿意。）
＊satisfying [`sætɪsˌfaɪɪŋ] *a.* 令人滿意的

3. **screw-up** [`skruˌʌp] *n.* 弄糟事情的人；笨手笨腳的人
screw up... / screw...up　　搞砸……

例: Luke is such a screw-up. He never does anything right!
（路克真是個笨手笨腳的人。他從沒做對過任何事！）

If we can't rent costumes for the show, it'll really screw everything up.
（如果我們不能租到這場表演要用的服裝，真的會把一切搞砸！）
＊costume [`kɑstjum] *n.* 服裝（尤指戲服）

4. **in reality**　　實際上
＝ in practice
in theory　　理論上

例: Kelly's idea sounds good in theory, but I doubt if it can be done in reality.
（凱莉的點子理論上聽起來很不錯，但我懷疑實際上是否可行。）

5. **imagine** [ɪ`mædʒɪn] *vt.* 想像

6. **customer** [`kʌstəmɚ] *n.* 顧客
client [`klaɪənt] *n.* 顧客，客戶（尤指大宗買賣的客戶）

例: That restaurant has a large number of regular customers.
（那家餐廳有很多老主顧。）

Jim is delighted because he just closed a deal with a big client.
（吉姆因為剛和一位大客戶完成一筆交易，所以很開心。）
＊delighted [dɪ`laɪtɪd] *a.* 開心的
close a deal　　完成一筆交易

7. **paycheck** [`peˌtʃɛk] *n.* 薪水支票（通常指薪水）

Tips and More

Index | Links | about | comments | Photo

August 26

I think I'm finally **getting the hang of** the job. Today was my best day ever for two reasons. **First off**, I got a really big tip from a group of seven people. Usually I just get the 10 percent service **charge**, but they **were** so **satisfied with** my service that they left me another 40 percent. That wasn't even the best part. One of my **regular** customers started **flirting** with me **like crazy**.

About me

Tom

Calendar

◄   *August*   ►

Sun	Mon	Tue	Wed	Thu	Fri	Sat
					1	2
3	4	5	6	7	8	9
10	11	12	13	14	15	16
17	18	19	20	21	22	23
24	25	26	27	28	29	30
31						

Blog Archive

- ► August (26)
- ► July
- ► June
- ► May
- ► April
- ► March
- ► February
- ► January
- ► December
- ► November
- ► October
- ► September

Tom at Blog 於 August 08.26. PM 10:16 發表 | 回覆 (0) | 引用 (0) | 收藏 (0) | 轉寄給朋友 | 檢舉

小費多多

August 26

我想我對這份工作終於上手了。今天可說是最棒的一天，原因有兩個。第一，我從一群 **7** 個人的手中拿到一筆可觀的小費。通常我拿到百分之十的服務費，但他們非常滿意我的服務，所以另外留給我百分之四十的小費。這還不是最棒的。有個常客還開始拼命跟我打情罵俏。

About me

Tom

Calendar

◄   *August*   ►

Sun	Mon	Tue	Wed	Thu	Fri	Sat
					1	2
3	4	5	6	7	8	9
10	11	12	13	14	15	16
17	18	19	20	21	22	23
24	25	26	27	28	29	30
31						

Blog Archive

▶ August (26)
▶ July
▶ June
▶ May
▶ April
▶ March
▶ February
▶ January
▶ December
▶ November
▶ October
▶ September

網誌作者歷經了工作上一些失誤後，終於覺得自己比較上手了，也就是 get the hang of the job。

hang [hæŋ] 當動詞時，有『懸、掛』之意，三態為：hang, hung [hʌŋ], hung。

例: I hung a picture on the wall.

（我在牆上掛了一幅畫。）

The wet clothes are hanging on the clothesline.

（那些濕衣服正掛在曬衣繩上。）

＊clothesline [ˋkloz͵laɪn] *n.* 曬衣繩

而 hang 當名詞時則有『訣竅、要領』之意，因此 get the hang of... 就是『掌握做……的訣竅、對……上手』之意。

get the hang of... 掌握做……的訣竅，對……上手
= get the knack of...

＊knack [næk] *n.* 竅門，本領

例: After playing the video game a few times, Meg was getting the hang of it.

（那個電動遊戲玩了幾次後，梅格開始掌握到訣竅了。）

另一個類似的用法 **get the feel of...** 則表『培養對……的瞭解／感覺』、『習慣……』。

例: It took Jim a month to get the feel of his new job.

（吉姆花了一個月的時間才習慣他的新工作。）

字詞幫幫忙！

1. **tip** [tɪp] *n.* 小費；秘訣 & *vt.* 給小費

   例: Monica gave the waitress a tip of NT$300 for her excellent service.

   = Monica tipped the waitress NT$300 for her excellent service.

   （莫妮卡給這名女服務生 3 百塊錢小費以酬謝她優質的服務。）

   Thank you for giving me some new tips on how to ski.

   （謝謝你告訴我一些新的滑雪訣竅。）

2. **First off, S + V** 首先，……
= First of all, S + V
> 例: There are many people I would like to thank. First off, I want to mention my husband, Eric.
> （我要感謝的人很多。首先，我想謝謝我的老公艾瑞克。）

3. **charge** [tʃɑrdʒ] *n.* 費用
a service charge 服務費

4. **be satisfied with...** 對……感到滿意
= be contented with...
= be content with...
> * content [kən'tɛnt] *vt.* 使滿足 & *a.* 滿足的（= contented
> [kən'tɛntɪd] / satisfied ['sætɪs,faɪd] ）
> satisfy ['sætɪs,faɪ] *vt.* 使滿意，使高興
> 例: Henry isn't satisfied with his new hairstyle.
> （亨利不滿意自己的新髮型。）
> Suzie did her best to satisfy her customers.
> （蘇西盡她所能來滿足她的顧客。）

5. **regular** ['rɛgjələ] *a.* 經常的；定期的
regularly ['rɛgjələlɪ] *adv.* 規律地，定期地
a regular customer 常客
on a regular basis 定期地，固定地（= regularly）
> 例: My mother said I should go to the dentist on a regular basis.
> （我媽媽說我應該定期去看牙醫。）
> I check my email regularly, so you can contact me anytime.
> （我定期檢查我的電子信箱，所以你隨時可以跟我聯絡。）
> * contact ['kɑntækt] *vt.* 聯繫，聯絡

6. **flirt** [flɜt] *vi.* 調情，打情罵俏
flirt with sb 和某人調情 / 打情罵俏
> 例: I can't believe you were flirting with Matt. He is Susan's boyfriend.
> （我真不敢相信妳剛剛跟麥特打情罵俏。他可是蘇珊的男朋友。）

7. **like crazy** 拼命地；瘋狂地
> 例: Mandy and I shopped like crazy and bought all our Christmas gifts in one afternoon.
> （曼蒂和我拼命血拼，一個下午就買完所有的聖誕節禮物。）

Unit 39

Out with a Bang

Index | Links | about | comments | Photo

August 27

As soon as I got used to being a waiter, I was fired. I was carrying a **tray** with plates and glasses on it and got **bumped**. Everything fell onto a customer's table, and the manager fired me right **on the spot**. Well, at least I went out with a bang. I got another job, but I'm a little **hesitant**. It's only part-time work at an **amusement park**, and I think I might have to wear one of those **furry costumes**.

About me

Tom

Calendar

◄ August ►

Sun	Mon	Tue	Wed	Thu	Fri	Sat
					1	2
3	4	5	6	7	8	9
10	11	12	13	14	15	16
17	18	19	20	21	22	23
24	25	26	27	28	29	30
31						

Blog Archive

- August (27)
- July
- June
- May
- April
- March
- February
- January
- December
- November
- October
- September

Tom at Blog 於 August 08.27. PM 07:17 發表 | 回覆 (0) | 引用 (0) | 收藏 (0) | 轉寄給朋友 | 檢舉

轟轟烈烈地走人

August 27

　　我才剛適應服務生的工作就被炒魷魚了。我手上端著有盤子和玻璃杯的托盤時被撞到了。所有的東西全都掉到一位顧客的桌上，經理當場就要我回家吃自己。嗯，至少我是『轟轟烈烈』的離開。我找到另一個工作，不過有些遲疑。那只是在遊樂園打工，而且我想我可能還得穿上毛茸茸的道具服。

Tom at Blog 於 August 08.27. PM 07:17 發表｜回覆 (0)｜引用 (0)｜收藏 (0)｜轉寄給朋友｜檢舉

155

bang 作名詞時表『碰撞聲、發出砰的一聲』，with a bang 原指『砰然一聲』之意。

例: The door slammed with a bang.

（門砰的一聲關上了。）

　＊slam [slæm] *vi.* 猛地關上

網誌作者說自己 went out with a bang，這是因為作者被撞到，托盤上的盤子和玻璃杯砰的一聲全掉到顧客桌上，因而自我解嘲說『自己乒乒砰砰的離開』，引申為『自己轟轟烈烈的離開』。

with a bang 除表『砰然一聲』外，亦可表『很成功地』，用於下列結構：

start off with a bang　　極為成功

= go off with a bang

例: The birthday party started off with a bang when a clown jumped out of the cake.

（這次的生日派有小丑從蛋糕裡蹦出來，因此辦得很成功。）

1. **tray** [tre] *n.* 托盤

   ashtray [`æʃ͵tre] *n.* 煙灰缸

2. **bump** [bʌmp] *vt. & vi.* 碰撞

   bump into sth　　撞到某物

   bump into sb　　與某人不期而遇

= come across sb

= run into sb

　例: I bumped my head on the bookshelf.

　　（我的頭撞到書架。）

　　Yvonne bumped into the vase and knocked it over.

　　（伊芳撞到花瓶而把它給打翻了。）

　　Shane bumped into his friend at the bookstore.

　　（尚恩在書店和他朋友不期而遇。）

3. on the spot 立刻，當場

be caught on the spot　當場被逮

例: Denise applied for a job at the restaurant and was hired on the spot.

（丹尼斯去餐廳應徵工作，當場就被錄用了。）

＊apply for...　應徵……

The shoplifter was caught on the spot.

（那名商店扒手當場被逮個正著。）

＊shoplifter [ˈʃɑpˌlɪftɚ] *n.* 在商店偷東西的扒手

4. hesitant [ˈhɛzətənt] *a.* 遲疑的，躊躇的

hesitate [ˈhɛzəˌtet] *vi.* 遲疑，猶豫（接 to 引導的不定詞片語作受詞）

hesitate to V　做……猶豫不決

例: Eric was hesitant to call Jane for a date because she used to go out with his friend.

（艾瑞克猶豫是否該打電話約阿珍出來約會，因為她曾經和他的朋友約會過。）

Brian hesitated to tell his father that he dropped out of school.

（布萊恩猶豫要不要告訴父親他休學了。）

＊drop out of school　休學，輟學

5. amusement park [əˈmjuzmənt ˌpɑrk] *n.* 遊樂園

6. furry [ˈfɝɪ] *a.* 毛茸茸的

7. costume [ˈkɑstjum] *n.* （節慶、戲劇、化裝舞會等的）特別服裝；戲服

I'm Dying in Here

Index | Links | about | comments | Photo

August 28

Humiliation and **exhaustion**. These are the feelings I had on my first and last day of work at the amusement park today. I was **suffocating** in the **giraffe** suit because it was more than 30 degrees **Celsius** outside. Also, by 2:00 p.m. I became so **irritated** that I was <u>**flying off the handle**</u> when little kids hit me. At 7:00 p.m., I told my boss that **I couldn't take it anymore** and threw the **sweaty** giraffe suit on his desk.

About me

Tom

Calendar

◄ *August* ►

Sun	Mon	Tue	Wed	Thu	Fri	Sat
					1	2
3	4	5	6	7	8	9
10	11	12	13	14	15	16
17	18	19	20	21	22	23
24	25	26	27	28	29	30
31						

Blog Archive

- ► August (28)
- ► July
- ► June
- ► May
- ► April
- ► March
- ► February
- ► January
- ► December
- ► November
- ► October
- ► September

Tom at Blog 於 August 08.28. PM 10:53 發表 | 回覆 (0) | 引用 (0) | 收藏 (0) | 轉寄給朋友 | 檢舉

我要窒息了

August 28

　　丟臉、疲憊。這些是我今天第一天，也是最後一天在遊樂園工作的感受。因為外面的溫度超過攝氏 30 度，我簡直要在長頸鹿道具服裡窒息了。還有，到下午兩點時我超級煩躁的，有小孩打我時，我對他們大發脾氣。晚上 7 點時，我跟我的老闆說我再也受不了了，然後就把溼透的長頸鹿道具服丟在他桌上。

About me

Tom

Calendar

◄ August ►

Sun	Mon	Tue	Wed	Thu	Fri	Sat
					1	2
3	4	5	6	7	8	9
10	11	12	13	14	15	16
17	18	19	20	21	22	23
24	25	26	27	28	29	30
31						

Blog Archive

- ▸ August (28)
- ▸ July
- ▸ June
- ▸ May
- ▸ April
- ▸ March
- ▸ February
- ▸ January
- ▸ December
- ▸ November
- ▸ October
- ▸ September

Tom at Blog 於 August 08.28. PM 10:53 發表｜回覆 (0)｜引用 (0)｜收藏 (0)｜轉寄給朋友｜檢舉

網誌作者在大熱天穿著道具服而熱到要中暑，所以心情煩躁，對想要親近他的小朋友大發脾氣，網誌裡用了 fly off the handle 這個說法。handle [ˈhændl̩] 表『手把、手柄』之意，試想若有人手握斧頭，但斧頭卻從斧頭柄上飛出去，誰要是正好倒楣站在旁邊的話，就有可能遭殃被砍傷，因此 fly off the handle 就引申為『大發雷霆、大發脾氣』，而旁人為此受罪。

fly off the handle　　大發雷霆，大發脾氣

例: I don't understand why Larry flew off the handle when I mentioned Monica.

（我不懂為什麼我提到莫妮卡時，賴瑞會發這麼大的脾氣。）

以下再介紹幾個類似的用法：

fly into a rage　　大發雷霆，勃然大怒

＊rage [redʒ] *n.* 憤怒

例: Sam flew into a rage when he learned that his wife had spent NT$30,000 on a purse.

（山姆知道他太太花了 3 萬元買了一個手提包後大發雷霆。）

hit the roof / ceiling　　大發雷霆

例: My father hit the ceiling when my younger brother came home at 2:00 a.m.

（弟弟清晨兩點才回家讓老爸大發雷霆。）

blow one's top　　氣炸了

例: Cathy's boss blew his top and yelled at her because she lost the client.

（凱西的老闆氣炸了對她大吼大叫，因為她丟了那個客戶。）

lose one's temper / cool　　失去冷靜，發脾氣

例: My brother lost his temper when his classmates called him a silly name.

（當同學用愚蠢的名子罵我老弟時，他發脾氣了。）

　＊call sb a silly name　　用愚蠢的名字罵某人

　　call sb names　　用各種綽號罵某人（如『王八蛋』、『混蛋』等）

1. **humiliation** [hjuˌmɪlɪˋeʃən] *n.* 丟臉，羞辱

2. **exhaustion** [ɪgˋzɔstʃən] *n.* 筋疲力竭

3. **suffocate** [ˋsʌfəˌket] *vi. & vt.* （使）窒息
   例: The baby nearly suffocated when a blanket got wrapped around her head.
   （這個小嬰兒的頭被毛毯纏住，差一點就窒息了。）
   The heavy smoke almost suffocated the firefighter.
   （這片濃煙差點讓這名消防員窒息。）

4. **giraffe** [dʒəˋræf] *n.* 長頸鹿

5. **Celsius** [ˋsɛlsɪəs] *n.* 攝氏溫度
   Fahrenheit [ˋfærənˌhaɪt] *n.* 華氏溫度
   例: Water freezes when the temperature drops to zero degrees Celsius.
   （溫度降到攝氏零度時水就會結冰。）

6. **irritated** [ˋɪrəˌtetɪd] *a.* 惱怒的，煩躁的
   irritate [ˋɪrəˌtet] *vt.* 激怒
   例: If you play a joke on Cindy, she may get irritated.
   （如果你對辛蒂開玩笑，她可能會生氣。）
   Paul's rude behavior really irritated me.
   （保羅無禮的行為真的惹毛我了。）

7. **I can't take it anymore.**　　我再也受不了了。
   = I can't bear it anymore.
   = I can't stand it anymore.
   = I can't tolerate it anymore.
   = I can't put up with it anymore.
   例: My boss yells at me all the time. I can't take it anymore.
   （我老闆一天到晚對我吼叫。我再也受不了了。）

8. **sweaty** [ˋswɛtɪ] *a.* 滿身大汗的

The Midnight Shift

Index | *Links* | *about* | *comments* | *Photo*

August 29

After the restaurant and amusement park **disasters**, I was hoping to find something a bit more **stable**. One of my online **buddies**, Robert, said they were **hiring** a clerk at the supermarket near his house. I went in and **had a meet-and-greet with** the manager, and they hired me. The only problem is that I have to work <u>the graveyard shift</u> from midnight to eight in the morning.

About me

Tom

Calendar

◀   *August*   ▶

Sun	Mon	Tue	Wed	Thu	Fri	Sat
					1	2
3	4	5	6	7	8	9
10	11	12	13	14	15	16
17	18	19	20	21	22	23
24	25	26	27	28	29	30
31						

Blog Archive

- ▸ August (29)
- ▸ July
- ▸ June
- ▸ May
- ▸ April
- ▸ March
- ▸ February
- ▸ January
- ▸ December
- ▸ November
- ▸ October
- ▸ September

Tom at Blog 於 August 08.29. PM 06:14 發表 | 回覆 (0) | 引用 (0) | 收藏 (0) | 轉寄給朋友 | 檢舉

值大夜班

August 29

經過了餐廳和遊樂園徹底的失敗後，我希望找個比較穩定的工作。羅伯特是我在網路認識的一位好友，他說他家附近的超市正在招募店員。我到店裡和經理會晤後被錄取了。但問題來了，我得上大夜班，從午夜 12 點到清晨 8 點。

About me

Tom

Calendar

◀ *August* ▶

Sun	Mon	Tue	Wed	Thu	Fri	Sat
					1	2
3	4	5	6	7	8	9
10	11	12	13	14	15	16
17	18	19	20	21	22	23
24	25	26	27	28	29	30
31						

Blog Archive

▸ August (29)
▸ July
▸ June
▸ May
▸ April
▸ March
▸ February
▸ January
▸ December
▸ November
▸ October
▸ September

Tom at Blog 於 August 08.29. PM 06:14 發表 | 回覆 (0) | 引用 (0) | 收藏 (0) | 轉寄給朋友 | 檢舉

標題及網誌中所提的 shift [ʃɪft] 表『輪班』之意，是可數名詞，the day / night / midnight shift 是『早／晚／大夜班』之意，而 work eight hours a day and in three shifts 就是『一天 3 班制工作 8 個小時』。以下介紹各種值班的說法：

work the day shift　　　值早班
= work day shifts（shifts 恆用複數）
work the night shift　　　值晚班
= work night shifts（shifts 恆用複數）
work the midnight / graveyard shift　　值大夜班
= work midnight / **graveyard shifts**（shifts 恆用複數）

＊midnight [ˋmɪd͵naɪt] *n.* 午夜，子夜
　graveyard [ˋɡrev͵jɑrd] *n.* 墓地

be on the day shift　　　上早班的
be on the night shift　　　上晚班的
be on the midnight / graveyard shift　　上大夜班的

例: I work the day shift this week.
（我這星期輪早班。）

Police officers work midnight shifts, and sometimes it's the busiest one.
（警方輪值大夜班，有時候這是最忙碌的時段。）

The person who was on the night shift last night forgot to lock the door when he left.
（昨晚上晚班的人離開時忘了鎖門。）

字詞幫幫忙！

1. **disaster** [dɪˋzæstɚ] *n.* 徹底的失敗；災難
   a natural disaster　　　天災
   例: My wedding proposal last night was a total disaster because May said no.
   （我昨晚的求婚徹底失敗了，因為阿梅拒絕我。）

   The natural disaster caused great damage to the country.
   （這場天災對該國造成極大的損失。）

2. **stable** [ˈstebl̩] *a.* 穩定的
   unstable [ʌnˈstebl̩] *a.* 不穩定的
   be in stable condition　　（病人）處於穩定的狀況
   be in critical condition　　（病人）處於危急的狀況
   例: Sam has had a stable income for several years.
   （山姆這幾年來收入穩定。）
   Shortly after the operation, the patient was in stable condition.
   （手術後不久，病人的情況就穩定下來了。）
   ＊operation [ˌɑpəˈreʃən] *n.* 外科手術（可數）
   We all think that the manager has seemed a bit unstable lately.
   （我們都認為經理最近似乎有點情緒不穩定。）

3. **buddy** [ˈbʌdɪ] *n.* 好朋友，死黨（口語，等於 a close friend / a good friend）
   例: Nick and I have been buddies since we were in elementary school.
   （尼克和我從小學開始就是死黨了。）

4. **hire** [haɪr] *vt.* 僱用
   = **employ** [ɪmˈplɔɪ] *vt.*
   例: Mr. Wang hired three new foreign laborers to work in his factory.
   （王先生僱了 3 名新的外籍勞工在他的工廠工作。）
   ＊laborer [ˈlebərɚ] *n.* 勞工
   a foreign laborer　　外籍勞工

5. **have a meet-and-greet (with...)**　　（和……）會晤，面談
   greet [grit] *vt.* 問候；迎接
   greet sb with a smile / hug　　用微笑／擁抱迎接或歡迎某人
   ＊hug [hʌg] *n.* 擁抱
   例: The CEOs of the two powerful companies had a meet-and-greet at the hotel.
   （這兩家大公司的執行長在那間飯店進行一場會晤。）
   The hostess warmly greeted me with a smile.
   （女主人給了我一個微笑，親切地迎接我。）

Covering for a Co-Worker

Index | *Links* | *about* | *comments* | *Photo*

August 30

I **was all set to** go to the movies with my new **sweetheart** when I got a phone call from my boss. He asked me if I could **cover a co-worker's shift** from 4:00 p.m. until midnight. **In my mind**, I **was torn** because I had been working a lot lately and hadn't seen my girlfriend for a while. In the end, though, I figured it was best to **cover the shift** and **score** some points at work.

About me

Tom

Calendar

◄   August   ►

Sun	Mon	Tue	Wed	Thu	Fri	Sat
					1	2
3	4	5	6	7	8	9
10	11	12	13	14	15	16
17	18	19	20	21	22	23
24	25	26	27	28	29	30
31						

Blog Archive

▸ August (30)
▸ July
▸ June
▸ May
▸ April
▸ March
▸ February
▸ January
▸ December
▸ November
▸ October
▸ September

Tom at Blog 於 August 08.30. PM 02:37 發表 | 回覆 (0) | 引用 (0) | 收藏 (0) | 轉寄給朋友 | 檢舉

幫同事代班

August 30

　　正當我準備好要和我的新女友去看電影時，卻接到了老闆的電話。他問我能不能替同事代班，從下午 **4** 點到午夜。我心裡很掙扎，因為我最近工作得很賣力，已經好一陣子沒見到女友了。但最後我想還是去代班來替工作加分好了。

Calendar

◄　　　　*August*　　　　►

Sun	Mon	Tue	Wed	Thu	Fri	Sat
					1	2
3	4	5	6	7	8	9
10	11	12	13	14	15	16
17	18	19	20	21	22	23
24	25	26	27	28	29	30
31						

Blog Archive

▸ August (30)
▸ July
▸ June
▸ May
▸ April
▸ March
▸ February
▸ January
▸ December
▸ November
▸ October
▸ September

Tom at Blog 於 August 08.30. PM 02:37 發表｜回覆 (0)｜引用 (0)｜收藏 (0)｜轉寄給朋友｜檢舉

我們常在電影槍林彈雨的場面中，聽到某人要別人 "Cover me!"，也就是要別人『掩護我！』之意。cover 本指『遮蓋、遮蔽』，在此則指『掩護』。但 cover 亦可表『代替某人工作、替某人代班』，其用法有兩種：

作及物動詞，**cover sb's / the shift** 表『代某人的班 / 代班』；
作不及物動詞，cover for sb 表『為某人代班』。

例: Andy: I have a parents' meeting tomorrow. Could you cover my shift?

　　　Mary: I'd like to, but I already promised Rita I'd cover for her.

（安迪：我明天要參加家長會。妳可以代我的班嗎？）

（瑪莉：我很願意，但我已經答應麗塔要幫她代班了。）

此外，cover for sb 也可表『照應某人、替某人找掩護或藉口』。

例: When the boss asked why John wasn't at the meeting, Hal covered for him and said that he had gotten sick.

（當老闆問阿強為何沒出席會議時，赫爾替他掩護，說他生病了。）

tear [tɛr] 原表『撕扯』，當我們說某人 be torn (between...) 是指某人『（在……之間）左右為難 / 難以取捨』，好比內心被兩種力量拉扯似的。此外，**be torn by sth** 則表某人『在情感上因某事而受折磨 / 煎熬』。

例: Kyle was torn between continuing his studies and working to support his family.

（凱爾掙扎要繼續升學還是工作養家。）

A lot of victims were torn by the memory of the disastrous typhoon.

（許多受災者都飽受那場災情慘重的颱風回憶的煎熬。）

　＊victim [ˈvɪktɪm] *n.* 受害人

　　disastrous [dɪˈzæstrəs] *a.* 造成災害的

字詞幫幫忙！

1. be all set + to V/for N　　　準備好要……
=　be ready + to V/for N
=　be prepared + to V/for N

例: We were all set to sign the contract when Mr. Lee changed his mind.
（我們已準備好要簽訂這份合約，這時李先生卻改變了心意。）

Are you all set for the meeting?
= Are you ready for the meeting?
= Are you prepared for the meeting?
（你準備好要開會了嗎？）

2. sweetheart [ˈswitˌhɑrt] *n.* 情人，戀人

例: Jimmy married his high school sweetheart.
（吉米娶了他高中時的女友。）

3. in one's mind　　在某人心中

例: I have no doubt in my mind that Mike wasn't telling the truth.
（我當時心中敢肯定麥克沒有說實話。）

4. score [skɔr] *vt.* & *vi.* 得分 & *n.* 分數；成績（常用複數）

score a point　　得一分

score high / low on a test / an exam　　考試得高分 / 低分

注意:
在 test, exam, quiz [kwɪz]（小考）等表『考試』的名詞之前置介詞 on，乃因在測驗卷上作答之故。

get a score of...　　得若干分

例: The baseball team scored eight points in the final minute of the game.
（該棒球隊在比賽的最後一刻得到 8 分。）

In order to score high on his TOFEL exam, Greg went to a cram school every night.
（為了考好托福，葛雷格每晚都去上補習班。）

That gymnast got a score of 19 from the judges.
（那名體操選手獲得評審給 19 分。）

*gymnast [ˈdʒɪmnæst] *n.* 體操選手

Did you find out all of your scores on your final exams?
（你知道你期末考所有的成績了嗎？）

The Seafood Section

Index | Links | about | comments | Photo

August 31

It's my second week at the supermarket, and all I know is it **smells awful**. My boss took me to the seafood section and said I have to work there until they hire someone else. I guess this is the way they **harass** the <u>**newbie**</u>. I've **been off work** for three hours and already **taken a shower**, but I still have the smell of fish in my **nostrils**.

About me

Tom

Calendar

◄   August   ►

Sun	Mon	Tue	Wed	Thu	Fri	Sat
					1	2
3	4	5	6	7	8	9
10	11	12	13	14	15	16
17	18	19	20	21	22	23
24	25	26	27	28	29	30
31						

Blog Archive

- ► August (31)
- ► July
- ► June
- ► May
- ► April
- ► March
- ► February
- ► January
- ► December
- ► November
- ► October
- ► September

Tom at Blog 於 August 08.31. PM 11:06 發表 | 回覆 (0) | 引用 (0) | 收藏 (0) | 轉寄給朋友 | 檢舉

薰死人的海鮮區

August 31

　　今天是我在超市工作的第二個星期，我只覺得這地方聞起來糟透了。我老闆帶我到海鮮區，說我得一直在這區工作，直到他們聘請到另一個人。我猜這是他們對待菜鳥的招數。我已經下班 3 小時了，而且還洗了澡，可是鼻子裡還是一直聞到魚腥味。

About me

Tom

Calendar

◄　　　*August*　　　►

Sun	Mon	Tue	Wed	Thu	Fri	Sat
					1	2
3	4	5	6	7	8	9
10	11	12	13	14	15	16
17	18	19	20	21	22	23
24	25	26	27	28	29	30
31						

Blog Archive

- ► August (31)
- ► July
- ► June
- ► May
- ► April
- ► March
- ► February
- ► January
- ► December
- ► November
- ► October
- ► September

Tom at Blog 於 August 08.31. PM 11:06 發表│回覆 (0)│引用 (0)│收藏 (0)│轉寄給朋友│檢舉

剛到新的工作環境，接下別人不願意做的工作是常有的事，不過身為新人也只好硬著頭皮做了。網誌中提到的 **newbie** [ˋnjuˏbɪ] 原指『使用網路遊戲或程式的新手』，但亦可表示某個領域的『新手』，也就是我們中文裡常說的『菜鳥』，英文裡相似的字彙尚有：greenhorn [ˋgrinˏhɔrn], newcomer [ˋnjuˏkʌmɚ], novice [ˋnɑvɪs], rookie [ˋrukɪ] 等。

例: Mary is a rookie in the office and quite often makes mistakes.

（瑪麗是辦公室裡的菜鳥，經常凸槌。）

要形容某個人沒有什麼經驗時，還可以用 be wet behind the ears 來形容。這個用法字面上的意思是『耳朵後面很濕』，這是因為小動物剛出生時，整個身體都是濕答答的，耳朵後面的這一塊也不例外，因此被引伸為『涉世未深、缺乏經驗』，就像我們中文說的『乳臭未乾』。

例: Kent is still wet behind the ears. He didn't even recognize the manager when he walked in.

（肯特的經驗還不夠。他甚至連經理走進來時都認不出來。）

學會了『菜鳥』，那『老鳥』又該怎麼說呢？最直接的說法是 old hand，或者是 veteran [ˋvɛtərən]，兩者皆用來表示『經驗豐富的人』。

例: You should just follow what Peter says. He is an old hand in this field.

（你應該照彼得說的話做。他是這一行的老鳥。）

字詞幫幫忙！

1. **seafood** [ˋsiˏfud] *n.* 海鮮（不可數）

2. **section** [ˋsɛkʃən] *n.* 單位，部門
   例: Lisa was promoted to head of the sales section.
   （麗莎被升為業務部門的主管。）

3. **smell** [smɛl] *vi.* 聞起來（其後接形容詞）& *n.* 氣味
   smell like + N　聞起來像是……
   例: The cake smells good and tastes even better.
   （這蛋糕聞起來很香，吃起來更棒。）

I like the bottle of perfume that smells like roses.
（我喜歡那瓶聞起來像玫瑰的香水。）
＊perfume [`pɝf jum] *n.* 香水

4. **awful** [`ɔfl̩] *a.* 可怕的；糟糕的
比較:
awesome [`ɔsəm] *a.* 棒極的
例: Many people nearly froze to death during that awful
blizzard.
（許多人在那場可怕的暴風雪中差點凍死。）
＊blizzard [`blɪzɚd] *n.* 暴風雪
It's a pity that you didn't go to the concert with us. It was
awesome!
（你沒有和我們一起去聽演唱會真可惜。那真是棒呆了！）

5. **harass** [hə`ræs] *vt.* 使煩惱；騷擾
harassment [hə`ræsmənt] *n.* 騷擾
例: I have warned Jim if he doesn't stop harassing me, I'll call
the police.
（我已經警告提姆，如果他不斷騷擾我，我就會報警。）
Albert was accused of sexual harassment by one of his
subordinates.
（艾伯特被他一名下屬指控性騷擾。）
＊be accused of...　　被指控……
subordinate [sə`bɔrdənɪt] *n.* 下屬

6. **be / get off work**　　下班
例: Jane has to get off work earlier today because she needs
to pick her son up from school.
（阿珍今天得早點下班，因為她要去學校接她兒子。）

7. **take a shower**　　沖澡，淋浴
take a bath　　泡澡

8. **nostril** [`nɑstrɪl] *n.* 鼻孔

I'm a Killer

Index | Links | about | comments | Photo

September 01

Today was not a fun day in the seafood section for me. A woman came to me and picked out a fish from the **tank**. Usually, my **co-worker is responsible for cutting** the fish **up**, but he was out for lunch. So I had to catch the fish and kill it. Once I got it out of the tank, I **was** very **nervous about** giving the fish a **death blow**. My hands were even **shaking**. The woman looked at me like I was a **sissy** until I finally killed the fish.

About me

Tom

Calendar

◀ September ▶

Sun	Mon	Tue	Wed	Thu	Fri	Sat
	1	2	3	4	5	6
7	8	9	10	11	12	13
14	15	16	17	18	19	20
21	22	23	24	25	26	27
28	29	30				

Blog Archive

- ► September (1)
- ► August
- ► July
- ► June
- ► May
- ► April
- ► March
- ► February
- ► January
- ► December
- ► November
- ► October

Tom at Blog 於 September 09.01. PM 05:03 發表 | 回覆 (0) | 引用 (0) | 收藏 (0) | 轉寄給朋友 | 檢舉

我殺生了

September 01

　　今天在海鮮區實在不是很有趣。有位女士走向我，並從水缸裡挑了一隻魚。通常是我的同事負責殺魚，但他出去吃中餐了。所以我必須抓魚並殺了牠。當我把魚從缸裡撈出來，然後要一刀宰了牠時我超緊張。我的手甚至在發抖。直到我動刀殺魚前，那名女士看著我，好像我是個娘娘腔似的。

About me

Tom

Calendar

◄　　*September*　　►

Sun	Mon	Tue	Wed	Thu	Fri	Sat
	1	2	3	4	5	6
7	8	9	10	11	12	13
14	15	16	17	18	19	20
21	22	23	24	25	26	27
28	29	30				

Blog Archive

- ▸ September (1)
- ▸ August
- ▸ July
- ▸ June
- ▸ May
- ▸ April
- ▸ March
- ▸ February
- ▸ January
- ▸ December
- ▸ November
- ▸ October

Tom at Blog 於 September 09.01. PM 05:03 發表 | 回覆 (0) | 引用 (0) | 收藏 (0) | 轉寄給朋友 | 檢舉

網誌作者對於自己要動手殺魚這件事粉緊張，在給那隻魚 a death blow 前手還發抖。a death blow 就是所謂的『致命的一擊』。blow [blo] 當名詞本身就有『一擊、打擊』的意思，a death blow 可指造成某人死亡的一擊，也可表對某件事造成毀滅性的影響。以下介紹相關的用法：

a death blow　　致命的一擊
= a fatal blow

give / deal...a death blow　　給……致命的一擊
= give / deal....a fatal blow

例: The villain gave the man lying on the floor a death blow at the end of the TV series.

（在影集最後，這名壞蛋給躺在地上的男子致命的一擊。）

＊villain [ˈvɪlən] *n.* 壞人

We dealt the enemy a fatal blow and won the battle.

（我們給敵軍致命的一擊，贏得了這場戰役。）

The boxer dealt his opponent a fatal blow.

（那名拳擊手給對手致命的一擊。）

＊opponent [əˈponənt] *n.* 對手，敵手

字詞幫幫忙！

1. **tank** [tæŋk] *n.* （儲水、油等的）箱，槽
   a fish tank　　魚缸

2. **co-worker** [ˈkoˌwɝkɚ] *n.* 同事
   = colleague [ˈkɑlig] *n.*
   例: Phil and Paul have been co-workers for five years.
   （菲爾和保羅已經共事 5 年了。）

3. **be responsible for...**　　負責……，對……負責
   responsible [rɪˈspɑnsəbḷ] *a.* 負責任的
   例: On weekends, my sister and I are responsible for doing the dishes.
   （姊姊和我週末時負責洗碗盤。）

4. cut...up / cut up...　　切開／切碎……

例: Please cut up the cucumbers and add them to the salad.
（把小黃瓜切一切，然後放進沙拉裡。）
＊cucumber [ˋkjukəmbɚ] *n.* 小黃瓜

5. be nervous about...　　對……感到緊張

nervous [ˋnɝvəs] *a.* 緊張的

例: I'm nervous about tomorrow's exam because I'm not prepared for it.
（我對明天的考試感到很緊張，因為我沒有準備。）

6. shake [ʃek] *vi.* 發抖，顫抖 & *vt.* 抖動；握（手）

三態為：shake, shook [ʃuk], shaken [ˋʃekən]。

shake hands with sb　　和某人握手（hands 恆用複數）

例: David was so angry that he couldn't help but shake.
（大衛氣到忍不住發起抖來。）

Matt shook hands with Mr. Lee and said it was a pleasure working with him.
（麥特和李先生握手，並說很高興跟他合作。）

7. sissy [ˋsɪsɪ] *n.* 膽小無用的男子；娘娘腔

tomboy [ˋtɑmˏbɔɪ] *n.* 男性化的女生，男人婆

例: Some boys in the class call Alan a sissy because he is afraid of spiders.
（班上有些男生說艾倫是娘娘腔，因為他怕蜘蛛。）

My little sister is a tomboy. She always wears jeans and a baseball cap.
（我的小妹是個男人婆。她總是穿牛仔褲，頭戴棒球帽。）

Unit 45

Rain on the Parade

Index | *Links* | *about* | *comments* | *Photo*

September 02

Just when I had **adjusted myself to** the seafood section, my boss **rained on my parade**. I was **gutting** fish when he started talking to me. He told me I needed to be more **amicable** to the customers. I wanted to tell him that it's pretty hard to be that way when you **smell like fish** 24 hours a day. I didn't, though. I just told him I'd try to **work** it **out**.

About me

Tom

Calendar

◄ September ►

Sun	Mon	Tue	Wed	Thu	Fri	Sat
		1	2	3	4	5	6
7	8	9	10	11	12	13
14	15	16	17	18	19	20
21	22	23	24	25	26	27
28	29	30				

Blog Archive

▸ September (2)
▸ August
▸ July
▸ June
▸ May
▸ April
▸ March
▸ February
▸ January
▸ December
▸ November
▸ October

Tom at Blog 於 September 09.02. PM 07:06 發表 | 回覆 (0) | 引用 (0) | 收藏 (0) | 轉寄給朋友 | 檢舉

澆冷水

September 02

就在我剛適應了海鮮區,老闆卻澆我冷水。我正在清魚內臟,這時他開始對我講話。他要我對顧客更友善一點。我想告訴他當一個人整天全身都是魚腥味時,實在很難做到這點。但是我沒說出口,只是告訴他我會設法改進。

About me

Tom

Calendar

◄ September ►

Sun	Mon	Tue	Wed	Thu	Fri	Sat
		1	2	3	4	5	6
7	8	9	10	11	12	13
14	15	16	17	18	19	20
21	22	23	24	25	26	27
28	29	30				

Blog Archive

‣ September (2)
‣ August
‣ July
‣ June
‣ May
‣ April
‣ March
‣ February
‣ January
‣ December
‣ November
‣ October

Tom at Blog 於 September 09.02. PM 07:06 發表 | 回覆 (0) | 引用 (0) | 收藏 (0) | 轉寄給朋友 | 檢舉

179

parade [pə`red] 作名詞時，表『遊行』之意。我們在遊行時若下起雨來，那就再掃興不過了。所以 rain on the / one's parade 的意思就是『掃某人的興、澆某人冷水』。

例: Our teacher rained on our parade when she gave us a pop quiz before we went home for the weekend.

（老師在我們回家度週末前，給了我們一個臨時小考，讓我們覺得很掃興。）

＊a pop quiz　　抽考，臨時小考

Andy: There isn't going to be a party tonight.

Beth: Well, that rains on my parade. I was really looking forward to it.

（安迪：今晚不會有派對了。）

（貝絲：啊，真是澆了我一盆冷水。我本來還真期待的。）

下列用法也有『掃興』之意：

put a damper on...　　掃……的興

＊damper [`dæmpɚ] *n.* 原本表『（鋼琴的）制音器、（銅管樂器的）減音器』，用來比喻『令人掃興的人 / 事物』

例: The typhoon put a damper on our plans to go to the beach.

（這個颱風打壞了我們去海邊的計劃。）

be a wet blanket　　掃興的人，潑冷水的人

注意:

名詞 blanket [`blæŋkɪt] 表『毯子』，wet blanket 原為『溼毯子』之意，試想若將溼毯子蓋在身上一定很難過，故以 a wet blanket 來比喻『掃興的人』。

例: Please don't bring Todd tonight. He's always a wet blanket and brings everyone down.

（今晚別帶陶德來。他總是潑大家冷水，讓每個人很不開心。）

1. adjust (oneself) to + N/V-ing　　使自己適應於……

= adapt (oneself) to + N/V-ing

= accustom oneself to + N/V-ing

=   get accustomed to + N/V-ing

=   get used to + N/V-ing

    * adjust [əˈdʒʌst] *vt. & vi.*（使）適應

      adapt [əˈdæpt] *vt. & vi.*（使）適應

      accustom [əˈkʌstəm] *vt.* 使習慣

    例: Having lived in Taipei for years, Harry still can't adjust (himself) to city life.

    （哈利在台北住了許多年，卻仍無法適應都市生活。）

2. gut [gʌt] *vt.* 取出內臟

    guts [gʌts] *n.* 內臟；勇氣（恆為複數）

    have the guts to V   有勇氣（做）……

=   have the courage to V

=   have the nerve to V

    * nerve [nɝv] *n.* 膽量，勇氣（不可數）

    例: My mother gutted the fish before cooking it.

    （我媽媽在料理魚之前，先把牠的內臟取出來。）

    Bill doesn't have the guts to ask Mary out on a date.

    （比爾沒有勇氣約瑪莉出去。）

3. amicable [ˈæmɪkəbḷ] *a.* 友善的，友好的

    例: I like that small town because the locals are amicable to visitors.

    （我喜歡那個小鎮，因為當地居民對遊客都很友善。）

4. smell like fish   聞起來像魚一樣；（喻）聞起來很臭

    例: Your feet smell like fish. You need to go wash them right now.

    （你的腳聞起來臭的像鹹魚。你得立刻去洗腳。）

5. work...out / work out...   解決……

    例: I hope you and your husband can work out your problems.

    （我希望妳和妳先生能解決你們的問題。）

Unit 46

Goodbye Seafood, Hello Survey

Index | Links | about | comments | Photo

September 03

Here we go again. The fish smell **drove** me **crazy**. **As a matter of fact**, if I had to choose between working in the seafood section and letting thousands of bees **crawl** all over my body, I'd probably want **the latter**. It's funny; I was walking home after telling my boss I couldn't take another day, and a pretty woman came up and asked me if I wanted to do a survey. Right then, <u>a light bulb went off in my head</u>.

About me

Tom

Calendar

◄ *September* ►

Sun	Mon	Tue	Wed	Thu	Fri	Sat
	1	2	3	4	5	6
7	8	9	10	11	12	13
14	15	16	17	18	19	20
21	22	23	24	25	26	27
28	29	30				

Blog Archive

- September (3)
- August
- July
- June
- May
- April
- March
- February
- January
- December
- November
- October

Index | Links | about | comments | Photo

September 03

　　又來了。魚腥味讓我快『起肖』了。事實上，如果要我選擇在海鮮區工作或是讓全身爬滿好幾千隻蜜蜂，我可能會選擇後者。好笑的是，我在告訴老闆我再也無法忍受多待一天後便走路回家，路上有個美女走上前來問我是否想做個問卷。就在當下，我腦海中閃過了一個念頭。

About me

Tom

Calendar

◄　　*September*　　►

Sun	Mon	Tue	Wed	Thu	Fri	Sat
	1	2	3	4	5	6
7	8	9	10	11	12	13
14	15	16	17	18	19	20
21	22	23	24	25	26	27
28	29	30				

Blog Archive

▸ September (3)
▸ August
▸ July
▸ June
▸ May
▸ April
▸ March
▸ February
▸ January
▸ December
▸ November
▸ October

Tom at Blog 於 September 09.03. PM 04:16 發表 | 回覆 (0) | 引用 (0) | 收藏 (0) | 轉寄給朋友 | 檢舉

您是否常在動畫中，看到卡通人物在瞬間想到了什麼主意，他的頭上就會有顆燈泡閃起的畫面？這就是所謂的 a light bulb moment（靈光一現的時刻，light bulb [ˈlaɪt ˌbʌlb] *n.* 燈泡）。因此 **"A light bulb goes off in one's head."** 常用來比喻『某人靈光一閃／靈機一動。』

例: Nike's founder saw the waffle maker and a light bulb went off in his head. Soon he invented the world-famous sports shoe.

（Nike 的創始人看見鬆餅機時靈光一閃。不久他便發明了世界著名的運動鞋。）

＊waffle [ˈwafḷ] *n.* 鬆餅

類似用法:

a eureka moment　　靈光一現的時刻

eureka [juˈrikə] 原是發現某件事物或真相時所用的感嘆詞，源自希臘，相當於中文『有了！』或『我找到了！』之意。據說古希臘學者阿基米德有一天在洗澡時，發現當他坐進浴盆裡時有許多水溢出來，而使他發現了浮力的原理。阿基米德不禁高興地從浴盆跳了出來，光著身體在城裡邊跑邊喊叫着 "Eureka! Eureka!"，企圖與城裡的民眾分享他的喜悅。後來才延伸出 a eureka moment 的說法。

例: After days of thinking, Eric had a eureka moment about what he should give his wife for her birthday.

（經過多日思考，艾瑞克靈光一閃想到要送他太太什麼生日禮物。）

字 詞幫幫忙！

1. **survey** [ˈsɝve] *n.* 調查
   do a survey　　做問卷調查
   conduct a survey　　進行調查
= carry out a survey
   ＊conduct [kənˈdʌkt] *vt.* 執行，實行
   例: The company conducted a survey in the market before they launched their new product.
   （這家公司在推出新產品前，進行了一項市場調查。）
   ＊launch [lɔntʃ] *vt.* 發表（新書、新作品、新產品等）

2. Here we go again. 又來了。又發生了。

注意:

"There you go again." 則是用來說別人又做了同樣的事,相當於『你又來這一套了。』或『你老毛病又犯了。』

例: Here we go again. My wife and I always fight over trivial things.

(又來了。我跟我太太老是為了小事情吵架。)

＊trivial [ˈtrɪvɪəl] *a.* 瑣碎的

John: I used to be the most popular guy in high school.

Anna: There you go again.

(約翰:我曾經是高中裡最受歡迎的男生。)

(安娜:你又來了。)

3. drive sb crazy 令某人抓狂

= drive sb nuts

＊nuts [nʌts] *a.* 發瘋的

例: The little kid's endless questions are driving Andy crazy.

(那小孩無止盡的問題快把安迪搞瘋了。)

＊endless [ˈɛndlɪs] *a.* 無窮盡的,不斷的

4. As a matter of fact, S + V 事實上,……

= In fact, S + V

例: I'm not wealthy at all. As a matter of fact, I can hardly pay my rent.

(我一點也不有錢。事實上,我連房租都快繳不出來了。)

5. crawl [krɔl] *vi.* 爬行

例: Betty screamed when she saw a cockroach crawling on her bed.

(貝蒂看到她床上有隻蟑螂在爬便尖叫了起來。)

6. the latter 後者

注意:

the latter 常與 the former 並用,形成下列用法:

the former...the latter... 前者……後者……

例: This is Larry and Bobby. The former is my brother, and the latter is my cousin.

(這是賴瑞和鮑比。前者是我兄弟,後者是我的表親。)

＊cousin [ˈkʌzn̩] *n.* 堂(表)兄弟姐妹

Survey Tips

Index | *Links* | *about* | *comments* | *Photo*

September 04

This survey job is not as easy as I thought it would be. Almost everyone I walked up to just **brushed me off**. Some people were **rude**, and some people just **ignored** me. I didn't know what to do, so I asked a co-worker, Sean, what I should do to get more people to take my survey. He's been at this for half a year, so he had some great tips for me.

About me

Tom

Calendar

◄　　September　　►

Sun	Mon	Tue	Wed	Thu	Fri	Sat
	1	2	3	4	5	6
7	8	9	10	11	12	13
14	15	16	17	18	19	20
21	22	23	24	25	26	27
28	29	30				

Blog Archive

▸ September (4)
▸ August
▸ July
▸ June
▸ May
▸ April
▸ March
▸ February
▸ January
▸ December
▸ November
▸ October

請前輩指點迷津

September 04

　　這份問卷調查的工作不如我想像中那樣簡單。幾乎我走向前的每個人都讓我碰了一鼻子灰。有些人很沒禮貌，而有些人則是根本不理我。我不知道怎麼辦才好，所以問我的同事尚恩，該怎麼做才能讓更多人接受我的問卷調查。他做這份工作已經半年了，所以給了我一些很棒的秘訣。

About me

Tom

Calendar

◄　　　　*September*　　　►

Sun	Mon	Tue	Wed	Thu	Fri	Sat
		1	2	3	4	5	6
7	8	9	10	11	12	13
14	15	16	17	18	19	20
21	22	23	24	25	26	27
28	29	30				

Blog Archive

▸ September (4)
▸ August
▸ July
▸ June
▸ May
▸ April
▸ March
▸ February
▸ January
▸ December
▸ November
▸ October

Tom at Blog 於 September 09.04. PM 06:37 發表 | 回覆 (0) | 引用 (0) | 收藏 (0) | 轉寄給朋友 | 檢舉

brush [brʌʃ] 可當名詞，表『刷子』，也可以作動詞，表『（用刷子）刷』。

例: Billy forgot to brush his teeth before he went to bed last night.

（比利昨晚上床睡覺前忘了刷牙。）

但網誌中主角抱怨路人 brushed me off，直譯為『把我刷掉』，也就是『不理睬我，讓我碰一鼻子灰』。而 brush off 也可以形成複合名詞 brush-off [ˋbrʌʃˏɔf]，表『拒絕、不理睬』之意。

brush sb off　不理睬某人，讓某人碰一鼻子灰

= give sb the brush-off

例: Rick thought Polly liked him, but when he asked her out, she brushed him off.

= Rick thought Polly liked him, but when he asked her out, she gave him the brush-off.

（瑞克以為波莉喜歡他，但當他約她出去時，卻碰了一鼻子灰。）

brush sth off / brush off sth 則是指『漠視／打發某事物；對某事物充耳不聞』。

例: If you hadn't brushed off my warning, you might not have gotten yourself into trouble.

（如果你當時沒有對我的警告充耳不聞，或許就不會惹上麻煩。）

其他表『拒絕』或『漠視』他人的類似說法如下：

give sb the cold shoulder　對某人冷漠以待／冷眼相待

例: I feel that Pam is difficult to get along with. Whenever I talk to her, she gives me the cold shoulder.

（我覺得阿潘很難相處，每次我跟她說話時，她總是對我冷眼相待。）

＊get along with sb　與某人相處（融洽）

give sb the run-around　找藉口搪塞某人

＊run-around [ˋrʌn əˏraʊnd] *n.* 搪塞，推託

例: Kent always gives us the run-around when we ask him for help.

（我們向肯特求助時，他總是找藉口搪塞我們。）

turn a blind eye to sb　　對某人視而不見

例: Ted has turned a blind eye to me ever since we had a quarrel last week.

（自從我們上禮拜吵架後，泰德一直對我視而不見。）

＊quarrel [ˈkwɔrəl] *n.* 爭吵

turn a deaf ear to...　　對……充耳不聞

= be deaf to...

例: David always turns a deaf ear to his wife's complaints.

（大衛總是對他老婆的抱怨充耳不聞。）

＊complaint [kəmˈplent] *n.* 抱怨

字詞幫幫忙！

1. **tip** [tɪp] *n.* 訣竅，秘訣

give sb some tips on...　　給某人……方面的秘訣 / 建議

例: Can you give me some tips on how to improve my English ability?

（你能就如何增進我的英文能力給我一些建議嗎？）

2. **rude** [rud] *a.* 粗魯的

例: I think you should apologize to Patty. It was rude of you to hang up on her.

（我想你應該向派蒂道歉。你掛她電話實在是很不禮貌。）

＊apologize [əˈpɑləˌdʒaɪz] *vi.* 道歉

hang up on sb　　掛某人的電話

3. **ignore** [ɪgˈnɔr] *vt.* 忽視，忽略

例: Simon tends to ignore his wife when she's nagging him.

（當賽門的老婆對他嘮叨時，他往往都不搭理她。）

＊nag [næg] *vt.* 對……嘮叨

To the Letter

Index | *Links* | *about* | *comments* | *Photo*

September 05

I've been following Sean's **advice** to the letter. He told me to make an **effort** to talk to **chicks** because girls are more **willing** to provide help. Besides, I can **flirt** with them and get their phone numbers. Today was great. A beautiful girl walked by, and I got her phone number. I think she might **be** a little **out of my league**, though.

About me

Tom

Calendar

◄ September ►

Sun	Mon	Tue	Wed	Thu	Fri	Sat
		1	2	3	4	5	6
7	8	9	10	11	12	13
14	15	16	17	18	19	20
21	22	23	24	25	26	27
28	29	30				

Blog Archive

- September (5)
- August
- July
- June
- May
- April
- March
- February
- January
- December
- November
- October

Tom at Blog 於 September 09.05. PM 03:27 發表 | 回覆 (0) | 引用 (0) | 收藏 (0) | 轉寄給朋友 | 檢舉

聽老鳥的準沒錯

Index | *Links* | *about* | *comments* | *Photo*

September 05

　　我一直嚴格遵照尚恩的建議。他跟我說要努力設法跟馬子說話，因為女孩子比較願意提供幫助。此外，我還可以跟她們打情罵俏，順便要到電話。今天相當不錯。有個漂亮女生經過，而我要到了她的電話。不過我覺得我可能配不上她。

About me

Tom

Calendar

◄　　*September*　　►

Sun	Mon	Tue	Wed	Thu	Fri	Sat
		1	2	3	4	5	6
7	8	9	10	11	12	13
14	15	16	17	18	19	20
21	22	23	24	25	26	27
28	29	30				

Blog Archive

▸ September (5)
▸ August
▸ July
▸ June
▸ May
▸ April
▸ March
▸ February
▸ January
▸ December
▸ November
▸ October

Tom at Blog 於 September 09.05. PM 03:27 發表 | 回覆 (0) | 引用 (0) | 收藏 (0) | 轉寄給朋友 | 檢舉

191

網誌作者遵照尚恩的建議，果然要到漂亮美眉的電話。不過他卻覺得自己配不上她，網誌中的 be out of one's league 就是用來形容這種情況。league [lig] 原意為『聯盟』，be out of one's league 字面上看來是『在某人的聯盟之外』，引申為『跟某人不屬同一類型』、『是某人高攀不上的』之意。

be out of one's league　　跟某人不屬同一類型，是某人高攀不上的

be in a different league from sb　　與某人等級／層次不同
= be not in the same league as sb

例: Sally is way out of your league. She is the head cheerleader at our school, and her dad is the chairman of a bank.
（你高攀不上莎莉的。她是我們學校的啦啦隊隊長，而她爸爸是銀行的董事長。）

＊cheerleader [ˈtʃɪrˌlidə] *n.* 啦啦隊隊員

Beth's new boyfriend is in a different league from her previous ones. He belongs to the Royal Family in Denmark.
（貝絲的新男友和她以前交往的男士等級不同。他是丹麥的皇室成員之一。）

類似用法:

be a cut above sb　　高某人一等
= be a lot better than sb

例: Mandy thinks she is a cut above the rest of us just because she hangs out with celebrities.
（只因為她常和名人在一起，曼蒂就認為她比我們都要高一等。）

＊hang out with sb　　和某人一起打發時間；和某人混在一起
celebrity [səˈlɛbrətɪ] *n.* 名人

字 詞 幫幫忙！

1. to the letter　　嚴格按照字面地；不折不扣地
= exactly [ɪgˈzæktlɪ] *adv.*
= precisely [prɪˈsaɪslɪ] *adv.*

例: The boss asked us to carry out his orders to the letter.
（老闆要我們完全按照他的指示去做。）

192

2. advice [əd'vaɪs] *n.* 忠告，建議（不可數）

    <u>an</u> advice (X)

→ <u>a piece of</u> advice (○)   一項忠告，一則建議

    some <u>advices</u> (X)

→ some <u>advice</u> (○)   一些忠告，一些建議

    follow one's advice   遵照某人的忠告／建議

    例: You should follow Karen's advice and quit smoking.
    （你應該聽凱倫的忠告戒菸。）

3. effort ['ɛfɚt] *n.* 努力

    make an effort to V   努力（設法）……

    make every effort to V   盡一切努力去……

= spare no effort to V

    例: Jack made an effort to win his ex-girlfriend back, but in vain.
    （傑克努力要追回前女友，但徒勞無功。）

    ＊in vain   徒勞無功，白費工夫

    I promised Julia that I would make every effort to help her.
    （我承諾茱莉亞我會盡一切力量來幫助她。）

4. chick [tʃɪk] *n.* （俚語）馬子，女孩子（原指『小雞』）

5. willing ['wɪlɪŋ] *a.* 樂意的，願意的

    unwilling [ʌn'wɪlɪŋ] *a.* 不願意的，不情願的

    be willing to V   願意做……

    be unwilling to V   不願意做……

= be reluctant to V

    ＊reluctant [rɪ'lʌktənt] *a.* 不情願的，勉強的

    例: The job may be difficult, but I'm willing to give it a try.
    （這工作也許很困難，但我願意嘗試。）

    John is unwilling to lend Mike money.
    （約翰不願意借錢給麥克。）

6. flirt [flɝt] *vi.* 調情，打情罵俏

    flirt with sb   和某人調情，和某人打情罵俏

    例: Robert enjoys flirting with his female co-workers.
    （羅伯特喜歡跟女同事打情罵俏。）

Getting More Data

Index | *Links* | *about* | *comments* | *Photo*

September 06

I called the girl today. I **pretended** that I needed to get more data about the survey. She **saw** right **through** my lie, but thought it was cute. I **asked** her **out** for a cup of coffee and she said yes. We met at the coffee shop, and she looked **drop-dead gorgeous**. She is too good for me, but we had so much fun that we are going to **see a movie** on Sunday night.

About me

Tom

Calendar

◀ *September* ▶

Sun	Mon	Tue	Wed	Thu	Fri	Sat
	1	2	3	4	5	6
7	8	9	10	11	12	13
14	15	16	17	18	19	20
21	22	23	24	25	26	27
28	29	30				

Blog Archive

- ► September (6)
- ► August
- ► July
- ► June
- ► May
- ► April
- ► March
- ► February
- ► January
- ► December
- ► November
- ► October

Tom at Blog 於 September 09.06. PM 09:29 發表 | 回覆 (0) | 引用 (0) | 收藏 (0) | 轉寄給朋友 | 檢舉

進一步探聽資料

September 06

　　我今天打電話給這個女孩。我假裝需要更多的調查資料。她馬上就看穿我的謊言，卻覺得這樣的舉動蠻可愛的。我約她出來喝杯咖啡，她也答應了。我們在咖啡廳見面，她看起來真是美呆了。她條件太好了，我配不上她，但是我們在一起時很開心，星期日晚上我們還要去看場電影。

About me

Tom

Calendar

◄　　　September　　　►

Sun	Mon	Tue	Wed	Thu	Fri	Sat
	1	2	3	4	5	6
7	8	9	10	11	12	13
14	15	16	17	18	19	20
21	22	23	24	25	26	27
28	29	30				

Blog Archive

▸ September (6)
▸ August
▸ July
▸ June
▸ May
▸ April
▸ March
▸ February
▸ January
▸ December
▸ November
▸ October

Tom at Blog 於 September 09.06. PM 09:29 發表 | 回覆 (0) | 引用 (0) | 收藏 (0) | 轉寄給朋友 | 檢舉

195

drop dead 原本表『猝死、暴斃』之意。

例: The talented actor dropped dead at the age of 30.

（那位才華洋溢的男演員在 30 歲時猝死。）

＊talented [ˋtæləntɪd] *a.* 有才華的

但網誌中的 drop-dead 則是副詞，表『極端地』，而 drop-dead gorgeous 即是用來形容一個人非常美麗、美到不行的意思。gorgeous [ˋgɔrdʒəs] 是『美麗的』，因此 drop-dead gorgeous 按字面來看，是說一個人美到讓人看了會忘記呼吸而暴斃之意，也就是用來形容一個人是超級大美女。

drop-dead gorgeous　　非常美麗的，美到不行的

例: I fell in love with the drop-dead gorgeous girl at first sight.

（我對那位美到不行的女孩一見鍾情。）

＊at first sight　　第一眼

形容女孩子的美麗時，還有下列用語：

attractive [əˋtræktɪv] *a.* 有魅力的，有吸引力的

例: Michelle is a very attractive woman.

（蜜雪兒是個很有魅力的女人。）

stunning [ˋstʌnɪŋ] *a.* 極美的，美到令人目瞪口呆的
a stunning beauty　　令人驚艷的美女

例: The new lipstick Gina is wearing looks stunning on her.

（吉娜擦的新口紅讓她看起來美極了。）

Molly's sister is a stunning beauty. By contrast, Molly looks like an ugly duckling.

（茉莉的姊姊是個絕世美女。相較之下，茉莉看起來像隻醜小鴨。）

＊by contrast　　相較之下

duckling [ˋdʌklɪŋ] *n.* 小鴨

an ugly duckling　　醜小鴨

1. data [ˈdetə / ˈdætə] *n.* 資料；數據（不可數）

例: A lot of scientific data has been proven wrong upon further research.

（經過進一步研究後，很多科學資料已被證實有誤。）

2. pretend [prɪˈtɛnd] *vt.* 假裝

pretend + that 子句　　假裝……

例: Mary has broken up with George, but he still pretends that they are boyfriend and girlfriend.

（瑪麗和喬治分手了，但他仍假裝他們是男女朋友。）

3. see through...　　　看透 / 看穿……

see through one's lie　　看穿某人的謊言

例: Judy saw through the flattery (which) the salesperson showered her with and left the store.

（茱蒂看穿店員對她的阿諛奉承，所以就離開了那家商店。）

  ＊ flattery [ˈflætərɪ] *n.* 諂媚，奉承

  shower sb with sth　　大量給予某人某物

4. ask sb out (on a date)　　約某人外出約會

例: My best friend is going to ask my sister out on a date next week.

（我最要好的朋友下星期要約我妹妹出去。）

5. see a movie　　看一場電影

＝ watch a movie

＝ take in a movie

  ＊ take in...　　觀賞……

  go to the movies　　（去）看電影

例: Julia and I went into town to take in a movie.

（茱莉亞和我到鎮上去看了場電影。）

  I feel like going to the movies tonight.

（我今晚想去看電影。）

Bedroom Eyes

September 07

I created a **singles profile** on www.loveintaiwan.com **for free**. I checked my account today and found that four women had **responded** to my ad. I had to pay to **access** their profiles, but it was worth it because of Sofia. She has bedroom eyes and likes to **surf**. I sent her a message asking her if she would be willing to teach me how to surf. We'll see what happens.

About me

Tom

Calendar

◄ September ►

Sun	Mon	Tue	Wed	Thu	Fri	Sat
		1	2	3	4	5	6
7	8	9	10	11	12	13
14	15	16	17	18	19	20
21	22	23	24	25	26	27
28	29	30				

Blog Archive

▸ September (7)
▸ August
▸ July
▸ June
▸ May
▸ April
▸ March
▸ February
▸ January
▸ December
▸ November
▸ October

Tom at Blog 於 September 09.07. PM 10:03 發表｜回覆 (0)｜引用 (0)｜收藏 (0)｜轉寄給朋友｜檢舉

眼睛會放電

September 07

　　我在 www.loveintaiwan.com（愛在台灣）這個網站上建立了免費的單身資料檔案。我今天查看了一下我的帳號，發現有 4 個女生回應我的廣告。我必須付費才能觀看她們的檔案，但因為蘇菲亞的關係，這一切都很值得。她有雙誘人會放電的眼睛，喜歡衝浪。我寫了一則訊息給她，問她願不願意教我衝浪。咱們且看事情會如何發展。

About me

Tom

Calendar

◄　　　September　　　►

Sun	Mon	Tue	Wed	Thu	Fri	Sat
		1	2	3	4	5	6
7	8	9	10	11	12	13
14	15	16	17	18	19	20
21	22	23	24	25	26	27
28	29	30				

Blog Archive

▸ September (7)
▸ August
▸ July
▸ June
▸ May
▸ April
▸ March
▸ February
▸ January
▸ December
▸ November
▸ October

Tom at Blog 於 September 09.07. PM 10:03 發表 | 回覆 (0) | 引用 (0) | 收藏 (0) | 轉寄給朋友 | 檢舉

網誌作者新看上的女生 Sofia 有雙會放電的眼睛，讓他想跟她有進一步的發展。網誌中所用的 bedroom eyes 字面翻譯為『臥室裡的眼睛』，想像一下，如果一個女生睡眼惺忪，那雙瞇瞇眼是不是有股吸睛的朦朧美呢？因此 bedroom eyes 就是用來形容某人的眼睛充滿魅力會放電，亦即有一雙性感的眼睛。

例: Robert's girlfriend has the most beautiful bedroom eyes. It is really hard not to be attracted to her.
（羅伯特的女友有雙超漂亮又會放電的眼睛。實在很難不被她吸引。）
＊be attracted to... 被……吸引

下列用法則可用來形容『對某人放電 / 拋媚眼』：
make eyes at sb 向某人放電 / 拋媚眼 / 眉目傳情
例: Look! Sandy is making eyes at Scott.
（你瞧！珊蒂在向史考特放電。）

1. **single** [ˋsɪŋgl̩] *n.* 單身（男子或女子）& *a.* 單身的
   bachelor [ˋbætʃələ] *n.* 單身男子，單身漢
   例: Mary has decided to remain single for the rest of her life.
   （瑪麗已經決定終身不嫁。）
   That movie star was chosen by the magazine as one of the most desirable bachelors in the UK.
   （那位影星被這本雜誌選為英國最富魅力的單身漢之一。）
   ＊desirable [dɪˋzaɪrəbl̩] *a.* 富有魅力的

2. **profile** [ˋprofaɪl] *n.* 人物簡介，概況
   keep a low profile 保持低調
   keep a high profile 引人注目
   例: Mike browsed through Jenny's profile before sending her an email.
   （麥克在寄送電子郵件給珍妮前，先瀏覽了她的簡介。）
   ＊browse [brauz] *vi.* 瀏覽
   browse through... 瀏覽……

That famous singer was trying to keep a low profile in public in order to avoid negative publicity.

（那位名歌星試著在公眾面前保持低調，以避免有負面名聲。）

＊publicity [pʌbˈlɪsətɪ] *n.* 名聲；媒體曝光

3. for free　　免費地

= free of charge

例: This coupon admits two people to the new movie for free.

（這張優待券可供兩人免費觀賞這部新上映的電影。）

＊coupon [ˈkupɑn] *n.* 優待券；折價券

4. respond [rɪˈspɑnd] *vi.* 回應，反應（與介詞 to 並用）

respond to...　　回應……

例: Several people responded to the company's want ad for an electrician.

（有好幾個人回覆那家公司應徵電工的徵人啟事。）

＊electrician [ɪˌlɛkˈtrɪʃən] *n.* 電工

5. access [ˈæksɛs] *vt.* 使用；存取（尤指電腦數據）& *n.* 接近（與介詞 to 並用）

have access to...　　接觸到……；有使用……的機會或權利

例: Bank customers can now access their accounts through the new online system.

（銀行顧客現在可以利用新的線上系統進入自己的帳戶。）

Students only have access to the library during the daytime.

（學生只有在白天才能使用圖書館。）

6. surf [sɜf] *vi.* 衝浪 & *vt.* 瀏覽（網路資料）

go surfing　　衝浪

surf the Internet　　上網

例: My friends and I decided to go surfing this weekend.

（我朋友和我決定週末一起去衝浪。）

Larry likes to surf the Internet in his free time.

（賴瑞空閒時喜歡上網。）

A Sporty Girl

September 08

Sofia **got back to** me right away. This means she **is** very interested in or **dying for** a date. She loves **tanning** at the beach, which is not really my thing, but I like **easygoing** girls. It's only been a day or two, and we've **messaged** each other five times. I think we could **be meant for each other** because we <u>**are on the same wavelength**</u>.

About me

Tom

Calendar

◄　　September　　►

Sun	Mon	Tue	Wed	Thu	Fri	Sat
		1	2	3	4	5	6
7	8	9	10	11	12	13
14	15	16	17	18	19	20
21	22	23	24	25	26	27
28	29	30				

Blog Archive

▸ September (8)
▸ August
▸ July
▸ June
▸ May
▸ April
▸ March
▸ February
▸ January
▸ December
▸ November
▸ October

Tom at Blog 於 September 09.08. PM 08:15 發表 | 回覆 (0) | 引用 (0) | 收藏 (0) | 轉寄給朋友 | 檢舉

202

運動型女孩

September 08

　　蘇菲亞立刻就回覆我的訊息。這表示她約會很有興趣，或者是她很渴望約會。她喜歡到海邊做日光浴，這可不是我喜歡做的事，但我喜歡隨和的女生。才一、兩天的時間，我們就通了 5 次訊。我想我們可能是天作之合，因為我們很投緣。

Tom at Blog 於 September 09.08. PM 08:15 發表 | 回覆 (0) | 引用 (0) | 收藏 (0) | 轉寄給朋友 | 檢舉

wavelength [ˈwevˌlɛŋθ] 是『波長』的意思，網誌中提到的 be on the same wavelength 就是說『波長相同』。試想，當兩個人的波長相同，是不是就很投緣、想法一致呢？所以 be on the same wavelength 這個片語可用來形容人與人『（思想）有交集、具有相同觀點』。

be on the same wavelength (as sb) （與某人）（思想）有交集，（與某人）很投緣

be on a different wavelength (from sb) （與某人）（思想）沒有交集，（與某人）不投緣

例: Tony and Nina are on the same wavelength, so they can finish each other's sentences.

（東尼和妮娜想法一致，所以他們能接對方要說的話。）

I'm on a totally different wavelength from Beth. I wanted to dress in all black, but she insisted on bright colors.

（我和貝絲完全沒有交集。我想穿一身漆黑，而她堅持要穿亮色系的衣服。）

類似的說法尚有下列：

like-minded [ˌlaɪkˈmaɪndɪd] *a.* 想法相同的，志趣相投的

例: The two like-minded businessmen decided to start a website design company together.

（這兩位志趣相投的商人決定共同開設一家網路設計公司。）

字詞幫幫忙！

1. **sporty** [ˈspɔrtɪ] *a.* 擅長運動的；喜歡運動的

2. **get back to sb**　　再與某人（於電話或網路上）聯絡；回某人電話

例: I'll have the lawyer review the contract and get back to you in three days.

（我會請律師審過合約，3 天內會再與你聯絡。）

＊review [rɪˈvju] *vt.* 復審；檢閱

3. be dying + for N/to V　　渴望得到 / 做……
= be longing + for N/to V
= be eager + for N/to V

例: After such a long walk, I'm dying for a cold drink.
（走了這麼一大段路之後，我超想來杯冷飲。）

I'm dying to know the ending of the story.
（我極欲知道故事的結局。）

4. tan [tæn] *vi.* 曬黑，曬成古銅色

例: Some people do not tan easily.
（有些人不容易曬黑。）

5. easygoing [ˈizɪˌɡoɪŋ] *a.* 隨和的

例: Jim is an easygoing guy.
（吉姆是個很隨和的人）

6. message [ˈmɛsɪdʒ] *vt.* 與……通訊聯絡 & *n.* 消息，口信
leave a message　　留信息；留言
take a message　　記下留話 / 留言

例: If Ms. Lin should call me while I'm out, ask her to leave a message.
（萬一林小姐在我外出時打電話找我，請她留言。）

Tom is not available to answer your phone. May I take a message?
（湯姆沒有空接您的電話。要不要我幫您留話？）

＊available [əˈveləbḷ] *a.* 有空的

7. be meant for each other　　彼此是天生一對，天作之合
be meant for sb　　注定和某人在一起

例: Pete and Laura are meant for each other. They have the same interests, and both are dog people.
（彼特和蘿拉是天作之合。他們有共同的興趣，而且倆人都是愛狗人士。）

Everyone knows Candy is meant for Anthony.
（每個人都知道肯蒂注定要和安東尼在一起。）

Unit 52

Our First Phone Call

Index | *Links* | *about* | *comments* | *Photo*

September 09

For a whole week, I've been either writing to Sofia by email or **chatting** with her on MSN. Today, I **suggested** that we **cut to the chase** and talk on the phone to **set up** a date. When I called, I was **pleasantly** surprised because her voice sounded **exactly like** I had **imagined**. Also, she told me she didn't like **mama's boys**. I think I may be her man.

About me

Tom

Calendar

◄   September   ►

Sun	Mon	Tue	Wed	Thu	Fri	Sat
		1	2	3	4	5	6
7	8	9	10	11	12	13
14	15	16	17	18	19	20
21	22	23	24	25	26	27
28	29	30				

Blog Archive

- September (9)
- August
- July
- June
- May
- April
- March
- February
- January
- December
- November
- October

Tom at Blog 於 September 09.09. PM 09:54 發表 | 回覆 (0) | 引用 (0) | 收藏 (0) | 轉寄給朋友 | 檢舉

第一通電話

September 09

一整個星期我不是寫 email 給蘇菲亞就是用 MSN 和她聊天。今天我建議我們直接進入重點,在電話中直接約個時間見面。當我打過去的時候,蘇菲亞的聲音就跟我想像中的一樣,讓我喜出望外。此外,她還跟我說她不喜歡離不開媽的男生。我想我或許就是她的真命天子。

About me

Tom

Calendar

◄   *September*   ►

Sun	Mon	Tue	Wed	Thu	Fri	Sat
		1	2	3	4	5	6
7	8	9	10	11	12	13
14	15	16	17	18	19	20
21	22	23	24	25	26	27
28	29	30				

Blog Archive

- ▸ September (9)
- ▸ August
- ▸ July
- ▸ June
- ▸ May
- ▸ April
- ▸ March
- ▸ February
- ▸ January
- ▸ December
- ▸ November
- ▸ October

Tom at Blog 於 September 09.09. PM 09:54 發表 | 回覆 (0) | 引用 (0) | 收藏 (0) | 轉寄給朋友 | 檢舉

chase [tʃes] 這個字有『追趕、追逐』之意，可作動詞或名詞。

例: The ferocious dog kept barking and chasing motorcycles down the street.

（那隻兇惡的狗不斷吠叫並追趕著街上的摩托車。）

＊ferocious [fəˋroʃəs] *a.* 兇惡的

I almost fell asleep watching the tedious film with the endless car chase scenes.

（那部無聊的電影盡是飛車追逐的畫面，我看得都快睡著了。）

＊tedious [ˋtidɪəs] *a.* 乏味的

而 **cut to the chase** 這個片語源自早期電影業的用語。一般人看動作片時，對冗長的對話大多沒太大興趣，因此 **cut to the chase** 就是指把那些無關緊要的畫面剪掉，直接跳到最精采的追逐場面之意。所以後來在口語中，**cut to the chase** 用來表示『言歸正傳，直接切入重點』，等同於 get to the point（進入重點）之意。

例: The boss cut to the chase at the beginning of the meeting, announcing that the company was in a crisis.

（老闆在會議一開始便切入正題，宣告公司已陷入危機。）

mama's boy 字面意思為『媽媽的男孩』，其實就是指離不開媽媽的男生，即使已成年人，仍無法在情感上或經濟上獨立自主，不管是生活、工作、戀愛全部都要向媽媽交代、聽從指示，也就是『極度依賴媽媽的男人』。

例: Ed is such a mama's boy. He runs home to his mother every time he has a problem.

（愛德簡直是離不開娘的孩子。他只要遇到問題就會跑回家找他媽媽。）

 字詞幫幫忙！

1. **chat** [tʃæt] *vi.* & *n.* 閒聊，聊天

   chat with sb　　和某人聊天

= have a chat with sb

   例: Becky often chats with her co-workers during her lunch break.

   （貝琪常在午休時間和同事閒聊。）

Nick and I had a pleasant chat over dinner last night.
（我和尼克昨晚邊吃晚餐邊聊得很愉快。）

2. **suggest** [səgˋdʒɛst] *vt.* 建議，提議

   suggest that + S + (should) + V　　建議……

   例: Mandy suggested this place for the class reunion.
   （曼蒂提議在這個地方辦同學會。）
   ＊reunion [riˋjunjən] *n.* 重聚
   　　a class reunion　　同學會
   The tour guide suggested that we should avoid street
   food if we didn't want to get sick.
   （導遊建議我們不想生病的話，就不要吃路邊攤。）

3. **set up...**　　安排……

   set up a date　　安排約會

   例: Gary was in charge of setting up the fundraiser.
   （蓋瑞負責籌辦這次的募款活動。）
   ＊fundraiser [ˋfʌndˏrezɚ] *n.* 募款活動
   Betty asked her brother to set up a date for her with his
   friend, Tom.
   （貝蒂要她哥哥幫她安排和他的朋友湯姆約會。）

4. **pleasantly** [ˋplɛzəntlɪ] *adv.* 愉快地

   例: The host and the hostess pleasantly greeted their guests
   at the party.
   （派對的男主人和女主人愉快地迎接他們的賓客。）

5. **exactly like...**　　完全像……

   例: Helen's nose looks exactly like her father's.
   （海倫的鼻子看起來完全像她父親的。）

6. **imagine** [ɪˋmædʒɪn] *vt.* 想像

   例: It is hard to imagine what it is like to lose your whole
   family in an accident.
   （在意外當中失去全家人的感覺令人難以想像。）

Surfing Nerves

Index | Links | about | comments | Photo

September 10

After we **got off the phone**, I realized that I **agreed to** try to surf with Sofia. I've **got butterflies in my stomach** because the only thing I've ever surfed is **websites**. **Besides** that, she's good and I'll probably **make an ass of myself** at the beach. Oh, well! I guess I've got to **take the bull by the horns** and learn quickly.

About me

Tom

Calendar

◄   *September*   ►

Sun	Mon	Tue	Wed	Thu	Fri	Sat
	1	2	3	4	5	6
7	8	9	**10**	11	12	13
14	15	16	17	18	19	20
21	22	23	24	25	26	27
28	29	30				

Blog Archive

► September (10)
► August
► July
► June
► May
► April
► March
► February
► January
► December
► November
► October

Tom at Blog 於 September 09.10. PM 08:27 發表 | 回覆 (0) | 引用 (0) | 收藏 (0) | 轉寄給朋友 | 檢舉

September 10

　　當我們講完電話後，我發現自己答應要和蘇菲亞去嘗試衝浪。我心裡七上八下，因為我唯一會做的只有上網。除此之外，她很厲害，而我大概會在海邊讓自己大出洋相。唉，好吧！我猜我只能鼓起勇氣面對挑戰，然後很快地學會才好。

About me

Tom

Calendar

◄　　*September*　　►

Sun	Mon	Tue	Wed	Thu	Fri	Sat
	1	2	3	4	5	6
7	8	9	**10**	11	12	13
14	15	16	17	18	19	20
21	22	23	24	25	26	27
28	29	30				

Blog Archive

▸ September (10)
▸ August
▸ July
▸ June
▸ May
▸ April
▸ March
▸ February
▸ January
▸ December
▸ November
▸ October

Tom at Blog 於 September 09.10. PM 08:27 發表 | 回覆 (0) | 引用 (0) | 收藏 (0) | 轉寄給朋友 | 檢舉

想追女孩子可沒那麼容易，為了投其所好，就算會 make an ass of oneself 也得硬著頭皮去做。ass [æs] 原本指『屁股』，也可以表『白痴、笨蛋、傻子』，所以這個俚語的意思就是某人做蠢事而『使自己出糗／出洋相』。

make an ass of oneself 　　使自己出糗／出洋相

例: Justin made an ass of himself when he spilled wine all over the woman's dress.

（賈斯汀把酒灑到那女子的洋裝上，讓自己大出洋相。）

對鬥牛士而言，當一頭怒氣衝天的公牛直衝而來時，其自衛反擊的辦法就是正面迎向地，雙手緊抓住它頭上的角，然後竭盡全力扭轉牛頭，使其失去平衡摔倒而被制服，這也就是為什麼英文裡有 take the bull by the horns 的說法。bull [bʊl] 就是『公牛』，而 horn [hɔrn] 就是『角』，所以此片語就用來表示鼓足勇氣、毅然決然地面對困難。

take the bull by the horns 　　挺身／勇敢面對困難；斷然採取行動

例: Ed was determined to take the bull by the horns even though he knew it was going to be tough for him to fight the big company on his own.

（即使艾德知道要靠他自己對抗那間大公司是件艱難的事，他仍決心要勇敢面對困難。）

＊determined [dɪˋtɜmɪnd] *a.* 下定決心的

　be determined to V　　下定決心做……

字詞幫幫忙！

1. **nerve** [nɝv] *n.* 神經焦躁，憂慮（恆用複數，如下列第 1 個片語）；勇氣（不可數）

   get on one's nerves　　使某人心神不寧，讓某人心煩（nerves 始終用複數）

   have the nerve to V　　有勇氣從事……

   = **have the courage to V**

   = **have the guts to V**

例: My mom's nagging really gets on my nerves.
（老媽的嘮叨實在搞得我心煩。）
＊nag [næg] *vi.* 嘮叨
I never had the nerve to talk back to my parents when I was a kid.
（我小時候從沒有勇氣跟父母頂嘴。）

2. get off the phone　　掛上電話，講完電話
＝ finish talking on the phone
例: When I got off the phone, I found that I'd forgotten to tell the deliveryman my address.
（當我掛上電話，才發現自己忘了告訴送貨員我家的地址。）
＊deliveryman [dɪˈlɪvərɪˌmæn] *n.* 送貨員

3. agree to V　　同意（做）……
例: Al would be willing to drop the charges if you agreed to pay for the broken window.
（如果你同意賠償打破的窗子，艾爾就願意撤銷對你的控告。）
＊be willing to V　　願意（做）……
charge [tʃɑrdʒ] *n.* 控告

4. get / have butterflies in one's stomach　　（某人）心裡
七上八下 / 緊張難安
butterfly [ˈbʌtəˌflaɪ] *n.* 蝴蝶
stomach [ˈstʌmək] *n.* 胃
例: I always have butterflies in my stomach before an exam.
（考試前我總會感到緊張。）

5. website [ˈwɛbsaɪt] *n.* 網站

6. besides [bɪˈsaɪdz] *prep.* 除……之外 & *adv.* 而且，此外
Besides + N/V-ing, S + V　　除……之外，還……
＝ In addition to + N/V-ing, S + V
Besides, S + V　　此外，……
例: Besides stamps, Frank likes to collect coins.
（除了郵票外，法蘭克還喜歡收集錢幣。）
I don't feel like going to the movies. Besides, it's raining outside.
（我不想去看電影。此外，現在外面正在下雨。）

Index | *Links* | *about* | *comments* | *Photo*

September 11

Sofia has told me she would be my **personal instructor** on our **surfing excursion**. I like that because it means we will be **getting up close and personal with** each other. Since I'm going to the beach tomorrow, I've been **starving** myself all day and doing **sit-ups**. Hopefully this will **pay off**, and she won't **make fun of** my <u>beer belly</u>.

About me

Tom

Calendar

◄ *September* ►

Sun	Mon	Tue	Wed	Thu	Fri	Sat
		1	2	3	4	5	6
7	8	9	10	**11**	12	13
14	15	16	17	18	19	20
21	22	23	24	25	26	27
28	29	30				

Blog Archive

- ► September (11)
- ► August
- ► July
- ► June
- ► May
- ► April
- ► March
- ► February
- ► January
- ► December
- ► November
- ► October

邁向親密接觸

September 11

　　蘇菲亞告訴我，她會在我們的衝浪之行中當我的私人教練。我喜歡這個主意，因為這就表示我們可以有近距離的接觸。由於明天就要去海邊了，所以我已經餓了一天肚子，還一直做仰臥起坐。但願這樣能有收穫，她才不會嘲笑我的啤酒肚。

About me

Tom

Calendar

◀　　*September*　　▶

Sun	Mon	Tue	Wed	Thu	Fri	Sat
		1	2	3	4	5	6
7	8	9	10	**11**	12	13
14	15	16	17	18	19	20
21	22	23	24	25	26	27
28	29	30				

Blog Archive

▸ September (11)
▸ August
▸ July
▸ June
▸ May
▸ April
▸ March
▸ February
▸ January
▸ December
▸ November
▸ October

Tom at Blog 於 September 09.11. PM 09:03 發表 | 回覆 (0) | 引用 (0) | 收藏 (0) | 轉寄給朋友 | 檢舉

相信很多男生都有網誌男主角的困擾，那就是大肚腩！鮪魚肚早就不再是中年男子的專利，由於男性的脂肪多半囤積在肚子（belly [ˋbɛlɪ]）這一塊，因此特別容易會有大肚子，而習慣喝啤酒（beer [bɪr]）的男生，肚子更加明顯，因此英文稱作 beer belly，跟中文的『啤酒肚』是一模一樣的。除了啤酒肚，以下介紹其他戲稱男生大肚腩的說法：

potbelly [ˋpɑtˏbɛlɪ] *n.* 大肚皮，啤酒肚；大腹便便的人
paunch [pɔntʃ] *n.* （男人的）大肚子
spare tire [ˏspɛr ˋtaɪr] *n.* 腰部贅肉，相當於中文的『游泳圈』（原意為『備胎』）

例: Mike's got a beer belly from drinking too much beer.
= Mike's got a potbelly from drinking too much beer.
= Mike's got a paunch from drinking too much beer.
（麥克因為喝太多啤酒而有啤酒肚。）

My dad always jokes that his spare tire could save him from drowning.
（我爸老是自嘲說他肚子上的游泳圈可以防止自己溺水。）

至於女生的腰圍一但過粗，一個不小心也會讓肚腩肥肉『春光外洩』，這時若又穿上緊身的褲子，就很容易擠出一圈游泳圈來，英文就叫作 "muffin top"。muffin [ˋmʌfɪn] 原是歐美常見的鬆糕（台灣又稱作『瑪芬』），長得就像我們的杯子蛋糕，只是 muffin 的上面看起來像是要溢出來的樣子，而非像杯子蛋糕平平的，因此用來形容女生被擠出來的肚腩，是不是還真有點傳神呢？

例: Britney's pants were so tight that she had a muffin top.
（布蘭妮的褲子緊到把她的肥肚腩都擠了出來。）

 字詞幫幫忙！

1. get up close and personal (with sb) （與某人）有親密的接觸

例: Kenny would never miss the chance to get up close and personal with his idol.
（肯尼絕不會錯過和他的偶像親密接觸的機會。）

2. personal [ˈpɝsənḷ] *a.* 個人的，私人的

3. instructor [ɪnˈstrʌktɚ] *n.* 教練；指導員

4. surf [sɝf] *vi.* 衝浪 & *vt.* 上（網）
surf the Internet　　上網

5. excursion [ɪkˈskɝʒən] *n.* 短途旅行；遠足
go on an excursion　　短程出遊；去遠足
例: The students went on an excursion to the beach last
　　Sunday.
　　（那些學生上星期日去海邊遠足。）

6. starve [stɑrv] *vt.* 使飢餓 & *vi.* 挨餓
be starving to death　　餓死了（誇張用語，喻『很餓』）
例: Lucy is trying to lose weight by starving herself.
　　（露西正嘗試用挨餓的方法來減肥。）
　　Since I didn't have time for breakfast, I was starving to
　　death by lunchtime.
　　（由於沒時間吃早餐，到了中午我肚子都餓扁了。）

7. sit-up [ˈsɪtˌʌp] *n.* 仰臥起坐
push-up [ˈpʊʃˌʌp] *n.* 伏地挺身
do 20 sit-ups at a time　　一次做 20 個仰臥起坐
do 20 push-ups at a time　　一次做 20 個俯地挺身

8. pay off　　取得成功，有代價
例: All of the time and effort that James spent on his research
　　paper finally paid off.
　　（詹姆士在他的研究報告上所花的時間與精力最後終於有了成果。）

9. make fun of...　　取笑 / 嘲笑……
例: Holly's friends often make fun of her hairstyle.
　　（荷莉的朋友經常嘲笑的她的髮型。）

Surf's Not Up

Index | *Links* | *about* | *comments* | *Photo*

September 12

I was so embarrassed that I wanted to **stick my head in a hole in the ground**. At the beach, I thought I would make a good **impression** by learning to surf, but I was **dead** wrong. As soon as I tried to get up on the **surfboard**, I **fell off** and **smacked** my head on some **coral**. I had blood **streaming** down my cheek, and we spent the afternoon in the **emergency room** waiting for the doctor to **stitch** me up.

About me

Tom

Calendar

◄   *September*   ►

Sun	Mon	Tue	Wed	Thu	Fri	Sat
	1	2	3	4	5	6
7	8	9	10	11	12	13
14	15	16	17	18	19	20
21	22	23	24	25	26	27
28	29	30				

Blog Archive

- ► September (12)
- ► August
- ► July
- ► June
- ► May
- ► April
- ► March
- ► February
- ► January
- ► December
- ► November
- ► October

Tom at Blog 於 September 09.12. PM 10:34 發表 | 回覆 (0) | 引用 (0) | 收藏 (0) | 轉寄給朋友 | 檢舉

帥不起來的衝浪初體驗

September 12

我真是糗到很想把頭鑽進地洞裡。在海邊時，我以為自己可以藉由學衝浪來讓人留下很好的印象，但我實在是大錯特錯。當我試著要站上衝浪板時，結果摔了下來，頭還撞到珊瑚。血從我的臉頰上流下來，我們整個下午都在急診室等醫生來幫我縫傷口。

About me

Tom

Calendar

◄　　September　　►

Sun	Mon	Tue	Wed	Thu	Fri	Sat
		1	2	3	4	5	6
7	8	9	10	11	12	13
14	15	16	17	18	19	20
21	22	23	24	25	26	27
28	29	30				

Blog Archive

▸ September (12)
▸ August
▸ July
▸ June
▸ May
▸ April
▸ March
▸ February
▸ January
▸ December
▸ November
▸ October

Tom at Blog 於 September 09.12. PM 10:34 發表 | 回覆 (0) | 引用 (0) | 收藏 (0) | 轉寄給朋友 | 檢舉

網誌作者本來以為可以在喜歡的女生面前好好表現，沒想到卻失足落水，出了個大糗，這時候難怪會想『把頭鑽進地洞裡』了！英文裡直譯的說法便是 **stick one's head in a hole (in the ground)**，也可以說成 hide one's head (in a hole) in the ground。

＊stick [stɪk] *vt.* 插，伸入

例: Jeff wanted to stick his head in a hole in the ground when he found that his zipper was down.
（傑夫發現自己拉鏈沒拉時，很想把自己的頭埋進地洞裡。）

另外相似的說法有 dig a hole to bury oneself in，dig [dɪg] 是『挖掘』，hole [hol] 表『洞』，而 bury [ˋbɛrɪ] 則是『埋藏』，整個語意為『挖個洞把自己埋進去』，同樣也是用來表示感到丟臉或尷尬。

例: I really wanted to dig a hole to bury myself in after I farted in the meeting this morning.
（我今天早上開會時放了屁，讓我很想挖個洞把自己埋進去。）

＊fart [fɑrt] *vi.* 放屁

但是另一個說法 bury one's head in the sand 就與丟臉或尷尬無關了。bury one's head in the sand 的字面意思為『將某人的頭埋在沙子裡』，是指一個人對危機逆境等視若無睹，猶如鴕鳥面臨危險時將頭埋在沙裡，以為看不見就安全了，也就是『持鴕鳥心態』，引申為『逃避現實』。

例: Don't try to bury your head in the sand when faced with problems. They won't go away.
（面對問題時不要逃避現實。這樣無法解決問題。）

字詞幫幫忙！

1. **impression** [ɪmˋprɛʃən] *n.* 印象
   make a good / bad impression (on sb)　（讓某人）留下好 / 壞的印象
   例: Mike made a good impression on his girlfriend's family.
   （麥克讓他女友的家人留下了好印象。）

2. **dead** [dɛd] *adv.* 全然地，完全地（= completely [kəm`plitlɪ] *adv.*）

be dead wrong 　　大錯特錯

be dead right 　　對極了

例: Kent admitted that his decision was dead wrong, but it's already too late.

（肯特承認自己做的決定大錯特錯，但為時已晚。）

3. **surfboard** [`sɜf,bɔrd] *n.* 衝浪板

4. **fall off (...)** 　　（從……）跌下來

例: David fell off the ladder. Fortunately, he wasn't hurt.

（大衛從梯子上摔下來。幸好，他沒受傷。）

5. **smack** [smæk] *vt.* 撞；用手掌打

例: Emily smacked her son in the face when he swore at the dinner table.

（當她兒子在餐桌上罵髒話時，艾蜜莉打了他一巴掌。）

6. **coral** [`kɔrəl] *n.* 珊瑚

7. **stream** [strim] *vi.* 流，淌 & *n.* 溪流

stream down... 　　沿著……流下

stream with tears 　　流下淚水

例: As Bill was delivering a speech on the stage, sweat streamed down his face.

（當比爾在台上演講時，臉上汗水直流而下。）

Amy's eyes streamed with tears at the end of the sad movie.

（愛咪在那部悲傷電影結束時，眼睛流下了淚水。）

8. **emergency room** [ɪ`mɜdʒənsɪ ,rum] *n.* 急診室（常縮寫成 ER）

9. **stitch** [stɪtʃ] *vt.* 縫 & *n.* 一針

stitch...up / stitch up... 　　縫合……

例: Mike started to cry when the doctor began stitching up his wounds.

（醫生開始幫他縫合傷口時，麥克哭了起來。）

A stitch in time saves nine.（諺語）

（及時一針可省下九針。喻：防微杜漸。）

A Real Sweetheart

Index | *Links* | *about* | *comments* | *Photo*

September 13

This girl Sofia might be a **keeper**. She called me today and asked how I was doing. She's such a sweetheart. She said that she was **impressed** that I tried to surf and sorry that I got **injured**. She **offered** to bring me over some chicken soup to make me feel better, but I **declined**. Then she asked if we could **go on a** real **date**. **I'm nobody's fool**, so I accepted it immediately.

About me

Tom

Calendar

◄   September   ►

Sun	Mon	Tue	Wed	Thu	Fri	Sat
	1	2	3	4	5	6
7	8	9	10	11	12	13
14	15	16	17	18	19	20
21	22	23	24	25	26	27
28	29	30				

Blog Archive

▸ September (13)
▸ August
▸ July
▸ June
▸ May
▸ April
▸ March
▸ February
▸ January
▸ December
▸ November
▸ October

Tom at Blog 於 September 09.13. PM 02:15 發表 | 回覆 (0) | 引用 (0) | 收藏 (0) | 轉寄給朋友 | 檢舉

真是個可人兒

Index | *Links* | *about* | *comments* | *Photo*

September 13

　　蘇菲亞這個女生實在值得好好把握。她今天打電話給我，問我感覺怎麼樣。她真是個可人兒。她說我嘗試衝浪讓她印象深刻，但對於我受傷這件事感到很遺憾。她提議要帶雞湯給我，讓我感覺好一些，但我婉拒了。她接著問我們要不要正式來個約會。我可不是傻瓜，所以馬上就接受了。

Tom at Blog 於 September 09.13. PM 02:15 發表 | 回覆 (0) | 引用 (0) | 收藏 (0) | 轉寄給朋友 | 檢舉

fool [ful] 當名詞時表『傻瓜、呆子』之意，網誌中所用的 be nobody's fool 照字面的意思來看，是指『不是任何人的傻瓜』，也就是『不笨、不傻』，亦可表『為人精明、精明能幹的』之意，與 be no fool 意思相同。

例: Terry will find out your secrets. He is nobody's fool. You'd better not cheat on him.
（泰瑞會發現妳的秘密的。他可不是傻瓜，妳最好還是不要給他戴綠帽子。）

Amy is no fool when it comes to money.
（愛咪對錢的事非常精明。）

fool 也可作動詞用，表『欺騙、愚弄』或『無所事事』，有下列重要用法：

fool sb into + V-ing　　欺騙某人從事……

例: David was fooled into believing that he had won the lottery.
（大衛被騙以為自己中樂透。）

fool around　　鬼混，游手好閒
= play around
= idle around
= horse around
= goof around

例: If you continue to fool around and waste your life, you will end up with nothing.
（如果你繼續游手好閒浪費生命的話，最後將一事無成。）

1. **sweetheart** [ˈswitˌhɑrt] *n.* 甜心；戀人

2. **keeper** [ˈkipɚ] *n.* 值得保留的人、事、物；看守人，管理者

3. **impress** [ɪmˈprɛs] *vt.* 使印象深刻
   be impressed with...　　對……留下深刻印象

例: The manager is impressed with the new employee's performance.
（經理對那位新員工的表現印象深刻。）

4. **injure** [`ɪndʒɚ] *vt.* 使受傷

injury [`ɪndʒərɪ] *n.* 傷害，受傷

例: David was seriously injured in the car accident.
（大衛在車禍中受重傷。）

Unfortunately, Eddie's injury was fatal.
（不幸的是，艾迪的傷勢足以致命。）

＊fatal [`fetḷ] *a.* 致命的

5. **offer** [`ɔfɚ] *vi.* 主動提議 & *vt.* 提供

offer to V   主動提議……

offer sb sth   提供某人某物

例: Bryan offered to help Jenny, but was turned down.
（布萊恩主動提議要幫忙珍妮，卻遭她拒絕。）

Thank you for offering me such a good opportunity.
（謝謝你提供我這麼一個好機會。）

6. **decline** [dɪ`klaɪn] *vi.* & *vt.* 婉拒（語氣比 refuse 客氣，refuse 表『拒絕』）

decline one's invitation   婉拒某人的邀請

＊invitation [ˌɪnvə`teʃən] *n.* 邀請

例: Peter asked me to join the party, but I declined because I was tired.
（彼得邀請我參加派對，但我因為很累所以便婉拒了。）

Audrey declined my invitation to dinner.
（奧黛莉婉拒了我一同晚餐的邀約。）

7. **go on a date (with sb)**   （跟某人）約會

例: Miranda came home in a good mood after going on a date with her new boyfriend.
（米蘭達跟新男友約完會回家時心情很好。）

The Do's and Don'ts of Dating

Index | *Links* | *about* | *comments* | *Photo*

September 14

James emailed me some advice for my first date. The first thing he wrote was not to **talk my head off**. He said that women loved to be listened to, so I should **keep** the talk about myself **to a minimum**. His next tip was that I should **go out of my way to** be **polite** not only to my date, but also to the waiters or waitresses. Finally, James told me that **the one thing I shouldn't do is go commando**. Hopefully, he was joking when he wrote that.

About me

Tom

Calendar

◄ *September* ►

Sun	Mon	Tue	Wed	Thu	Fri	Sat
		1	2	3	4	5	6
7	8	9	10	11	12	13
14	15	16	17	18	19	20
21	22	23	24	25	26	27
28	29	30				

Blog Archive

▸ September (14)
▸ August
▸ July
▸ June
▸ May
▸ April
▸ March
▸ February
▸ January
▸ December
▸ November
▸ October

約會守則

September 14

詹姆士伊媚兒給我一些關於初次約會的建議。他提到的第一件事是不要喋喋不休。他說女生喜歡被聆聽,所以我應該儘量少談論自己的事。他的下一招是我應該要禮貌周全,不僅是對女方,就連對服務生也是。最後,詹姆士告訴我千萬不要不穿內褲U///U(羞～)。希望他寫這個純粹是開玩笑。

About me

Tom

Calendar

◄　　*September*　　►

Sun	Mon	Tue	Wed	Thu	Fri	Sat
		1	2	3	4	5	6
7	8	9	10	11	12	13
14	15	16	17	18	19	20
21	22	23	24	25	26	27
28	29	30				

Blog Archive

▸ September (14)
▸ August
▸ July
▸ June
▸ May
▸ April
▸ March
▸ February
▸ January
▸ December
▸ November
▸ October

Tom at Blog 於 September 09.14. PM 04:35 發表 | 回覆 (0) | 引用 (0) | 收藏 (0) | 轉寄給朋友 | 檢舉

約會時非常忌諱滔滔不絕訴說關於自己的事，而完全無視對方的存在，網誌裡的 talk one's head off 就表示『某人喋喋不休／滔滔不絕』之意。

例: Jane: How was your blind date?

Tina: Not so good. He talked his head off all night.

（阿珍：妳昨晚的相親如何？）

（蒂娜：不怎麼樣。對方一整個晚上都喋喋不休。）

除了 talk one's head off，下列幾個用法亦可用來形容人愛說話：

a big mouth　　大嘴巴

motormouth [ˋmotɚ͵maʊθ] n. 滔滔不絕的快嘴

blabbermouth [ˋblæbɚ͵maʊθ] n. 大嘴巴，長舌男／婦

blabber [ˋblæbɚ] vi. 喋喋不休

例: You'd better not tell Jack your secret. He is a big mouth.

（你最好不要告訴傑克你的秘密。他是個大嘴巴。）

I wish Judy would stop blabbering about her boyfriend.

（我真希望茱蒂別再滔滔不絕談論她的男朋友。）

one's head off 之前亦常與下列動詞並用：

cry / laugh / scream one's head off　　大哭／大笑／驚聲尖叫

例: The hungry baby is crying its head off.

（那個饑餓的嬰兒哭得好厲害。）

The clown's funny tricks made all of the children laugh their heads off.

（那小丑的滑稽把戲逗得孩子們哄堂大笑。）

＊clown [klaʊn] n. 小丑

trick [trɪk] n. 把戲

My mother screamed her head off when she saw the rat.

（我媽媽看到那隻老鼠時發出驚聲尖叫。）

名詞 commando [kəˋmændo] 原為『突擊隊（員）』。**go commando** 乃源自於一些美國的突擊隊員怕行軍時，因為胯下和內褲長時間摩擦而發炎，所以乾脆不穿內褲，因此 go commando 就用來表示『不穿內褲』。網誌裡詹姆士怕他好友在約會那天沒穿內褲，要是石門水庫沒關好，可會嚇到人家，所以好心提醒他記得穿上內褲。

例: My four-year-old nephew likes to go commando.

（我 4 歲的外甥不喜歡穿內褲。）

1. do's and don'ts 該做與不該做的事；行為守則

例: It takes a while to get used to the do's and don'ts of the office.
（要適應辦公室規則得花上一點時間。）

2. keep...to a minimum 將……保持在最低限度

reduce...to a minimum 將……減少至最低限度

minimum [`mɪnəməm] *n.* 最低限度；最小量

maximum [`mæksəməm] *n.* 最大限度；最大量

例: Amy manages to reduce her budget for clothes to a minimum.
（愛咪設法將自己的治裝費減到最低額度。）

3. go out of one's way to V 某人竭盡全力（做）……

= go all out to V

= do one's best to V

例: Carol went out of her way to help us when we moved.
（卡蘿在我們搬家時竭盡全力幫忙我們。）

4. polite [pə`laɪt] *a.* 有禮貌的

impolite [ˌɪmpə`laɪt] *a.* 無禮的

be polite to sb 對某人有禮貌

例: You should be polite to your elders.
（你應該對長輩有禮貌。）

It's impolite to interrupt others while they are talking.
（打斷別人談話是很不禮貌的。）

＊interrupt [ˌɪntə`rʌpt] *vt.* 打斷，使中斷

5. the one thing sb shouldn't do is (to) + 原形動詞
某人不應該做的一件事就是……

the one thing sb should do is (to) + 原形動詞
某人應該做的一件事就是……

例: The one thing you shouldn't do is (to) chew gum in Mr. Wu's class.
（你絕不該在吳老師的課堂上嚼口香糖。）

Toning Up

Index | Links | about | comments | Photo

September 15

My date with Sofia is still three days away, and I'm going to the gym every afternoon. I'm hoping to tone my arms up and **get in** better **shape**. Maybe if I do some **aerobics**, my belly will **shrink** a little more. I'm no **muscleman**, but any way that **helps out** will be good. I should get a **haircut** pretty soon, too.

About me

Tom

Calendar

◄   September   ►

Sun	Mon	Tue	Wed	Thu	Fri	Sat
	1	2	3	4	5	6
7	8	9	10	11	12	13
14	15	16	17	18	19	20
21	22	23	24	25	26	27
28	29	30				

Blog Archive

▸ September (15)
▸ August
▸ July
▸ June
▸ May
▸ April
▸ March
▸ February
▸ January
▸ December
▸ November
▸ October

Tom at Blog 於 September 09.15. PM 06:29 發表 | 回覆 (0) | 引用 (0) | 收藏 (0) | 轉寄給朋友 | 檢舉

強健體格

September 15

離和蘇菲亞約會的時間還有 3 天，而我每天下午都會去健身房。我希望能讓手臂強健，並且讓身材好看些。或許我做一些有氧運動的話，我的肚子就可以消一點。我不是什麼肌肉男，但任何方式只要對我有幫助的就好。我也應該趕快去剪個頭髮。

About me

Tom

Calendar

◄   September   ►

Sun	Mon	Tue	Wed	Thu	Fri	Sat
	1	2	3	4	5	6
7	8	9	10	11	12	13
14	15	16	17	18	19	20
21	22	23	24	25	26	27
28	29	30				

Blog Archive

▸ September (15)
▸ August
▸ July
▸ June
▸ May
▸ April
▸ March
▸ February
▸ January
▸ December
▸ November
▸ October

Tom at Blog 於 September 09.15. PM 06:29 發表｜回覆 (0)｜引用 (0)｜收藏 (0)｜轉寄給朋友｜檢舉

tone [ton] 當名詞時，指樂器或聲音方面的音調、音色，在色彩方面則指色調，而用在人身上則表肌肉或皮膚的健康狀況。

例: From the tone of Kathy's voice, I knew she was angry with me.
（我從凱西的聲音語調知道她很氣我。）

Customer: What color do you think suits me?
  Stylist: I think a dark red would suit your skin tone.
（顧　客：妳覺得我適合什麼顏色？）
（髮型師：我覺得深紅色會適合您的膚色。）

tone 作動詞時，則表『使結實、使強健』，常與 up 並用，形成 "tone up..." 的用法，表『使……更結實／強健』。

例: Gary goes swimming every day to tone up his muscles.
（蓋瑞每天去游泳來鍛鍊肌肉。）

Lucy started exercising regularly to tone her body.
（露西開始規律運動來讓身體更結實。）

 ＊regularly [ˈrɛɡjələlɪ] *adv.* 有規律地

其他在健身或瘦身時常使用的字眼尚有下列：

build up one's muscles 鍛鍊某人的肌肉
strengthen one's muscles 增強某人的肌肉
 ＊strengthen [ˈstrɛŋθən] *vt.* 增強
sculpt one's muscles 雕塑某人的肌肉
 ＊sculpt [skʌlpt] *vt.* 雕塑；雕刻
tighten one's muscles 使某人的肌肉結實
 ＊tighten [ˈtaɪtn̩] *vt.* 使變緊
例: Jeff lifts weights to strengthen his muscles.
（傑夫練舉重來增強他的肌肉。）

1. **get in shape** 恢復身材；健身
 be in shape 身體／健康狀況良好
= be in good shape

be out of shape　　身體／健康狀況很差

= be in poor shape

例: Sandra decided to postpone her wedding until she got back in shape.
（珊卓拉決定將婚禮延期到她恢復身材為止。）

＊postpone [post`pon] vt. 使延期

Edward goes jogging each morning in the hope of getting in shape.
（艾德華每天晨跑就是希望身體健康。）

Since I exercise every day, I'm in pretty good shape.
（因為我每天運動，所以身體很好。）

Jim has been a little out of shape recently because he's been working overtime.
（吉姆因為最近常加班所以身體不太好。）

2. aerobics [ɛ`robɪks] *n.* 有氧運動

water aerobics　　水中有氧

3. shrink [ʃrɪŋk] *vi.* 收縮，變小 & *vt.* 使縮小

三態為：shrink, shrank [ʃræŋk], shrunk [ʃrʌŋk]。

例: My clothes shrank after they were washed.
（我的衣服洗過後縮水了。）

We were forced to shrink our production at the factory because of the lower market demand.
（市場需求減少迫使我們工廠縮減產量。）

＊factory [`fækt (ə) rɪ] *n.* 工廠

4. muscleman [`mʌsl͵mæn] *n.* 肌肉發達的男子

5. help out　　幫忙；分擔工作

help sb out / help out sb　　幫助某人，幫某人一把

例: Mike was too proud to ask anyone to help out.
（麥克太過驕傲而不願請任何人幫忙。）

Though I knew that Richard had been in financial trouble, there was not much I could do to help him out.
（雖然我知道李察有財務上的問題，但我能幫他的並不多。）

6. haircut [`hɛr͵kʌt] *n.* 理髮

The Super Stylist

Index | Links | about | comments | Photo

September 16

At the hair salon, I told the stylist that I wanted something special. She **came up with** a **phenomenal** look for me. My hair <u>is cut close on the sides and wavy on the top</u>. When I use some **gel**, I **feel like** a superstar. It wasn't only my hair she **fixed**. She took a **razor** and **shaved** between my **eyebrows** and even shaped them. I was **hesitant** at first, but I look much better with two eyebrows instead of one.

About me

Tom

Calendar

◄　September　►

Sun	Mon	Tue	Wed	Thu	Fri	Sat
	1	2	3	4	5	6
7	8	9	10	11	12	13
14	15	16	17	18	19	20
21	22	23	24	25	26	27
28	29	30				

Blog Archive

► September (16)
► August
► July
► June
► May
► April
► March
► February
► January
► December
► November
► October

超牛髮型師

Index | *Links* | *about* | *comments* | *Photo*

September 16

　　在美髮院裡，我告訴設計師我想要特別一點的髮型。她為我想出了一個超棒的樣子。我的頭髮兩側被剃平，上面的頭髮微捲。當我抹上點髮膠，感覺就像是個超級巨星。但她不只幫我用頭髮而已。她還拿剃刀剃掉我眉毛的中間，甚至修出眉形。我一開始有點猶豫，但我有兩條眉毛時比一條好看多了。

About me

Tom

Calendar

| | | | September | | | ▶ |
Sun	Mon	Tue	Wed	Thu	Fri	Sat
	1	2	3	4	5	6
7	8	9	10	11	12	13
14	15	16	17	18	19	20
21	22	23	24	25	26	27
28	29	30				

Blog Archive

Tom at Blog 於 September 09.16. PM 07:54 發表 | 回覆 (0) | 引用 (0) | 收藏 (0) | 轉寄給朋友 | 檢舉

想要改頭換面，上美髮院是最快的方法！雖然說男生大多是短髮的造型，但是也有不少的變化，像是網誌作者的髮型是 be cut close on the sides and wavy on the top（頭髮兩側被剃平，上面的頭髮微捲），wavy [`wevɪ] 指的就是頭髮呈波浪狀的樣子。以下介紹幾種男性髮型的說法：

make the top a bit spiky　　把頭頂剪成微尖的形狀
＊spiky [`spaɪkɪ] *a.* 尖尖的
cut off one's sideburns　　剪掉某人的鬢腳
＊sideburns [`saɪd͵bɝnz] *n.* 鬢腳
buzz cut [`bʌz ͵kʌt] *n.* 平頭
＊此名稱取自電動剃刀剃頭髮時唧唧叫的聲響（buzz），通常是指極短的平頭或光頭，又稱 skinhead cut。
faux hawk [`fo ͵hɔk] *n.* 貝克漢頭
＊這個字是由 faux（假的）和 Mohawk（美國原住民的一支）組合而成，指的是中間頭髮豎立且較兩側長的髮型。2002 年的世界盃中，貝克漢因為這個髮型而帶動一股風潮，因此大家便稱此髮型為貝克漢頭，又可直接稱作 Beckham。
bowl cut [`bol ͵kʌt] *n.* 西瓜皮頭
＊由英文便可得知，這種髮型類似碗（bowl）的形狀，中文大多稱為西瓜皮。

例: I've had a buzz cut for years, so I'm not used to my hair being long and wavy on the top now.
（我留平頭留了好幾年，所以現在不太習慣頭頂上的頭髮微捲的樣子。）

The stylist made the top of my hair a bit spiky, and I really like the way it looks.
（設計師幫我把頭頂剪成微尖的形狀，我真喜歡這髮型看起來的樣子。）

My girlfriend hopes I can get a faux hawk, which she thinks is a hip look.
（我女朋友希望我剪貝克漢頭，她覺得那樣很時髦。）
＊hip [hɪp] *a.* 時髦的

 字 詞 幫幫忙！

1. **stylist** [`staɪlɪst] *n.* 髮型設計師
2. **come up with...**　　提出／想出……

例: The manager came up with a way to solve the company's financial problems.
（經理想出一個解決公司財務問題的辦法。）

3. **phenomenal** [fəˈnɑmən̩l] *a.* 極好的；驚人的
   例: Kevin has been a phenomenal success in the world of business.
   （凱文在商界的成就非凡。）

4. **gel** [dʒɛl] *n.* 髮膠

5. **feel like + N**　　　感覺像是……
   feel like + V-ing　　想要……
   例: Annie felt like the luckiest girl in the world when she married Jack.
   （安妮嫁給傑克時，覺得自己就像是全世界最幸運的女孩。）
   Eric feels like eating at home, so he declined his colleague's invitation to dinner.
   （艾瑞克想在家裡吃飯，所以婉拒了同事的晚餐邀約。）
   ＊decline [dɪˈklaɪn] *vt.* 婉拒
   　decline one's invitation　　婉拒某人的邀請

6. **fix** [fɪks] *vt.* 修整／設計（頭髮）
   例: Alice doesn't like the way the stylist fixed her hair.
   （艾莉絲不喜歡造型師幫她設計的髮型。）

7. **razor** [ˈrezɚ] *n.* 剃刀，刮鬍刀

8. **shave** [ʃev] *vi.* & *vt.* 剃除，刮
   例: All new recruits must have their heads shaved before beginning basic training.
   （所有新兵都必須在基本訓練開始前理光頭。）
   ＊recruit [rɪˈkrut] *n.* 新兵

9. **eyebrow** [ˈaɪˌbraʊ] *n.* 眉毛

10. **hesitant** [ˈhɛzətənt] *a.* 遲疑的，猶豫不決的
    例: Brian was hesitant about telling his father the bad news.
    （布萊恩猶豫要不要告訴他父親那個壞消息。）

No Nose Hair

Index | Links | about | comments | Photo

September 17

My big date with Sofia **is fast approaching**. I want to look great on that day, so I asked James for his **opinions**. He **suggested** that we go shopping for a new pair of jeans and a shirt. I even got a new pair of **sneakers** to **match** my shirt. When we were at the sneaker store, I asked a girl if I looked cool and she said, "Yes, **except for** your nose hair." I was so embarrassed. I went home and **clipped** it right away.

About me

Tom

Calendar

◄ September ►

Sun	Mon	Tue	Wed	Thu	Fri	Sat
		1	2	3	4	5	6
7	8	9	10	11	12	13
14	15	16	17	18	19	20
21	22	23	24	25	26	27
28	29	30				

Blog Archive

► September (17)
► August
► July
► June
► May
► April
► March
► February
► January
► December
► November
► October

鼻毛不要來搗亂

Index | Links | about | comments | Photo

September 17

　　我跟蘇菲亞的約會日就快到了。我想在那天看起來很體面，所以就問了詹姆士的意見。他建議我們去逛街，買條新的牛仔褲和新襯衫。我還買了一雙新球鞋來搭配我的襯衫。我們在球鞋店時，我問了個女生我看起來酷不酷，她說：『你看起來是很酷，除了你的鼻毛以外。』我覺得超尷尬的，我回家後就馬上修剪了鼻毛。

About me

Tom

Calendar

◄　　　*September*　　　►

Sun	Mon	Tue	Wed	Thu	Fri	Sat
		1	2	3	4	5	6
7	8	9	10	11	12	13
14	15	16	17	18	19	20
21	22	23	24	25	26	27
28	29	30				

Blog Archive

▸ September (17)
▸ August
▸ July
▸ June
▸ May
▸ April
▸ March
▸ February
▸ January
▸ December
▸ November
▸ October

Tom at Blog 於 September 09.17. PM 09:13 發表│回覆 (0)│引用 (0)│收藏 (0)│轉寄給朋友│檢舉

網誌作者為了讓自己在約會時看起來帥氣無比，先去購買了些新行頭，但忘了修剪鼻毛，幸好有人提醒，不然到時就糗大了。以下就來介紹幾項約會前該注意的事：

clip your nose hair　　修剪鼻毛

＊clip [klɪp] *vt.* 修剪

clip your fingernails　　修剪手指甲

＊fingernail [ˈfɪŋɡəˌnel] *n.* 手指甲

clean your ears　　清理耳朵

floss your teeth　　用牙線清潔牙縫

＊floss [flɔs] *vt.* 用牙線潔牙 & *n.* 細線

dental floss　　牙線（不可數）

dental [ˈdɛntl̩] *a.* 牙齒的

make sure you don't have bad breath　　確定你沒有口臭

use breath spray / mints　　使用口腔清新噴劑 / 爽口薄荷糖

＊breath spray　　口腔清新噴劑

spray [spre] *n.* 噴劑

breath mints　　讓口氣清新的薄荷糖

mint [mɪnt] *n.* 薄荷糖；薄荷

例: Kent clipped his fingernails once a month.

（肯特每個月修剪一次手指甲。）

Helen: Your fingernails are too long and look dirty. Has your girlfriend ever complained about that?

Larry: No, never. But I always floss my teeth and use breath spray before I see her.

（海倫：你的指甲又長又髒。你的女朋友有沒有抱怨過啊？）

（賴瑞：從來沒有。但每次我見她之前，我都會用牙線清牙還有噴口腔清新劑。）

字詞幫幫忙！

1. **be fast approaching**　　即將來臨

= be around the corner

= be near at hand

approach [əˋprotʃ] *vi.* & *vt.* 接近

例: Winter is fast approaching, so I need to buy a new coat.
（冬天就要來了，所以我需要買件新外套。）

The soldiers silently approached the enemy fort.
（那些軍人靜悄悄地接近敵人的堡壘。）

＊fort [fɔrt] *n.* 堡壘，要塞

2. opinion [əˋpɪnjən] *n.* 意見

ask sb for his or her opinion　　詢問某人的意見

In sb's opinion, S + V　　某人認為……；依某人之見，……

= In sb's view, S + V

= sb is of the opinion + that 子句

例: Mindy knows a lot about Egypt, so I'm going to ask her for her opinion on my history report.
（明蒂知道很多有關埃及的事，所以我要去問她對我的歷史報告有什麼意見。）

In my dad's opinion, all of my boyfriends have been bad guys.
（我老爸認為我所有的男朋友都不是什麼好東西。）

3. suggest [səgˋdʒɛst] *vt.* 建議

suggest that + S + (should) + V　　建議……

例: Jennifer suggested that we (should) call off our meeting since everyone was so busy.
（珍妮佛建議既然大家都很忙，我們應該取消會議。）

＊call off...　　取消……

4. sneaker [ˋsnikɚ] *n.* 運動鞋

a pair of sneakers　　一雙運動鞋

5. match [mætʃ] *vt.* 和……相配 / 相稱

例: Your shirt really matches your green eyes.
（你的襯衫和你的綠眼珠真得很搭。）

6. except for...　　除了……之外

= with the exception of...

＊exception [ɪkˋsɛpʃən] *n.* 例外

例: Everything except for the piano is for sale.
（除了鋼琴以外，一切都待售。）

Unit 61

Play It Cool

Index | Links | about | comments | Photo

September 18

My fingernails are **trimmed. Check**. My nose hair is cut. Check. I'm wearing **deodorant**. Check. My haircut is **fashionable**. Check. Now, **all I have to do** to **make a** good **impression on** Sofia is to play it cool when we are talking. I'm pretty **smooth** chatting on the computer or talking on the phone, but it's **in person** that I **tend to** act **awkwardly**.

Tom at Blog 於 September 09.18. PM 03:31 發表 | 回覆 (0) | 引用 (0) | 收藏 (0) | 轉寄給朋友 | 檢舉

242

鎮定一點

September 18

指甲剪了，打勾。鼻毛修了，打勾。體香劑擦了，打勾。頭髮很有型，打勾。現在，我所要做的就是在我們交談時保持鎮定，讓蘇菲亞留下好印象。在電腦前和人聊天或講電話我都沒問題，但面對面時，我往往會表現得很彆扭。

About me

Tom

Calendar

◄　　*September*　　►

Sun	Mon	Tue	Wed	Thu	Fri	Sat
		1	2	3	4	5	6
7	8	9	10	11	12	13
14	15	16	17	18	19	20
21	22	23	24	25	26	27
28	29	30				

Blog Archive

▸ September (18)
▸ August
▸ July
▸ June
▸ May
▸ April
▸ March
▸ February
▸ January
▸ December
▸ November
▸ October

Tom at Blog 於 September 09.18. PM 03:31 發表│回覆 (0)│引用 (0)│收藏 (0)│轉寄給朋友│檢舉

網誌中的 **play it cool** 是『冷靜對待、鎮定處理』的意思。網誌作者平時和他人在網路上聊天時還挺溜的，但對於面對面聊天這件事很沒輒，所以要自己保持冷靜。

例: When Brian heard that Samantha liked him, he tried to play it cool, but deep down he was very excited.

（布萊恩聽到莎曼珊喜歡他時，他試圖冷靜以對，但其實內心非常興奮。）

以下介紹其他相關用法：

cool it　　冷靜下來，別衝動

= cool down

= cool off

例: Cool it! There is no point in getting so angry.

（冷靜下來！沒必要這麼生氣。）

keep one's cool　　某人保持冷靜

例: I tried to keep my cool while my teacher was handing out the exam papers.

（老師發考卷時我試圖保持冷靜。）

lose one's cool　　某人失去冷靜

例: David lost his cool when his wife said she wanted a divorce.

（大衛在老婆說要離婚時失去了冷靜。）

＊divorce [dəˋvɔrs] *n.* 離婚

1. **trim** [trɪm] *vt.* 修剪

例: My mother asked me to trim the bushes in the backyard.

（媽媽要我去修剪後院的樹叢。）

2. **check** [tʃɛk] *n.* （表示答案正確或某事項已處理的）勾號，已核對的記號

3. **deodorant** [diˋodərənt] *n.* 除臭劑

4. fashionable [ˋfæʃənəbḷ] *a.* 流行的；時髦的

5. All / What sb has to do is (to) + 原形動詞　　某人所必須做的
就是……

例: All Billy has to do to improve his grades is (to) spend less
time playing video games.
（比利想要使成績進步所必須做的就是少打電玩。）

6. impression [ɪmˋprɛʃən] *n.* 印象
make a good / bad impression on sb　　給某人留下好 / 壞印象
例: Beth made a bad impression on her teacher because she
fell asleep during the first class.
（貝絲讓老師留下壞印象，因為她在上第一堂課時打瞌睡。）

7. smooth [smuð] *a.* 順利的，沒問題的；順暢的
例: Peter was promoted to manager after his smooth
handling of the big event.
（彼得順利處理完那個大活動後被升為經理。）

8. in person　　親自地
例: The author enjoys going on book tours because she likes
to meet her fans in person.
（那位作者喜歡巡迴簽書會，因為她喜歡和書迷面對面接觸。）

9. tend to V　　往往會……；易於……
= be apt [æpt] to V
= be liable [ˋlaɪəbḷ] to V
= be prone [pron] to V
= be inclined [ɪnˋklaɪnd] to V
例: Candy tends to get nervous when speaking in front of a
group of people.
（肯蒂在一群人面前說話時往往會很緊張。）

10. awkwardly [ˋɔkwədlɪ] *adv.* 笨拙地
例: Hannah acts awkwardly whenever she is around Tom.
（漢娜每次在湯姆面前就會表現得很彆扭。）

The Third Wheel

Index | *Links* | *about* | *comments* | *Photo*

September 19

As soon as I got to the bar, Sofia walked in. She looked **fantastic**, but I was **shocked** because she brought her best friend, Gail, whom I immediately **nicknamed** the third wheel. **Talk about** a **party pooper**. I was so **upset** that I started to **drink heavily**. When I went to the bathroom, I said hello to a pretty girl. Gail saw this and told Sofia. Then they both **grabbed** their things and left.

About me

Tom

Calendar

◄   September   ►

Sun	Mon	Tue	Wed	Thu	Fri	Sat
	1	2	3	4	5	6
7	8	9	10	11	12	13
14	15	16	17	18	19	20
21	22	23	24	25	26	27
28	29	30				

Blog Archive

▸ September (19)
▸ August
▸ July
▸ June
▸ May
▸ April
▸ March
▸ February
▸ January
▸ December
▸ November
▸ October

Tom at Blog 於 September 09.19. PM 10:05 發表 | 回覆 (0) | 引用 (0) | 收藏 (0) | 轉寄給朋友 | 檢舉

大電燈泡

September 19

我一到了酒吧，蘇菲亞也走了進來。她看起來真是迷人，但她竟帶了她的好姊妹蓋兒，這使我十分震驚，我心裡立刻就幫她取了『大電燈泡』的外號。說到這兒，還有什麼比這更掃興的。我很不爽，所以便開始灌酒。當我去廁所的時候，我向一位漂亮美眉打招呼。蓋兒看到這一幕便向蘇菲亞打小報告。接著她們倆拿了東西就走人了。

About me

Tom

Calendar

◄　　　*September*　　　►

Sun	Mon	Tue	Wed	Thu	Fri	Sat
		1	2	3	4	5	6
7	8	9	10	11	12	13
14	15	16	17	18	19	20
21	22	23	24	25	26	27
28	29	30				

Blog Archive

- ► September (19)
- ► August
- ► July
- ► June
- ► May
- ► April
- ► March
- ► February
- ► January
- ► December
- ► November
- ► October

Tom at Blog 於 September 09.19. PM 10:05 發表 | 回覆 (0) | 引用 (0) | 收藏 (0) | 轉寄給朋友 | 檢舉

247

美語中電燈泡的表示方法可跟燈沒關係，而和自行車的輪子（wheel [wil]）有關。一般的自行車都只有兩個輪子，要是有 3 個輪子呢？沒錯，那第 3 個輪子就是多餘的。這也是為什麼美語中電燈泡就叫 **a third wheel**。

例: Jeff felt like a third wheel while his friends, Mary and John, were having a good time chatting with each other.

（傑夫的朋友瑪莉和約翰聊得很開心，讓他覺得自己像是個電燈泡。）

a party pooper [`pupɚ] 則指『掃興的人』。試想在派對裡，有人一副大便臉，看起來既不開心又不願意參與派對的遊戲，那不是掃大家的興致嗎？本網誌中，蓋兒的出現對網誌作者而言可以算是半路殺出的程咬金，大大掃了他和蘇菲亞同歡的興致。

例: Ben is such a party pooper that no one likes to invite him to any kind of activity.

（小班是個掃興鬼，所以沒有人喜歡邀他參加任何活動。）

1. **fantastic** [fæn`tæstɪk] *a.* 吸引人的；極好的

   例: The apartment looked fantastic, so Ted decided to rent it on the spot.

   （這棟公寓看起來棒透了，所以泰得當場就決定租下來。）

2. **shocked** [ʃɑkt] *a.* 驚愕的，感到震驚的

   例: Alice was shocked to learn that her best friend was pregnant.

   （艾莉絲得知她最好的朋友懷孕時感到十分震驚。）

3. **nickname** [`nɪk͵nem] *vt.* 給……取綽號 / 外號 & *n.* 綽號，外號

   例: The guitarist was nicknamed "Guitar God" due to his exceptional skill.

   （那名吉他手由於超凡的演奏技巧而有『吉他之神』的外號。）

   ＊guitarist [gɪ`tɑrɪst] *n.* 吉他手
     exceptional [ɪk`sɛpʃənl̩] *a.* 卓越的，非凡的

4. Talk about... 說到……（用來強調所談論的人或事物）

例: Talk about a muscleman. You should check out Randy's 20-inch biceps.

（說到肌肉男，妳應該去瞧瞧藍迪 20 吋的二頭肌。）

＊biceps [ˋbaɪsɛps] *n.* 二頭肌

5. upset [ʌpˋsɛt] *a.* 不快的；心煩意亂的

例: Hank's comments made me kind of upset.

（漢克的評論讓我有點不高興。）

＊comment [ˋkɑmɛnt] *n.* 評論

kind of + adj. = a little + aj. 有點兒……

Cindy was upset that she was tricked out of her money.

（辛蒂因被騙了錢而感到心煩意亂。）

＊trick sb out of... 騙走某人的……

6. drink heavily 大量地喝酒，豪飲

= drink like a fish

例: Every time Henry feels depressed, he drinks heavily until he pukes.

（亨利每次只要感到沮喪，他就會灌酒灌到吐為止。）

＊puke [pjuk] *vi.* 嘔吐

7. grab [græb] *vt.* 抓住，抓取

grab sb by the + 身體部位 抓住某人某部位

例: The thief grabbed my bag and ran away.

（那個小偷搶走我的皮包就跑走了。）

The little boy grabbed his mother by the arm and wouldn't let go.

（那名小男孩抓住他媽媽的手臂不讓她走。）

Unit 63

More Fish

Index | *Links* | *about* | *comments* | *Photo*

September 20

When I got home, I called Sofia **over and over again**, but she wouldn't **pick up the phone**. I called James, and he told me that **there were more fish in the sea** and not to worry about it. I told him that while I was **drowning my sorrows** about Sofia at the bar, the pretty girl came and sat next to me. **One thing** had **led to another**, and now we are going on a date tomorrow. I guess James was right.

Calendar

◄　　September　　►

Sun	Mon	Tue	Wed	Thu	Fri	Sat
	1	2	3	4	5	6
7	8	9	10	11	12	13
14	15	16	17	18	19	20
21	22	23	24	25	26	27
28	29	30				

Blog Archive

- ▸ September (20)
- ▸ August
- ▸ July
- ▸ June
- ▸ May
- ▸ April
- ▸ March
- ▸ February
- ▸ January
- ▸ December
- ▸ November
- ▸ October

Tom at Blog 於 September 09.20. PM 09:47 發表｜回覆 (0)｜引用 (0)｜收藏 (0)｜轉寄給朋友｜檢舉

天涯何處無芳草

September 20

　　我回到家後一直打電話給蘇菲亞，但她不肯接電話。我打給詹姆士，他告訴我天涯何處無芳草，不用太擔心這件事。我告訴他當我在酒吧為了蘇菲亞藉酒澆愁時，有個漂亮美眉進來坐在我旁邊。事情接二連三、一件接著一件發生，現在變成我們明天要去約會了。我想詹姆士說的是對的。

Tom at Blog 於 September 09.20. PM 09:47 發表 | 回覆 (0) | 引用 (0) | 收藏 (0) | 轉寄給朋友 | 檢舉

fish 表『魚』（單複數同形），sea 則是『海』，"There are more fish in the sea." 字面上的意思就是指『海裡有更多魚。』既然如此，就沒有必要為了一條魚，而放棄大海裡其它的魚，這跟中文在安慰失戀朋友時常說的『天涯何處無芳草，何必單戀一支花。』有異曲同工之妙，也可以說成 "There are plenty of fish in the sea."。

例: There are plenty of fish in the sea. Don't get so depressed just because one girl didn't pay attention to you.
（天涯何處無芳草。不要只因為一個女孩子不理你就這麼消沉。）

＊depressed [dɪˋprɛst] *a.* 消沉的

說到 fish，英文裡和魚相關的俚語可真不少，以下列舉數個常見的說法，學會用這些俚語，英文會更加道地！

a cold fish　　冷漠的人

a big fish in a small pond	小地方裡的大人物
drink like a fish	酒量很好；豪飲
teach a fish how to swim	班門弄斧
like a fish out of water	感到不自在；感到格格不入

例: Jeffrey looked like such a cold fish that no one at the party wanted to talk to him.
（傑佛瑞看起來很冷漠，所以派對上沒有人想跟他說話。）

Ed used to be a big fish in a small pond, but he feels like a nobody in the big city now.
（艾德曾經在小地方風光過，但現在在大城市裡他覺得自己卻像個無名小卒。）

Mandy is short and tiny, but actually she can drink like a fish.
（曼蒂看起來很嬌小，但其實她酒量很好。）

Larry drank like a fish at the party last night.
（賴瑞昨晚在派對上喝了很多酒。）

When Kent was suggesting improvements to the paintings in front of the artist, it was just like teaching a fish how to swim.
（當肯特在那名畫家面前建議這些畫作可如何改進時，就像是班門弄斧一般。）

＊improvement [ɪmˋpruvmənt] *n.* 改進之處

Angela felt like a fish out of water when she went to her ex-boyfriend's wedding.

（安琪拉參加她前男友的婚禮時，感到十分彆扭。）

字 詞幫幫忙！

1. **over and over (again)**　　一再地

例: I have drawn this picture over and over again, but it still looks awful.

（這幅圖我畫了又畫，還是畫不好。）

2. **pick up the phone**　　接電話

hang up the phone　　掛電話

例: Cindy doesn't pick up the phone when she doesn't recognize the number.

（辛蒂看到不認得的電話號碼就不會接電話。）

＊recognize [ˋrɛkəgˌnaɪz] vt. 辨認，辨識

It was very rude of Judy to hang up the phone without saying goodbye.

（茱蒂沒說再見就掛電話，真是沒禮貌。）

3. **drown one's sorrows**　　借酒澆愁

drown [draʊn] vt. 解（憂）；使溺斃 & vi. 溺斃

sorrow [ˋsaro] n. 悲傷

例: Paul has been drowning his sorrows at the bar every night since his girlfriend broke up with him.

（自從保羅的女友和他分手後，他就每晚在酒吧裡買醉借酒澆愁。）

The fisherman almost drowned when his boat overturned in the storm.

（那漁夫的船在暴風雨中翻覆時，他差點兒就淹死了。）

＊overturn [ˌovəˋtɜn] vi. 翻覆

4. **one thing leads to another**　　事情接二連三、一件接著一件發生

lead to...　　導致……

例: Excessive drinking could lead to liver problems.

（飲酒過度可能會導致肝臟方面的疾病。）

＊excessive [ɪkˋsɛsɪv] a. 過度的

liver [ˋlɪvə] n. 肝臟

Bitten by the Travel Bug

Index | Links | about | comments | Photo

September 21

My friend Alex **called** me **up** and said that he'd been bitten by the travel bug. He wondered if I could **afford** a trip to Thailand with him. I told him that this trip sounded **right up my alley**. I haven't had any time off work all year, and I'd love to **get away from it all** for a few days.

About me

Tom

Calendar

◄　　September　　►

Sun	Mon	Tue	Wed	Thu	Fri	Sat
		1	2	3	4	5	6
7	8	9	10	11	12	13
14	15	16	17	18	19	20
21	22	23	24	25	26	27
28	29	30				

Blog Archive

▸ September (21)
▸ August
▸ July
▸ June
▸ May
▸ April
▸ March
▸ February
▸ January
▸ December
▸ November
▸ October

September 21

　　我朋友艾力克斯打電話給我說他最近一直想去旅行。他想知道我能不能負擔得起跟他一起去泰國的費用。我跟他說這趟旅程聽起來很合我意。我今年都還沒有休假，我很想能有幾天將所有事都拋到九霄雲外。

Tom at Blog 於 September 09.21. PM 03:37 發表 | 回覆 (0) | 引用 (0) | 收藏 (0) | 轉寄給朋友 | 檢舉

bug [bʌg] 是名詞，表『蟲子』。在美語口語中也指『細菌』（germ [dʒɝm]）或『病毒』（virus [ˋvaɪrəs]），the flu bug 是『流感病毒』，pick up a bug 就是『感染病菌、染病』，a stomach bug 則引申為『腸胃不適』。

例: Sam picked up a stomach bug when he went to Bangkok to visit his friend.

（山姆到曼谷探訪他朋友時吃壞了肚子。）

bug 也可指『（一時的）狂熱、著迷』，the travel bug 就是指對旅行突如其來的一股狂熱。許多人出遊後都會對旅程念念不忘，一天到晚都還想要出國旅遊，這就是 **be bitten by the travel bug**。此外，也可用 have / get / catch the travel bug 來表示有這種想四處旅遊的狂熱。

例: Ever since Josh went backpacking in Italy last summer, he has been bitten by the travel bug and hungers for more.

（自從喬許去年夏天去了一趟義大利自助旅行，他便迷上了旅遊，一直渴望去更多地方。）

＊backpack [ˋbækˏpæk] *vi.* 背負簡便行李旅行

　hunger for...　　渴望……

As Chinese New Year is fast approaching, many people in my office have caught the travel bug.

（春節即將來臨之際，我們公司裡有許多人都有想去旅遊的念頭。）

除了 the travel bug，尚可與其他活動搭配使用，例如：

the ski bug　　　　　對滑雪著迷
the fitness bug　　　　對健身著迷

例: Maggie has the fitness bug and goes to the gym five times a week.

（梅姬對健身很狂熱，每個星期都會去健身房 5 次。）

1.　call sb up　　　打電話給某人

＝　give sb a call

= give sb a ring

= give sb a buzz

= phone sb

* ring [rɪŋ] *n.* （一通）電話；鈴響

buzz [bʌz] *n.* 電話；嗡嗡叫的聲音

例: Andy called Sally up and asked her out.

（安迪打電話約莎莉出去。）

Please give me a ring when you get home.

（回到家時請打個電話給我。）

2. **afford** [əˋfɔrd] *vt.* 負擔得起

注意：

afford 其前通常與助動詞 can 或 can't 並用，而不可單獨使用，其後則可接名詞或不定詞作受詞。

can / can't afford + N/to V　　負擔得起 / 負擔不起（做）……

例: Willie can only afford a secondhand car.

（威利只買得起二手車。）

Jenny couldn't afford to take piano lessons though she really wanted to learn.

（雖然珍妮很想學鋼琴，但是她無法負擔鋼琴課的費用。）

3. **right up one's alley**　　合某人的胃口 / 口味

alley [ˋælɪ] *n.* 小巷，巷道

例: I love extreme sports, so bungee jumping is right up my alley.

（我很愛極限運動，所以高空彈跳正合我胃口。）

4. **get away from it all**　　遠離塵囂，拋開一切煩惱

*get away from...　　原指『逃離……』之意。

例: You need to go on a vacation to get away from it all.

（你需要去度個假，擺脫一切煩惱。）

The robber managed to get away from the police.

（那名搶匪設法逃過警方的逮捕。）

Believe It or Not!

Index | Links | about | comments | Photo

September 22

I **made it to** Thailand with Alex, and it's even better than I **expected**. The **flight** was long, but **my day brightened up** as soon as we got to our five-star hotel. We have an **infinity** pool right outside our **bungalow**, and it looks like the water **vanishes** into the **horizon**. I've never seen a place so beautiful in my life.

About me

Tom

Calendar

◄   September   ►

Sun	Mon	Tue	Wed	Thu	Fri	Sat
	1	2	3	4	5	6
7	8	9	10	11	12	13
14	15	16	17	18	19	20
21	22	23	24	25	26	27
28	29	30				

Blog Archive

► September (22)
► August
► July
► June
► May
► April
► March
► February
► January
► December
► November
► October

Tom at Blog 於 September 09.22. PM 04:17 發表 | 回覆 (0) | 引用 (0) | 收藏 (0) | 轉寄給朋友 | 檢舉

信不信由你！

September 22

　　我和艾力克斯來到泰國了，而且這裡比我預期的還要棒。班機飛行時間還蠻久的，不過一到達我們投宿的五星級飯店，我一整天的心情都飛揚了起來。我們住的平房外面有座無邊際泳池，水面看起來就像是消失在地平線一般。我這輩子還沒看過這麼美的地方。

About me

Tom

Calendar

◄　　　September　　　►

Sun	Mon	Tue	Wed	Thu	Fri	Sat
		1	2	3	4	5	6
7	8	9	10	11	12	13
14	15	16	17	18	19	20
21	22	23	24	25	26	27
28	29	30				

Blog Archive

▶ September (22)
▶ August
▶ July
▶ June
▶ May
▶ April
▶ March
▶ February
▶ January
▶ December
▶ November
▶ October

Tom at Blog 於 September 09.22. PM 04:17 發表 | 回覆 (0) | 引用 (0) | 收藏 (0) | 轉寄給朋友 | 檢舉

259

brighten [`braɪtn̩] 原意為『發光、（使）明亮』或『（使）高興、（使）喜悅』，通常與介詞 up 並用，可作及物或不及物動詞片語。

例: Mother lit some candles to brighten (up) the house when the electricity went out.

（停電時，媽媽點了些蠟燭來照亮房子。）

＊electricity [ɪˌlɛk`trɪsətɪ] *n.* 電

Emily brightened up when her boyfriend came to the airport to pick her up.

（艾蜜莉的男友來機場接她時，她感到很開心。）

網誌作者經過漫長的飛行，終於到了下榻的五星級飯店，頓時覺得 "my day brightened up"，試想一下，一個人若整天處在明亮的狀態會是什麼樣的感覺？那當然是心情愉快、開心不已啦！

例: Kelly's day brightened up when she bought the pair of shoes she'd been longing for.

（當凱莉買到那雙她一直很想要的鞋子時，一整天的心情都好得不得了。）

＊be longing for... 渴望……

字詞幫幫忙！

1. **Believe it or not.** 信不信由你。

   Believe it or not, S + V 信不信由你，……

= Whether you believe it or not, S + V

   例: Believe it or not, this machine can make 100 copies in a minute.

   （信不信由你，這台機器一分鐘可以影印 100 張。）

2. **make it to +** 地方 （設法）到達／趕到某地

   例: Jerry got stuck in the traffic jam this morning and made it to the office an hour late.

   （傑瑞今早遇到塞車，晚了一個小時才到公司。）

3. **expect** [ɪk`spɛkt] *vt.* 期待，盼望

   例: The trip didn't measure up to what we had expected.

   （這趟旅行並不符合我們的期望。）

   ＊measure up to... 符合……

4. flight [flaɪt] *n.* 班機

5. infinity [ɪnˈfɪnətɪ] *n.* 無限，無窮

an infinity pool　　　無邊際泳池（視線感覺與大海連成一體的泳游池）

例: Mathematicians use the term infinity for a number that is limitless.

（數學家用無限大這個詞來代表無限大的數字。）

＊mathematician [ˌmæθəməˈtɪʃən] *n.* 數學家

limitless [ˈlɪmɪtlɪs] *a.* 無限的

6. bungalow [ˈbʌŋgəˌlo] *n.* 平房

7. vanish [ˈvænɪʃ] *vi.* 消失

vanish into thin air　　　　憑空消失

vanish without a trace　　　消失得無影無蹤

＊trace [tres] *n.* 痕跡

例: The beautiful woman vanished into thin air when the magician opened the box.

（當魔術師打開盒子時，那位美女憑空消失了。）

The deer we had been tracking in the mountains vanished without a trace.

（我們在山裡追蹤的那頭鹿就這麼消失得無影無蹤。）

＊track [træk] *vt.* 追蹤

8. horizon [həˈraɪzn̩] *n.* 地平線（單數）；範圍，眼界（恆用複數）

on the horizon　　　　　在地平線上

be on the horizon　　　　即將發生，迫近

broaden sb's horizons　　增廣某人的見聞

＊broaden [ˈbrɔdn̩] *vt.* 使變寬，使擴大

例: The customers could see the sun setting on the horizon from their rooms.

（房客可以從房間看到地平線上的落日。）

Economists expect that there might be a disaster on the horizon for the global economy.

（經濟學家預計全球經濟可能即將發生一場大災難。）

＊economist [ɪˈkɑnəmɪst] *n.* 經濟學家

Traveling abroad is a great way to broaden our horizons.

（旅遊是我們增廣見聞的好方法。）

My First Waves

Index | *Links* | *about* | *comments* | *Photo*

September 23

Since my last day of surfing didn't **end up** so well, I've **been longing to give it another shot**. Finally, I can say that I've <u>**caught some waves**</u>. Surfing was such a fun experience even though most of the time I fell off the surfboard as soon as I stood up. The **instructor** told me that <u>**practice makes perfect**</u>, so I **planned on** going surfing each morning for the rest of the summer. While it was a great day, I got a bit **sunburned** in the water.

Calendar

◀ *September* ▶

Sun	Mon	Tue	Wed	Thu	Fri	Sat
		1	2	3	4	5	6
7	8	9	10	11	12	13
14	15	16	17	18	19	20
21	22	23	24	25	26	27
28	29	30				

Blog Archive

▸ September (23)
▸ August
▸ July
▸ June
▸ May
▸ April
▸ March
▸ February
▸ January
▸ December
▸ November
▸ October

Tom at Blog 於 September 09.23. PM 05:18 發表 | 回覆 (0) | 引用 (0) | 收藏 (0) | 轉寄給朋友 | 檢舉

衝浪樂無窮

September 23

　　由於上一次衝浪的收場不太好，我一直很想再試一次。終於，我可以說我真的衝到浪了。雖然大部分時候我一站起來就從浪板上跌倒，但衝浪真的是很有趣的經驗。教練跟我說熟能生巧，所以我計劃今年夏天接下來的每一天早上都要去衝浪。今天過得很棒，但我在水裡把自己給曬傷了。

About me

Tom

Calendar

◄　　　*September*　　　►

Sun	Mon	Tue	Wed	Thu	Fri	Sat
	1	2	3	4	5	6
7	8	9	10	11	12	13
14	15	16	17	18	19	20
21	22	23	24	25	26	27
28	29	30				

Blog Archive

▸ September (23)
► August
► July
► June
► May
► April
► March
► February
► January
► December
► November
► October

Tom at Blog 於 September 09.23. PM 05:18 發表｜回覆 (0)｜引用 (0)｜收藏 (0)｜轉寄給朋友｜檢舉

網誌作者之前第一次衝浪就把自己搞得血流滿面，還進醫院縫了好幾針，因此很想再嘗試看看。這一次終於能 catch some waves，所以感到很高興。wave [wev] 當名詞表『波浪、海浪』之意，為可數名詞。而 catch some waves 照字面翻譯是『抓到一些海浪』，亦即『衝浪』之意。

catch (some) waves　　　衝浪
= ride (some) waves
catch one's first wave　　　某人衝浪時第一次跟到浪

例: Darren, would you like to come out and catch some waves with me this weekend?
（戴倫，你這個周末想不想出來和我一起去衝浪呢？）

Practice makes perfect.　　熟能生巧。

"Practice makes perfect." 字面意思為『練習能製造完美。』，也就是中文裡所說的『熟能生巧。』

practice [`præktɪs] *n.* 練習
perfect [`pɜfɪkt] *a.* 完美的

例: Don't worry about it; practice makes perfect. I'm sure you will get the hang of things pretty soon.
（別擔心，熟能生巧。我相信你很快就會上手的。）

　　＊get the hang of...　　對……上手；掌握……的訣竅

字詞幫幫忙！

1. end up　　結束

　　end up + 現在分詞 / 介詞片語　　結果 / 最後 / 到頭來……

　　例: Rachel often quarreled with her husband, so they ended up getting a divorce.
　　（瑞秋常和她先生爭吵，最後他們以離婚收場。）
　　＊quarrel [`kwɔrəl] *vi.* 爭吵
　　Gary's plan ended up in failure.
　　（蓋瑞的計劃結果失敗了。）

2. **be longing to V** 渴望要 / 從事……

= be dying to V

= be eager to V

*longing [ˈlɔŋɪŋ], dying [ˈdaɪɪŋ] 和 eager [ˈigɚ] 均為形容詞，表『渴望的』之意。

例: Sarah has been longing to learn how to drive a car for the past year.
（過去一年來莎拉一直渴望能學會開車。）

3. **give sth another shot** 再給某事一次機會；再嘗試某事一次

give sth a shot 試試看某事

= give sth a try

例: I know the job is difficult, but you should at least give it a try.
（我知道這項工作很難，但你至少應該試試看。）

4. **instructor** [ɪnˈstrʌktɚ] *n.* 教練，指導員

instruct [ɪnˈstrʌkt] *vt.* 教導；指示

instruct sb to V 指示某人做……

例: My brother, Tom, works as a fitness instructor.
（我弟弟湯姆是一位健身教練。）

Mom instructed me to clean the kitchen after cooking dinner.
（老媽指示我煮好晚餐後把廚房清理乾淨。）

5. **plan on + V-ing** 計劃 / 打算（做）……

= plan to V

= make a plan to V

例: Sandy and her boyfriend have been together for five years, and they plan on getting married next year.
（珊蒂和男友交往 5 年了，他們計劃明年結婚。）

6. **sunburned** [ˈsʌnˌbɝnd] *a.* 曬傷的

例: Light-skinned people get sunburned more easily than people with dark skin.
（膚色淺的人比膚色深的人更容易曬傷。）

Unit 67

The Massage

September 24

I had another great experience today. The hotel sent a **masseuse** up to the room, and for two hours, I had a great massage. This small woman had very strong hands, but she wasn't too **rough**. She **rubbed** my back and feet in a way that hurt so good. And the best part was that the massage was **dirt cheap**. I only paid 200 **baht** for two hours.

About me

Tom

Calendar

◄　　*September*　　►

Sun	Mon	Tue	Wed	Thu	Fri	Sat
		1	2	3	4	5	6
7	8	9	10	11	12	13
14	15	16	17	18	19	20
21	22	23	24	25	26	27
28	29	30				

Blog Archive

► September (24)
► August
► July
► June
► May
► April
► March
► February
► January
► December
► November
► October

Tom at Blog 於 September 09.24. PM 05:06 發表 | 回覆 (0) | 引用 (0) | 收藏 (0) | 轉寄給朋友 | 檢舉

266

馬殺雞

Index | *Links* | *about* | *comments* | *Photo*

September 24

我今天還有另一個很棒的體驗。飯店派了一位女按摩師到我房間，我享受了兩個小時舒服的馬殺雞。這位瘦小的女士有雙強壯的手，但力道卻不會太大。她按摩我的背部和雙腳，感覺雖痛卻很舒服。最棒的是這節馬殺雞非常便宜。這兩個小時我只付兩百泰銖而已。

About me

Tom

Calendar

◀ *September* ▶

Sun	Mon	Tue	Wed	Thu	Fri	Sat
		1	2	3	4	5
6	7	8	9	10	11	12
13	14	15	16	17	18	19
20	21	22	23	24	25	26
27	28	29	30			

Blog Archive

▸ September (24)
▸ August
▸ July
▸ June
▸ May
▸ April
▸ March
▸ February
▸ January
▸ December
▸ November
▸ October

Tom at Blog 於 September 09.24. PM 05:06 發表 | 回覆 (0) | 引用 (0) | 收藏 (0) | 轉寄給朋友 | 檢舉

網誌裡的 **dirt cheap** 就是 very cheap 的意思，因為 dirt 是『灰塵，塵土』，因此 dirt cheap 是一種強調說法，表『如塵土般一文不值的』，也就是『非常便宜的』或『不值錢的』之意。也可以說成 (as) cheap as dirt。

例: These watermelons are as cheap as dirt because they are in season right now.

（這些西瓜非常便宜，因為現在是盛產期。）

＊be in season 　（水果、漁產等）正當時令 / 盛產中

以下介紹其他表『便宜的』用法：

inexpensive [ˌɪnɪkˈspɛnsɪv] *a.* 價格低廉的
low-priced [ˌloˈpraɪst] *a.* 低價的
cost next to nothing 　便宜到不行
= cost almost nothing

例: It's impossible to find an inexpensive apartment in this neighborhood.

（在這社區內不可能找得到便宜的公寓。）

The hamburgers at this fast-food restaurant cost next to nothing because the restaurant is having a special sale.

（這家速食店的漢堡因為正在特價中，所以便宜到不行。）

字 詞 幫幫忙！

1. **massage** [məˈsɑʒ] *n.* & *vt.* 按摩；推拿

   a foot massage　　腳底按摩

   例: Mandy always gets a foot massage from her husband after a long day at work.

   （一整天漫長的工作後，曼蒂的老公都會幫她腳底按摩。）

   Would you massage my shoulders? They're sore after lifting all those boxes.

   （妳可以幫我按摩一下肩膀嗎？搬完所有這些箱子後我的肩膀好酸。）

2. **masseuse** [mæˋsɝz] *n.* 女按摩師

   masseur [mæˋsɝ] *n.* 男按摩師

3. **rough** [rʌf] *a.* 粗魯的，粗暴的

   例: Football is a rather rough game.

   （美式橄欖球是一種頗為粗暴的運動。）

4. **rub** [rʌb] *vt.* 摩擦；搓揉

   三態為：rub, rubbed [rʌbd], rubbed。

   rub one's eyes　　揉眼睛

   rub salt into one's wound　　在某人的傷口上灑鹽

   ＊wound [wund] *n.* 傷口

   例: Benny rubbed his eyes wearily after driving for three
   hours.

   （開了 3 小時的車後，班尼疲倦地揉了揉眼睛。）

   ＊wearily [ˋwɪrɪlɪ] *adv.* 疲倦地

   You're not helping by telling me what I've done wrong
   over and over. You are just rubbing salt into my wound.

   （你一直重複告訴我做錯了什麼，實在一點幫助也沒有。你只是在
   我傷口上灑鹽罷了。）

5. **baht** [bɑt] *n.* 泰銖（泰國的貨幣單位，複數形為 baht 或 bahts）

The Food on the Street

Index | *Links* | *about* | *comments* | *Photo*

September 25

In any country, some of the best food comes from the **stalls** on the street. Alex and I **ventured** out to the big market and tried everything. We even tried **cockroaches** on a **stick** because we were **in a daring mood**. Most of the food was **tasty**, but **by the time** I got to the hotel, I had a bad case of **diarrhea** and spent the rest of the night in the bathroom.

About me

Tom

Calendar

◄ September ►

Sun	Mon	Tue	Wed	Thu	Fri	Sat
			1	2	3	4	5	6
7	8	9	10	11	12	13
14	15	16	17	18	19	20
21	22	23	24	25	26	27
28	29	30				

Blog Archive

▸ September (25)
▸ August
▸ July
▸ June
▸ May
▸ April
▸ March
▸ February
▸ January
▸ December
▸ November
▸ October

Tom at Blog 於 September 09.25. PM 11:07 發表 | 回覆 (0) | 引用 (0) | 收藏 (0) | 轉寄給朋友 | 檢舉

探索街頭小吃

Index | *Links* | *about* | *comments* | *Photo*

September 25

在任何國家，有些最棒的食物是出自於街頭小吃。艾力克斯和我到一個大型市場裡探險，吃遍了每樣東西。因為有勇於冒險的精神，我們甚至還吃了一根蟑螂肉串。大部分食物都還蠻美味的，但回到飯店後，我嚴重腹瀉，整晚都在廁所裡度過。

About me

Tom

Calendar

◄　　*September*　　►

Sun	Mon	Tue	Wed	Thu	Fri	Sat
		1	2	3	4	5	6
7	8	9	10	11	12	13
14	15	16	17	18	19	20
21	22	23	24	25	26	27
28	29	30				

Blog Archive

▸ September (25)
▸ August
▸ July
▸ June
▸ May
▸ April
▸ March
▸ February
▸ January
▸ December
▸ November
▸ October

Tom at Blog 於 September 09.25. PM 11:07 發表│回覆 (0)│引用 (0)│收藏 (0)│轉寄給朋友│檢舉

網誌作者和朋友 Alex 因為 in a daring mood，所以大膽嚐試蟑螂肉串，但結果卻是拉肚子。daring [ˈdɛrɪŋ] 為形容詞，表『大膽的、勇於冒險的』，mood [mud] 則表『心情』之意，因此 be in a daring mood 就是某人『處於大膽／勇於冒險的心情』，願意嚐試新事物或做自己平時不敢做的事。

例: Mandy is in a daring mood right now, so she has agreed to go water skiing with Daniel.

（曼蒂現在充滿冒險精神，所以同意和丹尼爾一起去滑水。）

以下為 mood 的重要用法：

be in a good / bad mood　心情很好／很差

= be in high / low spirits

　＊spirits [ˈspɪrɪts] *n.* 情緒，心情（恆為複數）

be in the mood + for sth / to V　有做……的心情（多用於疑問句或否定句中）

例: You'd better leave Judy alone. She is in a bad mood because she got fired today.

（你最好讓茱蒂一個人靜一靜。她今天被炒魷魚所以心情很差。）

Are you in the mood to go for a ride?

（你有去兜風的興致嗎？）

I'm not in the mood for a walk today. It's too cold.

（我今天沒有心情去散步。天氣太冷了。）

Ryan just had a fight with his girlfriend, so he wasn't in the mood to play basketball with us.

（萊恩剛跟女友吵了一架，所以沒有心情和我們打籃球。）

字 詞幫幫忙！

1. **stall** [stɔl] *n.* 攤位

2. **venture** [ˈvɛntʃɚ] *vi.* 冒險從事（去某地或做某事）& *vt.* 冒……險

   例: Don't venture into that park after dark.

   （天黑之後不要冒然進入那座公園。）

Leo ventured in risky investments and eventually went bankrupt.
（里歐大膽從事冒險投資，結果破產。）

*risky [ˈrɪskɪ] *a.* 冒險的

Nothing ventured, nothing gained.

= If nothing is ventured, nothing will be gained.
（不入虎穴，焉得虎子。──諺語。）

3. **cockroach** [ˈkɑkˌrotʃ] *n.* 蟑螂（= roach [rotʃ]）

4. **stick** [stɪk] *n.* 棍子 & *vt.* 插；使困住 & *vi.* 堅守（與介詞 to 並用）

三態為：stick, stuck [stʌk], stuck。

be stuck in...　　　被困在……中，陷於……無法動彈

stick to sth　　　堅守某事物

例: Be careful not to stick the needle in your finger.
（小心不要讓針扎到手指。）

*needle [ˈnidl̩] *n.* 針

We were stuck in traffic for an hour this morning.
（我們今天早上被困在車陣中一個小時。）

You should stick to your principles.
（你應該堅守原則。）

*principle [ˈprɪnsəpl̩] *n.* 原則

5. **tasty** [ˈtestɪ] *a.* 美味的，可口的

= delicious [dɪˈlɪʃəs] *a.*

例: Dad is a great cook. Everything he makes is tasty.
（老爸很會做菜。他煮的東西樣樣好吃。）

6. **by the time...**　　　等到……時

例: By the time Sam woke up from his nap, it was dark outside.
（山姆小睡後醒來時，外面天色已暗。）

By the time you read this note, I will be long gone.
（在你看到這張紙條時，我已經離開很久了。）

7. **diarrhea** [ˌdaɪəˈrɪə] *n.* 腹瀉

have diarrhea　　　腹瀉，拉肚子

= have the runs

例: My mother said that I shouldn't drink milk when I have diarrhea.
（媽媽說我腹瀉時不應該喝牛奶。）

Unit 69

Ladyboys! Ladyboys! Ladyboys!

Index | Links | about | comments | Photo

September 26

While Alex and I were **window-shopping**, a beautiful woman came up to us and asked us to come in to see a show. We went in but **sensed** something was a little different. All the girls were tall and had bodies like models. It seemed like it **was too good to be true**, and it was. The whole bar **was full of** ladyboys! As soon as we finished our drink, we got out of there **quick as a flash**.

Tom at Blog 於 September 09.26. PM 10:58 發表 | 回覆 (0) | 引用 (0) | 收藏 (0) | 轉寄給朋友 | 檢舉

通通是人妖！

September 26

　　我和艾力克斯在逛櫥窗時，一名漂亮的女子走上前來，邀我們進去看秀。我們進去後，覺得苗頭不對。所有的女孩都很高挑，身材就像模特兒一樣。這似乎好得不像是真的，而且果然不是真的。整間酒吧裡都是人妖！我們一喝完酒，就迅速地逃離現場。

About me

Tom

Calendar

◄　　*September*　　►

Sun	Mon	Tue	Wed	Thu	Fri	Sat
		1	2	3	4	5	6
7	8	9	10	11	12	13
14	15	16	17	18	19	20
21	22	23	24	25	26	27
28	29	30				

Blog Archive

▶ September (26)
▶ August
▶ July
▶ June
▶ May
▶ April
▶ March
▶ February
▶ January
▶ December
▶ November
▶ October

Tom at Blog 於 September 09.26. PM 10:58 發表 | 回覆 (0) | 引用 (0) | 收藏 (0) | 轉寄給朋友 | 檢舉

網誌裡的 quick as flash 就是『迅速地』，因為 flash [flæʃ] 是『閃光』，因此 quick as a flash 是一種比喻用法，表『快如閃電一般』，也就是『速度很快』之意。

quick as a flash　　快如閃電一般；迅速地

= quick as lightning

= quick as a wink

＊lightning [ˈlaɪtnɪŋ] n. 閃電（不可數）

　wink [wɪŋk] n. 眨眼；眨眼的瞬間

例: The thief jumped out of the back window quick as a flash when he heard the police sirens.

（小偷聽到警笛聲，就迅速地從後窗跳出逃逸。）

　　＊siren [ˈsaɪrən] n. 警報器；氣笛

in / like a flash 則表『一瞬間、馬上』。

in / like a flash　　一瞬間，馬上

= in the blink of an eye

＊blink [blɪŋk] n. 眨眼

例: Computers can make big calculations in a flash.

（電腦可以在一瞬間完成大量的計算。）

　　＊calculation [ˌkælkjəˈleʃən] n. 計算

1. **ladyboy** [ˈledɪˌbɔɪ] n. 人妖

比較：

drag queen [ˈdræg ˌkwin] n. 男扮女裝的男子；變裝皇后

例: The girl you just danced with is a ladyboy.

（剛剛和你跳舞的女生其實是個人妖。）

Mike is a drag queen. He likes to dress up like Madonna.

（麥克是個變裝狂。他喜歡打扮成瑪丹娜的樣子。）

　　＊dress up　　裝扮

2. window-shopping [ˈwɪndoˌʃɑpɪŋ] *n.* 瀏覽商店櫥窗

go window-shopping　　逛商店櫥窗（純逛街但不花錢買）

例: When I'm bored, I usually go window-shopping at department stores.

（我覺得無聊時，通常會到百貨公司逛櫥窗。）

3. sense [sɛns] *vt.* 意識到，感覺到 & *n.* 意義

make sense　　有意義；有道理

例: I can sense my girlfriend is getting angry by her tone of voice.

（從我女友的語調我可以感覺到她正在生氣。）

＊tone [ton] *n.* 語氣；音調

Nothing David says makes sense when he gets drunk.

（大衛喝醉時所說的話都沒什麼意義。）

4. be too good to be true　　好得不像是真的；好到令人難以置信

例: The salary you offered me is too good to be true.

（您提供的薪資好到令我難以置信。）

5. be full of...　　充滿……

= be filled with...

例: The ocean is full of colorful fish.

（海洋中充滿色彩繽紛的魚兒。）

Unit 70

A Shopper's Paradise

Index | *Links* | *about* | *comments* | *Photo*

September 27

Alex and I went **souvenir** shopping because he needed to buy some things for his girlfriend. She was extremely mad that he went on a trip without her. I wanted to get my mom something she could **put up** on her wall. We found a market with cheap items, and we **haggled** with the **vendors** on everything. **Eventually**, we got some great bargains. I was very happy because I didn't go over my **budget** for this trip.

About me

Tom

Calendar

◀ September ▶

Sun	Mon	Tue	Wed	Thu	Fri	Sat
		1	2	3	4	5	6
7	8	9	10	11	12	13
14	15	16	17	18	19	20
21	22	23	24	25	26	27
28	29	30				

Blog Archive

- September (27)
- August
- July
- June
- May
- April
- March
- February
- January
- December
- November
- October

Tom at Blog 於 September 09.27. PM 07:23 發表 | 回覆 (0) | 引用 (0) | 收藏 (0) | 轉寄給朋友 | 檢舉

購物天堂

September 27

艾力克斯和我一同去採購紀念品,因為他得買點東西送他女友。他沒帶她一起出遊讓她氣炸了。我則想買給我媽可以讓她掛在牆上的東西。我們找到一個市集,裡頭賣的東西都很便宜,我們每樣東西都跟小販殺價。最後買到了一些不錯的便宜貨。這趟旅遊我沒有超支,讓我還滿開心的。

About me

Tom

Calendar

◄ *September* ►

Sun	Mon	Tue	Wed	Thu	Fri	Sat
		1	2	3	4	5
6	7	8	9	10	11	12
13	14	15	16	17	18	19
20	21	22	23	24	25	26
27	28	29	30			

Blog Archive

► September (27)
► August
► July
► June
► May
► April
► March
► February
► January
► December
► November
► October

Tom at Blog 於 September 09.27. PM 07:23 發表 | 回覆 (0) | 引用 (0) | 收藏 (0) | 轉寄給朋友 | 檢舉

到了觀光勝地的市集，當然得拿出氣勢來好好殺價一番，但也別忘了應有的分寸與禮貌，可別殺紅了眼而不歡而散。以下就為各位介紹與殺價有關的常用說法：

haggle [ˋhæɡl] *vi.* 討價還價
bargain [ˋbɑrɡɪn] *vi.* 講價，討價還價
haggle with sb　　與某人討價還價
= bargain with sb
haggle over the price　　殺價
bargain for a better / lower price　　殺價

例: After haggling with the shop clerk over the price, Emma bought a 42-inch plasma TV at less than NT$30,000.
（在和店員殺價後，艾瑪以不到 3 萬塊台幣的價錢買了一台 42 吋的電漿電視。）

＊plasma [ˋplæzmɑ] *n.* 電漿
My mother bargained with the vendor over a few dollars.
（我媽為了幾塊錢和那攤販討價還價。）

bargain 也可作名詞用，表『便宜貨、特價商品』。

例: It's quite easy to get some good bargains during the clearance sale.
（在清倉大拍賣的時候很容易買到不錯的便宜貨。）

＊clearance [ˋklɪrəns] *n.* 清倉
a clearance sale　　清倉大拍賣
Sally always shops around for the best bargains so she won't get ripped off.
（莎莉總是貨比三家找最划算的東西，以免吃虧上當。）

＊get ripped off　　被敲竹槓，吃虧上當

覺得東西買得很划算時則可以這麼說：

That's a good bargain.
= That's a good buy.
= That's a good deal.

例: Sandy: The shoes only cost me NT$199.
　　Kathy: Wow. That's really a good bargain.
（珊蒂：這雙鞋只花了我 199 元台幣。）
（凱西：哇，那真的很便宜耶。）

1. paradise [ˈpærəˌdaɪs] *n.* 天堂，樂園

例: Hawaii is a paradise for surfers.
（夏威夷是衝浪者的天堂。）

2. souvenir [ˈsuvəˌnɪr] *n.* 紀念品

3. put up... （在牆上）張貼／懸掛……

例: The list of personnel changes is going to be put up on the bulletin board next week.
（人事異動的名單將於下週張貼在佈告欄上。）

＊personnel [ˌpɜsəˈnɛl] *n.* 全體職員
bulletin board [ˈbʊlətɪn ˌbɔrd] *n.* 佈告欄

4. vendor [ˈvɛndɚ] *n.* 小販

5. eventually [ɪˈvɛntʃʊəlɪ] *adv.* 最後，終於

例: Donna eventually forgave her husband for forgetting their anniversary.
（唐娜最終還是原諒她老公忘了他們結婚週年紀念日一事。）

＊anniversary [ˌænəˈvɜsərɪ] *n.* 週年紀念（日）

6. budget [ˈbʌdʒɪt] *n.* 預算

go over one's budget　　超出某人的預算
stay under (the) budget　在預算內
on a tight budget　　　　預算吃緊

例: Clair was afraid that she would go over her budget after she found out that everyone was bringing their families to her party.
（克萊兒發現每位賓客都攜家帶眷出席她的派對，她擔心這場派對會超出預算。）

The director was required to stay under the budget for the movie.
（該導演被要求在預算內拍出那部電影。）

We have to carry out the project on a tight budget.
（我們必須在有限的預算下完成這件案子。）

Waiting in the Wings

Index | Links | about | comments | Photo

September 28

At the World Trade Center today, my buddy and I went to the **Comic** and Cartoon **Exhibition**. It was very **crowded** because a famous supermodel was there. Everyone **gathered** around her to take a picture with her, and we did, too. **It turned out that** we waited in the wings for nearly two hours just to take one picture. I think it was **worth** it because now I have a picture of us that I can post on Facebook, and she even **gave me a hug**. This was **definitely** the best exhibition I've ever been to.

About me

Tom

Calendar

◄ September ►

Sun	Mon	Tue	Wed	Thu	Fri	Sat
		1	2	3	4	5	6
7	8	9	10	11	12	13
14	15	16	17	18	19	20
21	22	23	24	25	26	27
28	29	30				

Blog Archive

▸ September (28)
▸ August
▸ July
▸ June
▸ May
▸ April
▸ March
▸ February
▸ January
▸ December
▸ November
▸ October

Tom at Blog 於 September 09.28. PM 05:26 發表 | 回覆 (0) | 引用 (0) | 收藏 (0) | 轉寄給朋友 | 檢舉

為伊排隊等候

September 28

今天我和麻吉到世貿參觀動漫展。因為來了一位超級名模，現場人山人海。大家都聚集到她身邊，要和她一起拍照，而我們也是。結果我們在舞台邊等了快兩個小時只為了拍一張照片。我覺得很值得，因為我有了跟她合照的照片，就可以放在我的 Facebook 上，她甚至還給我一個擁抱。這絕對是我去過最棒的展覽了。

About me

Tom

Calendar

◄ *September* ►

Sun	Mon	Tue	Wed	Thu	Fri	Sat
	1	2	3	4	5	6
7	8	9	10	11	12	13
14	15	16	17	18	19	20
21	22	23	24	25	26	27
28	29	30				

Blog Archive

- ► September (28)
- ► August
- ► July
- ► June
- ► May
- ► April
- ► March
- ► February
- ► January
- ► December
- ► November
- ► October

Tom at Blog 於 September 09.28. PM 05:26 發表 | 回覆 (0) | 引用 (0) | 收藏 (0) | 轉寄給朋友 | 檢舉

283

wing [wɪŋ] 原指『翅膀』，亦可表『舞台的側面』之意，一般都是讓準備上場表演的人等候的地區。而 **wait in the wings** 除了字面上『在舞台側面等待』的意思外，尚可引申為『時時刻刻準備著 / 等待著』或『（物品）隨時可以使用』之意。

例: The dancer suddenly passed out while she was waiting in the wings to go on stage.

（那位舞者在舞台邊等待上台時，突然暈倒了。）

＊pass out　暈倒

Kathy was waiting in the wings, hoping she would be chosen for the leading role in the play.

（凱西時時刻刻在等待，希望能被選為這齣戲的主角。）

We have a backup plan waiting in the wings if this plan doesn't work out.

（要是這項計劃行不通，我們還有一個備用計劃隨時可用。）

＊backup [ˈbækˌʌp] a. 備用的

字詞幫幫忙！

1. **comic** [ˈkɑmɪk] n. 連環漫畫
   cartoon [karˈtun] n. 卡通

2. **exhibition** [ˌɛksəˈbɪʃən] n. 展覽
   be on exhibition　　展出中
= be on display
   ＊display [dɪˈsple] n. 陳列，展出
   例: The artist's latest sculptures are on exhibition at the museum.
   （那位藝術家最新的雕刻作品正在這間博物館展出中。）
   ＊sculpture [ˈskʌlptʃɚ] n. 雕刻品

3. **crowded** [ˈkraʊdɪd] a. 擠滿人群的
   be crowded with...　　擠滿……
= be packed with...

例: The new department store was crowded with shoppers on its opening day.
（那家新百貨公司在開幕當天擠滿了購物人潮。）

4. **gather** [ˈɡæðɚ] *vi.* 聚集 & *vt.* 使聚集；蒐集

例: All the children gathered on the playground to play tag.
（所有的小孩聚集在運動場上玩捉人遊戲。）
＊tag [tæɡ] *n.*（兒童的）捉人遊戲
We need to gather information for the project before working on it.
（我們必須先蒐集與這項專案相關的資訊再著手進行。）

5. **It turns out + that** 子句　　結果（竟然）……

例: It turns out that James is the person who stole the money from my wallet.
（結果詹姆士竟是那個從我皮夾裡偷錢的人。）

6. **worth** [wɝθ] *prep.* 值得

be worth it　很值得（= be worthwhile）
be worth + N/V-ing　值得……

例: This restaurant is quite expensive, but the food is worth it.
（這家餐廳很貴，但那裡的菜值得這種價格。）
From what I've heard, this movie is very interesting and well worth seeing.
（據我所知，這部電影非常有趣，很值得一看。）

7. **give sb a hug**　給某人一個擁抱

hug [hʌɡ] *n.* 擁抱

例: Jenny's boyfriend gave her a hug before she got on her flight to Greece.
（珍妮上飛機去希臘前，她的男友給了她一個擁抱。）

8. **definitely** [ˈdɛfənɪtlɪ] *adv.* 絕對地

例: When it comes to baseball, Shawn is definitely a big fan.
（說到棒球，尚恩絕對是個大球迷。）

Disappointment Runs Deep

Index | *Links* | *about* | *comments* | *Photo*

September 29

I've had it up to here today. I spent NT$2,000 on tickets for the baseball game with my family. We wanted to be front and center to see our favorite pitcher **kick** the other team**'s ass**. However, the pitcher ended up **giving up** seven **runs** in the first **inning** and got **pulled**. I **was** so **disappointed at** this team and the pitcher that I may never watch a baseball game again.

About me

Tom

Calendar

◄   September   ►

Sun	Mon	Tue	Wed	Thu	Fri	Sat
	1	2	3	4	5	6
7	8	9	10	11	12	13
14	15	16	17	18	19	20
21	22	23	24	25	26	27
28	29	30				

Blog Archive

► September (29)
► August
► July
► June
► May
► April
► March
► February
► January
► December
► November
► October

失望透頂

September 29

　　我今天真是受夠了。我花了兩千塊買全家人的棒球賽門票。我們想坐在前面中間的位置，才可以看到我們最喜愛的投手痛宰對手。結果這名投手卻在第一局掉了 **7** 分，所以被換下場了。我對這個球隊和投手感到非常失望，或許我再也不會看任何一場棒球賽了。

About me

Tom

Calendar

◄　　　*September*　　　►

Sun	Mon	Tue	Wed	Thu	Fri	Sat
	1	2	3	4	5	6
7	8	9	10	11	12	13
14	15	16	17	18	19	20
21	22	23	24	25	26	27
28	29	30				

Blog Archive

▸ September (29)
▸ August
▸ July
▸ June
▸ May
▸ April
▸ March
▸ February
▸ January
▸ December
▸ November
▸ October

Tom at Blog 於 September 09.29. PM 09:43 發表 | 回覆 (0) | 引用 (0) | 收藏 (0) | 轉寄給朋友 | 檢舉

網誌作者為了最喜愛的棒球投手，花了大錢去看棒球賽，結果卻非常掃興，因為投手的表現實在太差勁。以下是幾個常見的棒球詞彙：

umpire [ˋʌmpaɪr]（裁判）、**pitcher** [ˋpɪtʃɚ]（投手）、**catcher** [ˋkætʃɚ]（捕手）、**batter** [ˋbætɚ]（打擊者）、**outfielder** [ˋaʊtˏfildɚ]（外野手）、**infielder** [ˋɪnˏfildɚ]（內野手）。

strike [straɪk]（好球）、**ball** [bɔl]（壞球）、**a foul ball**（界外球，**foul** [faʊl] *a.* 犯規的）、**fastball** [ˋfæstˏbɔl]（快速球）、**change-up** [ˋtʃendʒˏʌp]（變化球）、**curve ball** [ˋkɝv ˏbɔl]（曲球）、**a fly ball**（高飛球）。

hit [hɪt]（安打）、**a home run**（全壘打）、**walk** [wɔk]（保送）、**a double play**（雙殺）、**strike out**（三振）、**strike sb out / strike out sb**（將某人三振）

run [rʌn] *n.*（棒球比賽中的）一分
inning [ˋɪnɪŋ] *n.*（棒球比賽中的）一局
base [bes] *n.*（棒球）壘
first / second / third base 一 / 二 / 三壘

例: Taylor hurt his ankle when he tried to catch a foul ball.
（泰勒試圖要接住一個界外球時弄傷了自己的腳踝。）

Since Jimmy hit a home run in the ninth inning, his team won the game.
（因為吉米在第 9 局擊出全壘打，所以他那隊贏得這場比賽。）

I can't believe that my favorite pitcher allowed eight runs in the first inning.
（我真不敢想信我最喜愛的投手在第一局就丟了 8 分。）

字 詞幫幫忙！

1. **disappointment** [ˏdɪsəˋpɔɪntmənt] *n.* 失望
   To sb's disappointment, S + V　令某人失望的是，……
   例: To our disappointment, it rained on the day of our company trip.
   （令我們失望的是，公司旅遊那天下雨了。）

2. have had it up to here 感到很生氣；感到受夠了

be up to here with... 對……感到氣憤

例: I really have had it up to here with your nonsense about aliens.

（我真是受夠了你那些關於外星人的胡說八道。）

＊nonsense [ˈnɑnsɛns] *n.* 胡說八道（不可數）

alien [ˈelɪən] *n.* 外星人

Judy was up to here with Larry's constant complaints and decided to get a divorce.

（茱蒂對賴瑞不斷的抱怨感到很氣憤，決定走上離婚一途。）

＊constant [ˈkɑnstənt] *a.* 不停的，持續的

complaint [kəmˈplent] *n.* 抱怨

3. kick one's ass （輕而易舉地）打敗某人

ass [æs] *n.* 臀部

例: With Kyle on our team, we're definitely going to kick the other team's ass and win the championship this year.

（有凱爾在我們隊上，我們一定會痛宰另一隊，贏得今年的冠軍。）

＊championship [ˈtʃæmpɪənˌʃɪp] *n.* 冠軍地位／稱號

4. give up... （棒球）失……分；放棄……

例: Ed blamed Darren for losing the game because he gave up five runs in the final inning.

（艾德把輸掉比賽怪罪在戴倫頭上，因為他在最後一局失掉 5 分。）

Mary refused to give up her job after getting married.

（瑪麗拒絕婚後放棄她的工作。）

5. pull [pʊl] *vt.* 使退出；拉，拖

例: The coach decided to pull the ineffective pitcher.

（教練決定把這名無能的投手換下場。）

＊ineffective [ˌɪnəˈfɛktɪv] *a.* 無能的；不起作用的

I can't pull the drawer open. Something must be stuck in there.

（我拉不開這個抽屜。裡面一定有東西卡住了。）

＊drawer [ˈdrɔɚ] *n.* 抽屜

6. be disappointed at... 對……失望

disappointed [ˌdɪsəˈpɔɪntɪd] *a.* 失望的

例: A lot of people were disappointed at the results of the election.

（許多人對選舉結果感到失望。）

＊election [ɪˈlɛkʃən] *n.* 選舉

Unit 73

Overrated Art

Index | *Links* | *about* | *comments* | *Photo*

September 30

    Usually, I love art. The last time I went to an art exhibition, I was so happy to see Andy Warhol's paintings up close. Today was **a** totally **different story**, though. The art was overrated. I couldn't even remember the artist's name. Besides that, there were kids running around and **knocking over** things. It seemed that the **museum was** more **focused on making a killing instead of** giving the **audience** good art.

About me

Tom

Calendar

◄   *September*   ►

Sun	Mon	Tue	Wed	Thu	Fri	Sat
		1	2	3	4	5	6
7	8	9	10	11	12	13
14	15	16	17	18	19	20
21	22	23	24	25	26	27
28	29	30				

Blog Archive

- September (30)
- August
- July
- June
- May
- April
- March
- February
- January
- December
- November
- October

Tom at Blog 於 September 09.30. PM 07:28 發表 | 回覆 (0) | 引用 (0) | 收藏 (0) | 轉寄給朋友 | 檢舉

名不符實的藝術

Index | *Links* | *about* | *comments* | *Photo*

September 30

　　我通常都是喜愛藝術的。上一次我去看一場藝術展，很高興能近距離觀賞到安迪‧沃荷的畫作。但今天卻另當別論。人們給那些藝術品的評價過高了。我甚至連藝術家的名字也記不起來。除此之外，還有小孩跑來跑去、撞翻東西。我覺得這間美術館比較在意大撈一筆，而不是提供觀眾好看的藝術品。

Tom at Blog 於 September 09.30. PM 07:28 發表 | 回覆 (0) | 引用 (0) | 收藏 (0) | 轉寄給朋友 | 檢舉

story 除了表『故事』，尚有『內情、詳情』的意思。而網誌裡的 a different story 正是『情況並非如此』、『另當別論』之意。

例: Usually, I love going to Costco, but today was a different story.

（我通常喜歡到好市多購物，但今天卻另當別論。）

以下介紹 story 的幾個相關用法：

but that's another story　　那是另一回事了；那是題外話了

＊用於說話者談到一件事情時，順口提到的事，但卻不願再繼續往下說時。

It's the same old story.　　　　老樣子，一切都沒變。

It's a long story.　　　　　　　說來話長。

To make a long story short, ...　長話短說，……

例: So those were the things we did this weekend. I've got a new job on Monday, but that's another story.

（那就是我們這個週末所做的事情。我星期一找到新工作了，不過那是題外話了。）

Our team lost again. It's the same old story every week.

（我們球隊又輸球了。老樣子，每個星期都這樣。）

　Tony: My divorce and remarriage? That's a long story.

Jenny: I've got time.

（湯尼：關於我離婚與再婚的事？說來話長啊。）

（珍妮：我有的是時間。）

To make a long story short, we decided to cancel our trip and stay at home.

（長話短說，我們已經決定取消旅遊，待在家裡。）

字 詞幫幫忙！

1. **overrate** [ˌovəˈret] *vt.* 對……評價過高

   例: I think the magazine reviewer overrated the singer's new album. It's awful.

   （我覺得那本雜誌的樂評對這名歌手的新專輯評價過高。那真有夠難聽的。）

   ＊reviewer [rɪˈvjuə] *n.* 評論家

2. knock over... / knock...over　　撞倒……，撞翻……

knock [nɑk] *vt.* 碰撞，撞擊

例: Turning around, I knocked over the vase and broke it to pieces.
（我轉身時撞倒一個花瓶，然後它就碎了。）

3. museum [mjuˋzɪəm] *n.* 博物館

4. be focused on...　　重點被放在……

focus on...　　重點在……

例: Our supervisor's factory inspection tour will be focused
on fire prevention.
（我們督察員這次視察工廠的重點放在防火措施上。）
＊supervisor [ˋsupɚͺvaɪzɚ] *n.* 監督人
inspection [ɪnˋspɛkʃən] *n.* 檢查
This week, our law professor is focusing on contract law.
（這個星期，我們的法律教授講課的重點是合約法。）

5. make a killing　　發橫財，大賺一筆

= make a big fortune

例: Tony made a killing in the stock market.
（湯尼進出股市大賺了一筆。）

6. instead of + N/V-ing　　而非……

例: Julie decided to buy an apartment instead of renting one.
（茱莉決定買公寓而不租公寓。）

7. audience [ˋɔdɪəns] *n.* 觀眾，聽眾（集合名詞，不可數）

an audience of + 數字　　若干位觀眾 / 聽眾
a large audience　　一大群觀眾 / 聽眾
a small audience　　一小群觀眾 / 聽眾

例: The concert drew an audience of more than 10,000.
（演唱會吸引了一萬多名聽眾。）
A large audience came to watch the musical.
（一大群觀眾前來觀賞這齣音樂劇。）

國家圖書館出版品預行編目(CIP)資料

跟他學部落格職場生活英語/ 賴世雄總編審--初版
臺北市：智藤，2010.08
面： 公分--(常春藤職場生活英語系列；EF02)

ISBN 978-986-7380-62-3 (平裝附光碟片)

1. 英語 2. 職場 3. 讀本

805.18   99015681

常春藤職場生活英語系列 **EF02**

跟他學部落格職場生活英語

總 編 審：賴世雄
編輯小組：黃文玲・林明仕・柯乃文・鄭佩姍・柯沛岑
　　　　　Marcus Maurice・Rebecca A. Fratzke
封面設計：姚映先
電腦排版：王玥琦
顧　　問：賴陳愉姍
法律顧問：王存淦律師・蕭雄淋律師

出 版 者：智藤出版有限公司
　　　　　台北市忠孝西路一段33號5樓
　　　　　行政院新聞局出版事業登記證
　　　　　局版臺業字第 16024 號 J000081-3376

服務電話：(02)2331-7600　　服務傳真：(02)2381-0918
信　　箱：臺北郵政8-18號信箱
定　　價：**300**元（書＋1 CD）

＊如有缺頁、裝訂錯誤或破損　請寄回本社更換

常春藤叢書系列
讀者回函卡

✎ 感謝您的填寫，您的建議將是公司重要的參考及修正指標！

我購買本書的書名是		編碼	
我購買本書的原因是	☐ 老師、同學推薦　　　☐ 家人推薦　☐ 學校購買 ☐ 書店閱讀後感到喜歡　☐ 其他 _____		
我購得本書的管道是	☐ 電視購物　☐ 書展　　　☐ 學校／機關團訂 ☐ 書店名稱 _____　☐ 大型量販店名稱 _____ ☐ 其他 _____		
我最滿意本書的三點依序是	☐ 內容　　　☐ 編排方式　☐ 雙色印刷　☐ 試題演練 ☐ 解析清楚　☐ 封面　　　☐ 售價　　　☐ 促銷活動豐富 ☐ 信任品牌　☐ 廣告　　　☐ 其他 _____		
我最不滿意本書的三點依序是	☐ 內容　　　☐ 編排方式　☐ 雙色印刷　☐ 試題演練 ☐ 解析不足　☐ 封面　　　☐ 售價　　　☐ 促銷活動貧乏 ☐ 廣告　　　☐ 其他 _____		
我有一些其他想法與建議是			
我發現本書誤植的部份是	☐ 書籍第_____頁，第_____行，有錯誤的部份是 _____ ☐ 書籍第_____頁，第_____行，有錯誤的部份是 _____		

✎ 我的基本資料

讀者姓名		生　　日		性別	
就讀學校／公司行號		科系年級／職　稱			
聯絡電話		E-mail			
聯絡地址					

☐ 我願意　　☐ 我不願意　收到常春藤優惠活動訊息。

請您填寫完後寄至：

台北市忠孝西路一段 33 號 5 樓　　　　　智藤出版有限公司　　發行組收

填寫日期：西元_____年_____月_____日